THE ANGEL
STRIKES

Volume 1 of the Brandt Family Chronicles

The Napoleonic Wars

Oliver Fairfax

Revised Edition 2017

www.oliverfairfax.com

ISBN 13:9781545145937

Library of Congress Control Number 2016910254

CreateSpace Independent Publishing Platform

North Charleston, South Carolina

Enter a World that will change your view of History.

The Angel Strikes is the first in a series of epic novels that portray the saga of the Paul Brandt family across the centuries. The series challenges our understanding of history and gives us a glimpse of what lies ahead. These novels show the grandeur of the times, and the ugliness. You will enter forbidden territory.

History is written by the winner and from ace to knave it's a pack of lies. Endure misery in occupied territory to find new perspectives. You are not a pampered winner. To prosper you must survive. To survive you must fight. To win you must think.

But this is no crusty history! Ride in a rickety coach full of amazing characters driven at a maniacal speed to its conclusion—or doom.

In these family chronicles, you will experience history as it was—not how it is taught or sold. You will revel with larger-than-life characters spilling wine on their shirts and pouring fuel on the fire.

Step aboard—why not? Do you want to know what really happened? By the end, you'll know why we're where we are today and where we're going.

You'll meet aristocrats, strategists, politicians, statesmen, liars, double-crossers, secret policemen, spies and seducers. You'll meet innocence and honour. You'll enjoy humour and wit on your trip through time.

Enter *The Angel Strikes* and come to the woods south of Berlin in 1804. It's the dead of winter and people are hungry, cold and miserable. Yet if anyone is in this position, it's their own fault. They know it and they'll escape from it. Join them now and thrive, because this is the time Germany was conceived.

3

HISTORICAL NOTE. The French Revolution and its aftermath.

The French Revolution (1789-99) was possibly finally caused by crop failure and subsequent famine. The Revolution metamorphosed through many stages accompanied by high-flying principles, aims and claims.

But by 1793, France had collapsed into a 'Reign of Terror' during which time arbitrary executions, running into the tens of thousands, suppressed dissent, eliminated competence and eradicated infant democracy. Financial collapse, never far away, followed.

Like all European government collapses, real power eventually, but inevitably, fell to the most ruthless contestant. In 1799 it was Napoleon Bonaparte. The French exchanged king for dictator.

France was nothing more than a bankrupt association of regions, hardly recognizable as one nation. Central government did not function and unemployment was rife.

To correct these deficiencies, Bonaparte raised a huge army and trained it near Boulogne in the north-east of France, close to England, with the objective of invasion across the channel. The spoils of war would restore his treasury, his victory would subdue his enemy and warfare would employ his workforce.

However, the Royal Navy, under The Lord Nelson, sank a substantial part of the French and Spanish invasion fleet at the Battle of Trafalgar on 21st October 1805 and Bonaparte's invasion of England became impossible.

Assuming it took a week for the news of Nelson's victory to reach Bonaparte, he would have known by 28th October 1805.

He marched his army of approximately two hundred thousand men, fourteen hundred kilometres in thirty-five days, nigh on forty kilometres a day without rest days, while fighting at Ulm (20th October) and taking Vienna (12th November) to fight the

Battle of Austerlitz against a joint force from The Holy Roman Empire and Russia on 2nd December 1805. It was a stunning victory fulfilling all Bonaparte's objectives, except in one respect.

The scene is now set for Bonaparte's pillage of continental Europe. He is superlative on the battlefield and driven by an addiction to conquest.

It won't take him long to turn his gaze to the north and King Frederick III of Prussia.

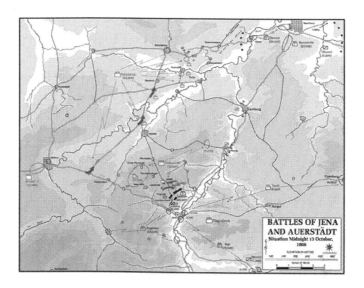

FICTITIOUS CHARACTERS

Appearing, or referred to, in **The Angel Strikes** in (approximate) order of appearance.

Uncle Franz and Uncle Albert – whatever names they may have lived by before they left Russia, these are the names they lived by in this story. They are Paul's uncles and his surviving relatives on this journey.

Anna – A waif, apparently, and in the charge of Rosina.

Rosina – Anna's protector.

Anstruther – the Englishman traveling in Thuringia and who was owner of the coach.

Gaston Dumarque – A member of Napoleon's Imperial police. Dreaded and unaccountable.

De Launcy – a cavalry officer.

Determined Servant. A person ordered by the Tayny Prikaz (see below) to complete a task.

Martin – an agent in the employ of the English government.

Charles Le Foy -Chef d'Escadron, a senior cavalry officer.

Lt. Brodeur. The aide to Le Foy, but also ...

Jerome Rickard. The factor of His Grace, the Duke.

The Duke. Possibly a senior member of the line of Saxe-Coburg-Saalfeld.

Frederica Storch, a seamstress to be avoided by young men.

Father Pym, a priest to be avoided by young men.

Susannah, the widow of a Prussian army officer, a guide and refuge for our hero.

Beatrice, a predatory soul wandering the castle corridors in search of solace.

Claude Fougas, a sometime assassin and 'go-fetch' servant for Bonaparte's Imperial police.

Henri du Vallois, Apparently, a senior member of Bonaparte's Imperial police.

Marie Delbarde and her husband Daniel, an ordinary Frenchman and his wife caught up in the tribulations of the times.

Henri Castel, a member of the innermost circle of the French government.

Catherine de Brunswick. A mysterious woman, whose true name is unknown, just as her birth date is unknown. She was the Tsar Alexander's first love. Kremlin plotters schemed to kill her to prevent any challenge to the succession to the Imperial throne. Friends tried to smuggle Catherine away, but it is not known if they succeeded.

HISTORICAL CHARACTERS AND INSTITUTIONS

Many historical institutions and characters appear, or are referred to, in The Angel Strikes and the author hopes readers will accept that they might, or could, have behaved as they are portrayed in the action of this story.

Von Dreyse – 1761-1815 a locksmith in Thuringia and father of Nicolaus

Nicolaus von Dreyse 1787-1868– became a famous gunsmith and invented the first reliable bolt-action breech loader.

Winchester – Franz and Alert think this is a person. They are yet to discover Winchester is a town in the south of England.

Robert – Robert Stewart – the Viscount Castlereagh, (1769-1822) the English Foreign Secretary, a man charged with the defeat of Bonaparte. He is also known in the action of the book as **Mr Brown of the Board of Control and Mr. Talbot of Canada.** Viscount Castlereagh was an Anglo-Irish statesman. He was widely experienced and far-sighted. An able diplomat and visionary, it was said of him that he failed to understand the means he required to achieve the ends he planned.

Author's note: There is no evidence the author is aware of that indicates Viscount Castlereagh ever travelled to Thuringia.

Graeme - a friend and confidant of Castlereagh. Unfortunately, Graeme remains well hidden in the shadows, but he did exist.

James Fox (Charles) (1749-1806) An English politician and leader of the House of Commons. He would be, in modern terms, a socialist believing in equality and the end of exploitation. He was slow to recognise France and Bonaparte as a threat. A man of conflicts and contrasts. His career was unsuccessful.

Yarmouth Third Marquis of Hertford. (1777-1842). A sportsman and wastrel. He eloped with an heiress and lived in Paris where he fell into the whirlpool of scheming stirred by Le Prince de Talleyrand. He was recalled to London in 1804.

Talleyrand, Charles Maurice (1754-1838) French politician and Foreign Minister. A study of this man is to engage in deceit, finesse, bribery, duplicity, cunning and (almost) magic. He exploited all humanity, but he served France's interests.

The Philadelphi. One of a host of secret societies within the French army devoted to the destruction of Bonaparte.

Colonel Oudet, 1775- was killed at the Battle of Wagram July 1809. He was the first chief of the Philadelphi, and dismissed the French army, but recalled for this battle. Grievously wounded he had been strapped to his horse, but was ambushed with his troop and, having been injured again, fell and was covered by the bodies of twenty-two of his comrades. He was found and survived for three days, during which time he arranged his affairs for the benefit of his son. He was never unmasked as the leader of the Philadelphi.

The Philopoemen. A Greek statesman and general (BC 253-183), but here used to indicate (but not to identify) the leader of the Philadelphi.

The Sequanese Republic. Sequana was the goddess of the River Seine and the Sequanese Republic would be founded in this area.

Tayny Prikaz. The department in the Kremlin, directly answerable to the tsar, dealing with confidential matters.

Lord Mulgrave (1755-1831). British soldier and politician who served as Foreign Secretary under William Pitt the Younger.

Saxe-Coburg-Saalfeld (1735-1826) One of the noble dynasties of the times. But, constant shifts of alliance and sovereignty changed responsibilities and territories and this house ceased in this form in 1826.

Mr Talbot from Canada -yet another persona of Viscount Castlereagh

Mr Smythe from The United states of America another persona for Graeme, Castlereagh's companion.

Georg Hegel (1770-1831) a leading and great philosopher whose original thought laid the foundations for many succeeding philosophers. Possibly the most elevated mind of the times.

Gebhard Blücher. (1742-1819) A Prussian aristocrat and Field Marshal at the time of Waterloo (1815). A count (Graf) and later Prince (Fürst). He returned to active service in 1813, (age 71) for the Prussian drive to rid the German speaking states of Napoleon and his new army.

Carl von Clausewitz (1780-1831) Prussian General, military theorist and strategist, author and reformer.

August Graf Neidhardt von Gneisenau (1760-1831) was the son on an army lieutenant. He rose through diligence with a penchant secret service overseas. He was a subordinate of Blücher's and one of the five reformers of the Prussian army.

Gerhard David von Scharnhorst (1755-1813). A Prussian General, and one of the leading reformers of the Prussian army. He died from a wound to the foot at the Battle of Lützen.

Hermann von Boyen (1771-1848) A Prussian aristocrat and general and one of the five reformers of the Prussian army.

General Ludwig Yorck von Wartenburg. (1759-1830). A highly principled and competent Prussian general who assumed leadership of the Prussian auxiliary column attached to the French army for the invasion of Russia. He was a Francophobe and was responsible for The Convention of Tauroggen that declared Prussian troops neutral in Bonaparte's campaign. He went on to fight to Paris in 1814.

President James Madison (1751-1836) was an American statesman and a Founding Father. As Secretary of State he oversaw the Louisiana Purchase in 1803 that doubled the size of the U.S. He served as President between 1804-13. He declared war against England in 1812 for several reasons, not all of which were obvious. He was hugely ambitious for the United States of America.

The Worshipful Company of Gunmakers. The company is one on the Livery companies of the City of London receiving its Charter in 1637 and being seventy third in order of precedence. The Gunmakers remain active in their trade, proofing barrels and decommissioning firearms.

The Proofing House was established in the City of London in 1637, but an explosion in 1673 demolished part of the City wall and the council required the Proof House to relocate outside the City limits, where it remains in Commercial Road to this day.

To proof a barrel the weapon is examined minutely and an oversize charge is fired twice. That having been done the weapon is re-examined for defect. If a barrel bursts or if it, or any part of the mechanism, shows distortion or degradation the barrel is not proofed, but the fee remains payable.

Contents

Chapter One: Time to Stand and Defend—1804

We came out of the east. Not Poland: that was bad enough. In Poland, children died for lack of food. We came from further east: Russia. Wagons heading west threw up pyres of dust. Day after day you saw them groaning across the plain and leaving their trail smeared in the sky. When the wind blew, the sun turned into an angry red sore erupting on a putrid grey skin. The few feeble plants holding onto life were unable to prevent the soil from climbing into a choking, stinging grit. The wagons rumbled on, pulled by skinny horses and led by defeated men. Each wagon was laden with a hungry family and a few paltry possessions. But the men carried despair.

The empty barns, waiting for the harvest, filled with dust from the fields. And no one was left to close the creaking doors.

When children died of hunger in Russia, they were buried quickly and secretly, for fear of what others might do. The word in Russian is *lyudoyedy*, and it means an animal that feasts on the flesh of its own kind. And humans are the most cunning of all the hunters. They can lurk in any band of smiling travellers. In Russia news travels slowly and warnings are never in time. The population is small and scattered and it is prey. Strangers become suspect, but before they arrive, there are stories and before them there are rumours. First there are distraught families looking for a loved one, possibly lost in the woods.

It is thought that the *lyudoyedy* move in bands living deep in the forest. No one goes to look for them for fear of finding them. So no one goes hunting alone.

People fear to leave their shelters. They fear to work in their master's fields or to sow grain. They fear for their children. The fear of cannibals finally broke our fragile existence.

We were serfs, bonded farmers, but what do you grow when there's no seed to plant and no fertilizer to spread? We had watched the columns grow on the road. We had spoken with them. We had looked into their eyes that said everything. They were afraid of the retribution that lay behind them just as they were afraid of the dangers in the unknown world that lay ahead. How could we survive here when they could not?

We had to leave. When a serf leaves the land he has nothing, except memories. He carries nothing. He can do nothing. But we survived. As a family, we survived—most of us—for a while.

We knew hunger followed crop failure, and starvation followed hunger. The *lyudoyedy* hunted the hungry.

When my parents finally decided to abandon everything we— our fathers and their fathers before them—had ever known and head west, we joined a group of neighbours. We would just desert our serfdom, the plot of land we worked, our tiny shelter and Russia with its privation, backwardness and cruelty. It was unreal—loading the wagon with what we would take and just leaving aside all the other things we knew. The moment our cart rolled away I felt torn from safety and terrible fear became real.

Tears streaked down my dirty face as I stared at our hut from the back of the squealing cart. Our home just shrank into the ground as the distance grew. The only link between me and home were wheel tacks in the dust and they would be gone soon enough. When the road turned into the alien forest, suddenly our home was gone from sight: together with our lives up to that moment. Only memories lingered and even our hens stopped clucking in the deepening shadows. We entered a new world, a world without permanence, a shifting, rumbling, rattling world. We never knew what we would find next. It was time to look at the view to the front of the wagon. The occasional litter of broken wheels and spars told us of the difficulties others had faced. Roadside graves testified that they had not always prevailed. There was no certainty now, certainly none of the kind that comes with having your own bed.

There were bands of robbers on the road and many of us met our end early, including my mother and father. I remember their deaths and it hurts today as much as it did when it happened.

Papa and I used to play *malen'kiy sharik*. We called it *myach* for short. It means little ball or ball and when Papa said, "Myach," I had to hide and make myself as small as a ball. Later, Papa would come to look for me, so I had to be absolutely quiet. It was a game, sort of, because if Father gave up he would give me a reward. But if he found me, he would cuff me around the ear, sometimes quite hard. I was quite good at *myach*.

We had been on the road for weeks, maybe months, when we stopped in the normal way. That night, Papa shook me awake and whispered, "Myach." So off I ran and hid very well, but he didn't come looking for me. I heard shouting and noise and the horses screaming, but still he didn't come. I waited until there was silence and still I hid. It was against the rules, but eventually I crept through the dark back to camp.

At first I thought everyone had left without me because the horses and carts were gone and the camp was quiet. I could hear a dog bark, but it wasn't one of ours. I walked to the fire and saw Mama and Papa lying beside each other on the grass. I ran over to them not realizing. I didn't realize, even when I saw the blood. I couldn't understand. Hands grabbed me.

"Don't look, Paul. We'll bury them tomorrow with the others." Uncle Franz took me in his arms and dragged me away.

The next day, my uncles, Franz and Albert, buried Mama and Papa and two of the neighbours. I watched them lowered into the ground, only realizing what it meant for me when Franz shovelled earth onto my parents' bodies. I felt I had been torn in half and overflowed with despair to find true loneliness. I sobbed into Uncle Albert's waistcoat.

When we left that place we set off on foot. From that moment we carried everything we needed. I often rolled up into a ball after that, but it wasn't to play *myach.*

We had been sheltered on the wagon, but now we walked, even as winter beckoned. The rain soaked us and the wind chilled us. My *valenki* were not waterproof and my feet became frozen. My uncles had leather soles on their *valenki,* but mine didn't because I was still growing. When I couldn't keep up, because my feet hurt so much, we stopped to earn money to buy boots.

That was in 1804, when I was twelve or thirteen, I think. Uncle Franz and Uncle Albert became my new parents.

We moved westwards. We stole. We smuggled and we were not alone in doing that.

We tried to keep moving, but some can't. In winter, the women and children can't and our little group began to break up. I was lucky—if you consider survival is lucky. Refugees who stayed in one place became prey and we often heard stories—terrible stories. That made us cautious of others and we relied on no one except ourselves. Even though we mixed with other travellers from time to time, we never joined their groups because, like us, they were in need and had nothing to trade. By that time, we had separated from our neighbours, who had stopped for winter.

Townsfolk drove us out. We tried to learn German and we knew enough to be understood, but we were Russian and our accent gave us away. It was as though we brought the plague.

They never allowed us to join their guilds and even their churches were closed to us. They wouldn't give us work and many just shut their doors in our faces. The changing seasons did little to ease the unending misery.

We moved west throughout 1805. Uncle Franz fretted that we were still on the road so late in the year, but we had been unlucky. Last year, just after we had set out on our own, we had found a sanctuary for winter. Perhaps this year we asked the impossible, because we had been unable to find anyone who would exchange winter lodgings for work. There was no alternative to going on, but winter would force her choice on us soon. I thought of the roadside graves, and of my parents, of how harsh last winter had been and trudged on.

Three is a good number if you're travelling, but September is not a good time to do it. The roads became a thick, clinging mire that gripped our boots and tried to trap us. Carts slid and broke their axles, while horses plunged and hurt themselves. We kept to the verges when we could. If there were devil strips—a cleared area between the road and the forest—so highwaymen could not lie in wait, we would walk on those. We each carried a quarterstaff. It's about one head longer than a tall man standing and it's strong without being heavy. I carried the leather collar. You put the three staves together, slip the collar over the ends (about one hand from the top), and then spread the other ends in a triangle as far apart as a man lying down. That makes the frame for our shelter. We each carried a three-cornered canvas with a stitched eye in one corner. The eye fitted over the top of a staff and we used thongs to tie the cloths together around the poles. Inside was dry and wind proof, unless the wind changed, of course.

Then we might lose the whole thing. Uncle Albert thought that was very funny when it happened once.

We would pitch our shelter and stop for several days. The idea was to rest from walking and catch food to cook. It's difficult to do that while you're on the move. Usually our shelter was left alone. But there were always people on the road who were worse off than us and sometimes we would find them sleeping in our tent when we returned from hunting. That's why we hid our tools a way off. On the second evening at this place we found people sleeping inside. On the first night, we had been lucky because Uncle Franz had shot a young stag. We had gutted it where it fell and carried the carcass home to joint for cooking and salting.

"It's not raining and it's not too cold. Let them sleep for a while. They'll wake when they smell the food," suggested Uncle Franz. I made up a fire and arranged the stand before recovering the iron pot from the branch where we had hidden it and hung it over the flames. The stew would taste better tonight.

Usually it was Uncle Albert who carried the cooking pot.

"At least you know where he is," Uncle Franz smiled. And it was true. You could always hear the clanking noise.

We each carried our bedding roll. They're easy when they're empty. I stuffed them with fresh heather or bracken when we pitched our shelter. There were also our Brown Bess muskets. To this day, I don't know why they're called that. Their real name is Land Pattern muskets and they come from England. For whatever reason, they were common on the road in the German-speaking states. We also carried some basic tools—a billhook, an axe, a honing stone and a flensing knife— but not much more. It was all weight and someone had to carry it. We crept into the forest to collect our traps and to see if we had snared anything we could trade.

When you set traps for food you don't know what you're going to catch—that is, if you catch anything. It's worse if some animal reaches your catch before you do. Nothing is assured in the forest. But my uncles were good at their work and we were often successful. Uncle Albert was our cook. He would joint the meat and sear it with a small amount of precious oil. Then he would pour in water and let it stew for a long time. I carried salt and dried herbs for preserving and to add flavour.

Just as our shelter attracted lodgers, Albert's cooking attracted the hungry. We seldom had bread or vegetables, only stew.

It was also my job to collect firewood that lay all round us. "Not too much, young Paul. You don't want to boil it. Let it cook slowly," Uncle Albert would say.

But it was such a temptation to build up the fire. I was so very hungry and it smelled so good as it heated. Instead, I concentrated on turning the pile of soaking bracken. You must gather it first and then dry it at the fireside. Once it was dry, I could stuff our palliasses for the night. It had to be bone dry, or I would get complaints of rheumatics in the morning.

"Instead of putting more wood on the fire, why don't you put more water in the pot?" Uncle Albert suggested.

And so it went on until finally it was time to eat. I returned with an armful of wood to see a woman, two boys—a little younger than me—and a man with a splint on his forearm. These were the people who had been sleeping in our shelter.

Uncle Albert felt tenderly for the bone in the offered arm and asked the man to make a fist.

"It's broken, all right and the splint isn't set right," he explained.

While the food bubbled, Uncle Albert adjusted the splint. I watched as his thick, strong fingers manipulated the broken bone as gently as anyone could wish. Once the splint was back in place, the man stopped wincing and nodded his thanks. We had no idea where they'd come from or what language they spoke between themselves, but it wasn't Russian.

We ate nearby, but in two separate groups and talking in quiet asides. You never get as much as you want, but you need to make sure you get as much as you need. With four extra mouths that evening, my greed went unassuaged, but everyone's needs were met. We had fed the strangers, but we only had one shelter. They would have to move on before dark. We would not allow them to camp near us.

We had all but finished eating when we heard a musket shot. There are only two sorts of people who shoot in forests: those who hit their target and those who don't. We didn't hear the ball pass by. It sounds like a hornet, so you know, but the gun had sounded as though it was pointed in our direction.

"Come, Paul. Get your musket." Franz was already loading his, while Albert took time selecting a flint from his pouch. He held one at arm's length. His sight was getting worse. I dismissed a worry about him using a musket and handed him mine. It was already loaded with the flint safely lowered. The trouble was the frizzen was loose on Albert's musket and the powder in the flash pan would spill or blow away. A cloth pad kept it in the pan and the loose frizzen held the cloth in place—usually. Albert nodded his thanks and trotted off after Uncle Franz. I loaded Albert's musket, but couldn't find the cloth pad, so I lowered the frizzen onto an empty pan and set off at a lope after the others. The family stayed by the fireside, eating. In their place, so would I.

We ran towards a bend in the track where there was no devil strip. As we approached we heard a horse whinny in fright. A man shouted. We burst from the trees into the afternoon sunlight to see an attack on a coach and a big smart rig it was.

The coachman slouched, flopping back and forth on his perch, as his horses struggled. They squealed with fright, trapped in the mud and held in their harnesses. The traces lay slack. Even as I watched, the coachman tumbled from his box and fell face down in the mud. I ran to him, sinking up to my calves in mire, to turn him over. My hand came away bloody. His face was slack and the front of his coat ripped by the ball that had killed him. Uncle Franz grappled with an attacker who had opened the coach door and who was wrestling with the person inside. Albert struggled with another bandit trying to unhitch the horses. He was thrashing them, even though they were stuck.

I had just bent down to lift the coachman when a musket fired nearby and a ball buzzed over my head. I looked up to see a third robber standing under the trees. He wore a dark cloak and, in the shadows, was easily overlooked. He started to reload. I waded desperately through the mud. My life depended on every second, even as the mud sucked at my legs, trying to hold me in the open as a perfect target. I grabbed Albert's Brown Bess and prayed the charge had not taken damp while it lay on the grass. I cocked it and primed the pan even as the robber rammed home a ball. I took aim, fired and immediately regretted it. The man was standing in front of his horse and if the ball went through him, it might injure the animal. Instead, my shot killed the man outright and flung him back onto the horse making it snort and sidle.

I reloaded. The first lesson to learn is that an empty weapon is of no use to anyone.

I turned my attention to the battle. Albert had felled the robber by the traces. He lay face down in the mud and he didn't lift his head. Uncle Franz still fought with the man who then stood on the step of the coach kicking at him while he tried to pull the occupant out. I saw the passenger's blade enter the robber's chest. He lurched backwards onto Uncle Franz and both men fell into the roadway. Only Franz rose.

Albert quietened the horses. I heard the man in the coach groan and drop his dagger.

"Look at the coachman." Albert nodded in the direction of the body lying beside the wheel. I waded over and stole his dark-green cloak and boots. I checked his pockets and took his papers. Even though we couldn't read, they might be useful somehow. Albert dragged the two robbers off the road and dumped them on the verge. Their boots weren't worth stealing. We left the three bandits and the coachman for a passing patrol to bury.

"For pity's sake get me to a hostel, a hostel with a doctor!" cried the man in the coach. He was bleeding from his mouth and had a cut over his eye.

It was all very well for him to say, but his coach was stuck in the mud. That's why the robbers had caught him in the first place. It's clearly stated in "The Regulations" how many horses must pull a coach in winter, because of the risk of becoming stuck. Every traveller on the road learns the regulations as time passes, but this man had ignored them to his cost.

Albert backed the robbers' horse and roughly hitched it ahead of the two at the pole. Franz and I each stood by one of the coach horses. I stroked its nose and talked to it, calming it. When they were ready, we turned the snorting team away from the mud. Once they stood on the grassy verge they could pull. The smaller steering wheels lifted and the coach followed. Uncle Albert stayed with the horses, but Uncle Franz and I searched our surroundings. Often musket fire will draw a crowd because there would be something to pillage, but that evening we remained alone on the verge. The muddy track was empty in both directions and when we reached the open ground, between track and forest, we saw no one.

The weather became overcast as the day drew to its close. I thought I heard thunder, but some way away, across the forest tops—where the clouds were darker.

The man in the coach spoke German as badly as we did and it took a little time for Franz to understand where he wanted to go and that he was English. I thought that might be why he didn't know the regulations.

Just on nightfall, with me riding on the robbers' horse—which was something I had little experience of doing—and with Albert sitting beside Franz on the box, we arrived at the inn on the *Kreuzung*. That's where the roads meet. The inn's lanterns were already lit, spreading a welcoming yellow glow across the yard and along the water-filled ruts in the churned-up track. I could smell the wood smoke. The main door opened and the innkeeper emerged followed by his servant and a lively conversation started. The ostlers arrived from the stables carrying another lantern to lead the coach to the barn. To avoid the mud as much as possible my uncles turned the coach at the inn's door and carried the Englishman, who was very fat, over the hard-standing and inside. They saw him as comfortable as they could, but the innkeeper didn't know of any doctor nearby. "There isn't even an apothecary and the monks won't come out after vespers." He shook his head. "We can send for one, but not until tomorrow."

The traveller looked very grey and coughed blood.

The ostler was not pleased to see us at that hour, especially when we said we wanted to sleep in his stables. However, he was mollified when he saw how Albert looked after the horses. He lifted the hoof of the robbers' horse.

"Is there a blacksmith hereabouts?" he asked.

"Not here," replied the ostler. "There's one that comes from time to time, but none that lives here." He looked at us speculatively. "I've got a forge. You can use it if you want. If you have the shoe."

Albert cleared out the frog and examined the hoof. "I'm not a skilled blacksmith and you can do more harm than good."

"That's true," the ostler agreed.

We groomed, fed and watered the horses and noted the sores on the robbers' animal. The ostler produced a tub of liniment and we spent time attending to her. She tossed her head and whinnied but submitted nonetheless.

We were allowed to sleep in the hay so we could be near the horses, but I was instantly asleep and never heard a snort.

The next morning, I awoke to a commotion. The innkeeper was calling for us and a chambermaid was screaming hysterically that he was dead.

"So I went up to his room and it's true," the innkeeper explained waving his arms to emphasize the drama. "Your master is dead. He died in the night. And I want paying for the room and the laundry, for he coughed up blood and it will stain the linen. And I want paying for the stabling for three horses and a coach."

"How much?" asked Franz.

The innkeeper mentioned a sum so large I thought my uncle would lose his temper. But he went up to the room and returned with money, which he held out in his calloused hand. The innkeeper poked about with his finger and helped himself. Franz pocketed the rest.

My uncles carried the body downstairs again, past gaping staff, and after lugging him across the courtyard to the stables, heaved him into the coach. Once his luggage was in there with him we hitched up and drove away.

We made our way to the roadside where we'd pitched our shelter the evening before. Mostly, people would leave a person's shelter alone. But that family, even with the father's broken arm, had stolen everything: shelter and cooking pot.

I dismounted and walked across the autumn bracken to make sure we were in the right place. Sure enough, I found the fire site and cautiously placed my hand on the ashes. I wiggled my fingers into the pile. It was cold. The family must have robbed us as soon as we'd left.

I stood back and looked around. We might leave our shelter, when hunting for instance, but we always hid our implements a way off. They're precious because they're difficult to replace. Ours still lay under some brambles where I had hidden them. They hadn't found those, nor had they found the carcass of the cerf hanging in a tree. We retrieved them to stack in the coach with the body.

I remounted the horse and looked over the empty space. In terms of one of life's trades we really couldn't complain.

On the byway, the going was firmer because it was not so much used. Uncle Franz shook the reins gently as the coach rocked and squeaked its way into the gloomy forest. There were many clearings there and in them, buildings. Often, they're left empty in winter. In times like those, many stood abandoned.

Franz drove slowly for an hour or so until we found a cluster of huts standing away from a spinney of pine trees and turned the coach into the clearing before them. We listened to hear only the scuttling sounds of the watching forest and the hiss of the wind in the branches above. We studied the cold dilapidation. You could smell the mould.

To our left stood a dingy hut with a brick chimneystack. That was good. The front wall was of wooden planks, many of them split, and the door was wedged shut with a broken branch. One of the shutters hung limply from a remaining hinge and I dismounted to peer into the dark interior. The smell of mould was the strongest sensation. Ahead of us were the remains of a wooden cart-standing, but one end had collapsed entirely, leaving only one open bay intact. That end was kept up by a bay with a closed end making a secure shed. To the right and further back was a small barn that looked to be in reasonable condition, but on the right side was the big barn. Its doors, which were arranged as bottom half and top half and not left and right, stood open showing animal pens inside. They were draped in remnants of sacking and ends of rope and other odd bits and pieces, but were devoid of any animals. The ground before us lay strewn with the litter of the forest: pine needles and cones, fallen twigs and branches. There was no clear path to the hut door.

No one lived here.

"Find water, Paul," Albert ordered as he dismounted.

I ran into the woods to do as I was bidden. When I returned, empty-handed, I saw the coach horses drinking from their buckets and the robbers' horse with its nose in a trough that Albert tipped water into.

"Usually, Paul, they keep water at the bottom of the hill. If you want to find it, it's sensible to look there," Uncle Albert teased me.

"But maybe you found some up there?" asked Uncle Franz, mocking. Both men laughed. I shook my head.

"When they've drunk, take the horses to that barn and rub them down." Albert unbuckled the traces.

"What about the coach?" I asked.

"Horses first."

With a certain amount of nudging and coaxing, the horses entered the big barn. It wasn't bad, but it needed repair. There was some fodder, but a lot of it had got wet because of a hole in the roof. In truth, the entire roof sagged.

I took rough hay and groomed the horses as I'd been taught and dressed the sores on the robbers' mare. I tethered and settled them for the night. We managed to close the bottom half of the barn door after a deal of lifting and pulling, but the top half sagged terribly once we tried to move it.

"What next?" I asked looking at the abandoned cluster of huts.

It seemed everything had to be attended to and we were last on the list. Franz chose the hut with the chimney for our shelter and the small barn to hide the coach in. Everything we did took effort and time. It was quite dark when we closed the hut door to the world with ourselves inside. The action of lighting a fire made a difference to me. It was a kind of ceremony marking our new home and I watched the light flicker into flame as the twigs caught fire and the bigger branches began to smoke. But it yielded only a slight amount of heat because the far-end wall had collapsed.

26

I woke last and heard the sharp hiss of a grindstone. Outside, Franz sharpened blades as Albert turned the wheel.

"Sorry to wake you, Paul," Albert laughed. It was a booming noise that issued from his black beard as he threw his head back.

"I'm sorry. I'll do the horses," I offered.

"Already done, Paul," Uncle Franz replied, smiling. Albert was big and strong, just as Franz was thin and sinewy. Also Franz was clean-shaven and his face had the look of leather. His eyes searched, just as Albert's saw. Albert stopped the wheel as Franz fingered the blade.

"Then what do you want me to do?" I asked.

"Well, you can stay here and talk with us about what we do next. How about that?" Albert offered.

"Look what we found in the shed." Franz placed a gleaming scythe against the wall and took up a sickle. He showed it to me and asked, "How'd you hone a sickle on a wheel?"

"You need a stone," I answered.

Franz nodded. "Look for one. Not now—later. Albert's saying this place looks good for winter."

"That is, if the real owners don't come back," Albert added.

"It'll be good to stop," I thought out loud.

"But it has its dangers," Albert warned.

I nodded. "I know."

"So if you agree, we'll start work for winter." Albert raised his bushy eyebrows as he asked the question.

"A winter that's already late and will be on us all too soon." Franz looked at the grey scudding sky. "So we have work to do."

I nodded. "What do you want me to do?"

Albert laughed. "Where do you want to begin?"

After everything we had been through, it was good to hear a laugh. Even Franz's smile meant a change in our fortunes, it seemed to me.

The list of things to do seemed endless and included some gruesome tasks. We prised the rings from the Englishman's fingers and stripped him of his clothes. We buried him behind the little barn while we could. When the ground froze, digging a grave would be impossible.

The more we searched the huts, the more we became convinced they'd been abandoned. The occupants had left their family homes as my parents had left ours. Were people moving west, even from here?

There was fodder enough in the barn and the stream flowed into the River Vippach, not that we knew it at the time. For food, there was game in the forest, fish in the river and plenty of wood for fires. We wouldn't have left such a place. There were possibly other reasons than hunger and we became cautious. But if we were to stay, we would enter a race against the onset of winter and it was a race we had to win.

I heard Franz laugh one morning as I cleared our food dishes and stepped out into the wind to find out why. "Listen." He chuckled.

I could hear Uncle Albert singing, his baritone voice echoing in the trees.

"He's singing to the forest, telling it he knows its laws and he'll only take what he needs."

I smiled. "Do you think these trees know Russian?"

"I hope so and I think we're here for winter. My brother's a woodsman at heart. He's not really a farmer." Franz slapped his leg. "No time to waste. If Albert's not a farmer, then we must do the farm work. Get the horses. There's an old plough. It isn't good, but it's all we have and there's a plot that needs it."

"But what'll we plant?"

"That, young Paul, is a good question. I've not seen any seed here, so we'll buy some and grow a crop. Then we can be thankful. But if we don't plough, we'll have nowhere to sow, so we'd never have a crop even if we did buy seed."

I led the horses back and forth across the clearing in the forest. It didn't look much until you came to plough it. Then it was quite big. Steam rose from the animals' nostrils as they pulled the creaking share through the soft earth. It was sandy with patches of sticky clay.

My happiness, when we had arrived here and decided to make it our home, collapsed into a time of despair and hard work. Each evening, I mixed a tub of clay with water at the stream, even as the weather grew colder and the wind rose in the trees. I sprinkled ash on the hearth to stop the clay from sticking and pressed the mix into frames made from stones. The mud baked overnight. Each morning I had six coarse bricks. Usually they were still warm and I rebuilt the back wall of our hut with them. The first bricks all but disappeared on the ground and it took three days to cross the hole to ankle height. I stood with my arms outstretched and the hole was wider than that and higher than me. It was soul destroying but, by that time, water no longer seeped onto our floor from outside, so we were dry underfoot. Unless it rained, that is.

When the ploughing was done, the horses dragged the timber that Albert felled. They pulled the logs and saplings as they pulled the plough. Franz listed the timber he needed and Albert found and cut it.

Uncle Franz was like a spider. Every day he worked up on the barn roof. His task was dispiriting too, because he demolished it.

"You have to understand, Paul. It's not keeping rain out that's the problem. It's keeping snow out. Snow's heavy and if it breaks the roof, it'll fall and maybe kill the horses."

I understood. But watching the hole grow larger as Franz worked to cut out the rotten timbers was enough to make tears chill my cheeks, especially as our roof had to wait until the horses were safe.

The work was endless and every day was shorter. But with my help, Uncle Franz erected whole trunks to support the new roof. They were to lie from one sidewall to the other, two on each side of the pitch, and one higher than the other of course.

You may ask how a tree trunk can be raised to the height of two men, by two men, or even a man and a boy. The two of us could just carry it, so you can judge its girth. Its length was about that of six men. We laid it on the ground with one end against the sidewall and the other end directly away from it. We laid the end furthest away from the barn on a stout plank that itself stretched further away. We tied that end of the beam to pegs so it could not slide along the plank.

We lifted the end that touched the wall and placed an *H*-frame under it. We went on lifting it little by little and each time we placed a longer *H*-frame under it until the *H*-frame was almost as high as the wall. It touched the trunk halfway between standing up and lying down. The frame's foot was against the wall and the top was about quarter of the way down the beam. We supported the *H*-frame so it could not fall flat, by which I mean away from the wall.

We were both blowing hard by this time and I sat down.

"No time to rest, young Paul. Look where the beam is. If it falls we must do all this work again. So we don't stop until it's safe."

I nodded and pushed my hair away from my face.

The next job was to lift the furthest end of the plank. We untied the beam to allow it to slide along the plank as we lifted it. We placed one of the *H*-frames we had used at the beginning under the farthest end of the plank and held it in place. We then pushed another *H*-frame under the plank to make it rise higher and that made it push the great beam up into the sky and over the top of the wall.

We came to the point when the first *H*-frame was vertical against the wall again and the beam was more than halfway to being level. About one-third was over the barn, or would be if it was flat and the rest stuck out to the side.

We had come nearly to the end of the plank and Uncle Franz let the beam rest on the wall. We moved the *H*-frames so the beam was horizontal and supported on the wall and at both ends.

It could all go wrong, but using an *H*-frame outside the barn, the wall itself and two *H*-frames inside, we walked the beam into place and at last the first purlin touched and rested on the far wall as well as the near one.

"Now we can rest, Paul, and while we do, I'll tell you this: I want us to do this three more times before nightfall today."

I was panting with exertion and I must have looked at him as though he'd gone mad.

Uncle Franz laughed. "Winter is coming and will not wait. You know also, young Paul, that winter will not spare the unready."

I nodded and fetched water. We drank.

"Understand, Paul, we do this work. There's no one else and we share it equally." I looked at the barn with its open roof. It stood in a trampled clearing surrounded by moaning forest and it demanded work. It was useless as it was. I rose, and we assembled the timbers for the next purlin.

We were both so tired by the last one that I made a mistake and Uncle Franz had to grapple to keep the great trunk from falling into the barn. He held the beam in his cupped hands as he stood on an *H*-frame. I pushed a plank across the two lower purlins and he lowered the rogue beam on it.

We rested for some time as Uncle Franz walked amongst the fallen leaves. He blew hissing through clenched teeth and rubbing his stomach.

Finally, we raised the beam again and started it on its journey to the far wall. It wasn't difficult, but it had been so nearly a whole lift to do again.

The next four days' ration of my bricks was used to keep the purlins in place on the sidewalls.

At the top of the roof is the ridge. It doesn't bear much weight, unlike the purlins, so it's lighter and not difficult to fit, except it's higher.

Uncle Franz laid saplings across the purlins from the front and back walls up to the ridge as rafters and held them in place on the purlins with wooden pegs. Before that, he had to make the holes for the pegs with a homemade bradawl. Only when all this work had been completed could the new roof take shape.

I made, and Uncle Franz hoisted, layer upon layer of chestnut and willow thatch all cut to an arm's length. The thick end of each stick was gripped between two battens lashed together that lay across the roof and which he lashed to the rafters. The battens were about the length of two men and as soon as one pair was up Uncle Franz would call for the next with each laid a little higher so it all overlapped.

The work went on all day and into the evening. Finally, I realized we were coming to the end of this major work and Uncle Franz called out. "Paul, tonight, even though I know you haven't finished our wall, I want you to fire ridge tiles and not bricks."

Ridge tiles turned out to be really difficult because they crack very readily. They are a square about one arm's length in each direction but folded nearly in half so they make a ridge tent shape. The trick, as I learned, is not to make them too thick. In all, I made twenty-five. When they were ready, Uncle Franz crawled up to the pitch of the roof with a bucket of clay and a tile. It was my job to bring him more—without breaking them.

I spent all day fetching buckets of clay and tiles. But that night saw the barn roof finished completely.

I should add that curing the ridge tiles was made more difficult because the wind had gone around to the east, which made the fire smoke. I saw Albert look at his brother with his eyebrows raised and Franz nod, understanding the omen.

"Snow won't be long now. That's a cold wind," Franz remarked, looking at the sky.

But first came slashing rain that made it wet and cold in our hut.

When there was nothing else to do, there were always logs to cut. We burned a fire to cook by each night and also to cure the bricks. We were thankful for its warmth too.

Albert set traps for fish and game and he was successful. He understood the forest and its ways.

I was told to finish the plough with only one horse because Albert took the others to haul lumber and by then he was hauling from some distance.

By December 1805 mayhem reigned in the northern states. The old order was swept aside after the French victory at Austerlitz and they struck down every authority they didn't control. They took what they wanted: particularly food and fuel. So many people were displaced that the roads were crowded with refugees and highwaymen became fat.

Franz washed himself and dressed in the Englishman's clothes, even though they were too big, and rode the robbers' horse to town to barter and find a blacksmith. He sold the Englishman's rings and retuned laden with a huge two-man saw, precious iron nails and a host of other things, including salt and seed. He had bought more than he could carry at one time and had to return to collect the rest the next day. I saw the horse had a new shoe.

When the days became bright again, they were clear and cold. The sky had been washed empty of dust and the weak sun stood low, cowering behind the bare boughs.

The two-man saw accelerated both work and exhaustion. I still could only make six bricks a day but my uncles cut boards straight from trunks. The north wall of the barn was wooden, unlike the stone-built back and sides, and it had gaping holes in it. With the new planks we sealed it up tight in just a few days and we mended the doors so they closed firmly. We also repaired the front wall to our hut.

"Now the horses will be safe from wolves," announced Uncle Franz.

"Yes, and unless Paul finishes his wall, they'll only have boy to eat, not horse," said Uncle Albert, laughing.

"I can only make six bricks a day," I protested.

"Tell that to the wolves."

Though absolutely exhausted as usual that night, I finally went to sleep staring at the hole in the wall and expecting to see a pair of yellow eyes blink at me. At least it was bricked up to waist height now. Franz had supported the roof and begun work on it to stop the leaks and protect us against the coming winter.

I was bidden to squeeze clay into the gaps on the plank walls my uncles had built on the barn and the hut and I did a good but messy job. The result was a dry barn, protected from wind, rain and wolf. It was a safe barn—a winter-proof barn—and we'd done it.

I stood inside it and looked at the roof and walls with true satisfaction.

Although there were days when the holes in our roof looked bigger, its quality improved from the fireplace end of the hut. But Uncle Franz took my bricks to build the chimney higher. "You don't want to be smoked out, do you?" he asked.

I shook my head and watched three days' worth of precious bricks used up on the chimney top.

Uncle Franz laid overlapping planks across the rafters and nailed them into place. On top, he laid woodland thatch. Soon we were weatherproof, except at the end where the wall had fallen down.

At six bricks a day my wall grew and the gap became smaller. But the hole seemed to have a life of its own because it devoured every brick I made for much longer than I had expected. It would not close up. The last day was my triumph when I finally sealed it with two bricks left over and my uncles tied the repaired roof into the top course of bricks.

That night, for the first time, the warmth from the fire was held captive inside our hut and we slept deeply. When I woke once, I realized we snored loudly too!

My next job was to sow the winter wheat Uncle Franz had bought, along with a bigger shirt for me.

We had achieved the necessities for life and during the long evenings we had time to call our own. We turned our attention to the Englishman's property. We had his cases, his clothes, money, a coach and horses and his dictionary. We also had the robbers' supplies, which didn't add up to much. We didn't know how much money the Englishman's banknotes represented and we didn't know what his papers meant because we couldn't read. Instead of rummaging through these possessions, as we had done quickly at the beginning, we went through them again carefully.

His papers showed drawings of iron and brass locks and in his luggage were examples. Some of the locks were for keeping things closed so they could only be opened with a key. But some were for holding flints that would spark powder in the flash pan of a musket or cannon.

During the following days, Franz became agitated and distracted as he thought. Eventually, he told us of his conclusions, "When spring comes we can either leave here as we arrived—vagabonds and lawbreakers—or we can be different people. If only we can take the opportunity the Englishman's papers offer."

"Then we need someone to teach us to read," said Uncle Albert, musing.

"But we can't pay for lessons," I pointed out.

"No. I don't know what we can offer." Uncle Franz blew noisily though his teeth as he thought. He shook his head. "There's no point going to the village. I don't suppose there's anyone there who would teach us even if we could pay."

"And I wouldn't want to leave this place empty every day," said Albert.

The two brothers looked at each other. "No, Albert. I agree with you. That could cause us trouble," answered Franz.

"What about the road?" I asked.

"What do you mean, young Paul?" queried Albert.

"Perhaps a traveller might want to stop or something."

Again, my uncles looked at each other. "It's worth trying," suggested Albert.

And so it was agreed.

Each day, once the traps for fish and game had been set, two of us would pick our way through the forest back to the main road and watch from the gloom of the pines.

We learned early on not to approach large groups. They would become defensive and make ready to fend us off. After that there was no chance of dialogue. Small groups were also hostile because they retaliated against even the mildest approach. Single travellers offered the best chance. But there were few.

When Franz and I had been waiting for most of a cold, damp day and had taken to stamping on the grass and blowing through our hands to stop shivering, we watched an old man splash towards us and hailed him. He listened to us with his head hung low and his damp black cloak clinging to him. He stood in the cold mud for a long time before answering. "I would do anything for warmth and shelter," he finally replied. "I would do anything to spare myself further exposure to this accursed journey. In truth, I can read, but my eyes are now so poor that I can hardly do so and, if I stopped with you, I would never be able to discover what happened to my wife and two darling daughters." He looked up, his face streaked with dirt. "I have led a virtuous life, certainly compared to some, and now I am cast adrift with nothing and no one." He smiled slightly and lowered his head with its fog-wet hair. "Thank you for the temptation. I shall savour it, but I shall not succumb to it."

With that, he splashed through a puddle and continued his lonely way and, eventually, out of sight. Each day we watched and waited, even as winter deepened and the muddy road was used less. We spent many days watching our breath drift into the branches and stamping our feet on the sodden turf to keep the creeping cold at bay. We took our positions under the pines where the Englishman's coach had been attacked. At least the robbers weren't still there. We couldn't see where they'd been buried, though.

We built a small fire. It was better than nothing and feeding it was something to do. Towards the end of a soggy winter afternoon, we watched a well-organized party pass by. It had wagons and three men on horseback. The women and children watched us from the wagons, where they sat, well wrapped up and protected. We made no move towards them because their horsemen were armed. They stared at us as we stared at them.

We watched them continue slowly down the sticky track and out of sight. The groaning noise of their carts faded until we were left in the silence of the dripping pines.

I heard it first and stood stock-still with my mouth open to hear better. A woman and a girl, I thought. One voice was harsh and the other plaintive. "Uncle Franz, listen."

"I hear, Paul." He cupped his ear and frowned. "They're speaking Russian."

The voices came from the far side of the bend. There was no devil strip there and the trees came right to the edge of the track.

The plaintive voice came again, "I must rest. I must. I can't go on. I don't mind if I die. I want to lie down."

"We must catch up. It's dangerous. We cannot stop here and I mind if you die," the other voice answered urgently.

"No, no. Please. I must rest. No more. I can go no further."

A woman and a girl appeared from the trees struggling and staggering through the shallower mud at the verge. The woman held the child, about ten years old, by the arm. They were trailing the travellers, but hoping for protection from them by proximity, we supposed. We concluded they were no part of that group.

The woman saw us and stopped. She drew the child close and put her arm around her. They stood on the verge of the foul track in their grey dresses, lank and cold, like wraiths. I could see wisps of vapour rise from them to be lost against the pitiless grey sky. Either side of the track stood the dark forest.

She made to cross the road, but that meant wading through the water-filled ruts.

"You have nothing to fear from us," Uncle Franz spoke out loud and he spoke in Russian. "What do you want?"

She stopped and looked at us with interest. "The child is exhausted. We must catch up with the wagons."

"They're already well ahead of you."

"I can't go on," wailed the girl.

"How far?" asked the woman.

"Some time. They'll be lucky to make the village before nightfall."

"How far is the village?"

"Maybe three hours walking. At your speed, three hours."

They looked at each other and the child implored again, "No more. I must stop."

"We have shelter nearby." Uncle Franz tempted her.

"Please. I am so tired I could die." It was the girl. The woman looked seriously at Uncle Franz.

"We have a fire and food," he continued.

"Please," the girl whined.

The woman's eyes narrowed as we came closer. "And what else do you have? We cannot pay."

Uncle Franz stood still. "I told you—you have nothing to fear."

The woman raised her chin. "Give me cause to regret my decision and I will give you cause to regret your actions."

Uncle Franz asked, "Can you read?"

I watched her eyes as she summed up my uncle. Her hand was at her side, but even in the dull light, I saw the blade glint as she drew it from a fold in her skirt. The blade was slender as a needle. I raised the muzzle of my Brown Bess until it pointed at her stomach, with my hand on the lock.

Though she might have been able to stab at Franz and possibly me, she would not be able to strike given the musket. A Brown Bess fires an iron ball about the size of a small walnut. From that range the woman would have been virtually torn in half and thrown back some distance.

"She has a knife," I warned and watched Franz back away.

She slid the blade out of sight and I lowered the musket.

Those eyes of hers were everywhere, even as she moved her hands to comfort the child and draw her closer.

Franz waved a paper and asked again, "Can you read?"

She nodded, but when she saw the writing, she cried out, "But I don't know this! I think it's English."

But obviously she could read.

Franz turned to the girl and asked, "Can you walk a little further?"

She nodded shyly.

"Would you like me to carry you?"

As though suddenly struck dumb she merely shook her head. Uncle Franz offered her his hand, but she slunk behind the woman.

"What's your name?" he asked.

"Anna." She peered up at him.

"We don't know much German," Franz admitted to the woman. "Tonight you can eat and dry yourself, get warm and rest. Tomorrow we can talk. And if you want to, you can go on your way. Where is that, by the way?"

"We're going south," the woman replied.

She looked down the empty road. Only the sagging pines, dripping with moisture, and the black, sticky track met her gaze. No one had turned back for her. There was no lantern held aloft and no returning horseman. She lowered her head in sadness. Relenting, she declared, "Lead on." She took the girl by the hand and they turned to follow Franz.

"What's your name?" Franz turned to ask.

"Rosina," she answered simply.

"I'm Franz. I'll lead the way." He started off, speaking even as he walked. "My brother is at the hut. He's Albert and the boy here is Paul. We're looking for someone to teach us to read." He stopped, turned and said smiling, "We have a way to go and we must be home before dark."

We didn't know what was in her mind, but she was obviously ready to fight and as the walk home dragged on she became hostile, demanding to know how much further it was. I think she had begun to suspect that we were false and was about to break away, but she was already in a desperate situation. By then it was near dark and, even though there might not be a frost that night, it would be so cold that they would perish in the open. It was at that moment we all smelled the wood smoke from our chimney that carried a waft of welcoming stew in it.

"We're home," Franz announced smiling as we entered clearing. He opened the door and called out, "Albert we're home with our teacher!"

Once she was inside, Rosina felt the warmth, smelled the food and seemed to relax. It was a beginning. They sat beside the fire and ate. They felt comfort for the first time in a long time, I think. In the firelight they looked so tired and wet, to say nothing of being pale, thin and muddy.

Franz and Albert made a great deal of noise in the back of our hut moving things about—not that we had much to move—but what they did impressed Rosina. They created a room with a waxed canvas draped over a taught rope and moved a bed frame into it with straw for bedding and a huge feather quilt the Englishman had travelled with. Whatever the woman's expectations had been, they were still alive, warm and fed. Soon they would be dry too.

They ate like boys. We often had stew. Albert cooked it. "Slowly, slowly" was his motto and it always tasted good. I don't think the women savoured it much that night, even if it was mainly deer meat, my favourite. They gulped it down.

43

As they dried by the fire, they stretched their legs and that was when Albert saw their feet. Their shoes were worn completely through and the skin around their ankles was blue-black with dull-red weals and sores. Their feet were black with mud.

You must understand the mud on the roads was foul and any cut to a foot would likely fester and possibly ulcerate and that could easily lead to suppuration, fever and even death.

"I'll take off your shoes," offered Albert, "and attend to your feet."

"We'll do it in the morning."

"No, now's the time. When you're cold it's one thing, but when you're warmer, it's quite another."

They relented. But the little girl squealed with pain as the remnants of her shoes were taken from her tiny feet. They were black underneath.

"Fetch vinegar and hot water," Albert ordered me. I hurried to the stream with the kettle and returned with it full and the vinegar flask, which we had found in the shed, to see the two men bent over four very small and dirty feet. It was almost Biblical. I hooked the kettle over the iron and pushed it hissing over the flames.

We didn't have fine cloth as we do today. The softest material we possessed was hay and it was hay that Albert dipped into the bowl of warm water and vinegar. Gently he wiped at their feet as he examined their cuts and bruises. He was a countryman and he treated them as he would an injured animal. When he'd finished, most of the dirt had been removed and the women sat by the fire with their feet immersed in bowls of the warm mixture.

"We must find new shoes." Albert held up the tatters of their old ones. Once they had been fine, but now they were just shreds of leather and hardly recognizable for what they had been.

"I'll go tomorrow to see what's available. Maybe the French don't have the same appetite for women's shoes as they do for everything else," offered Franz.

He became pensive and left for the shed returning with a night pail. "They'll not want to go outside without shoes."

The little girl was asleep when Albert lifted her feet from the vinegar and dried them. He appeared satisfied. He took her up in his arms and carried her behind the screen. Rosina dried her own feet and rose, smiling slightly. But she winced with pain as she stood. She hobbled off after the girl to sleep. The worst had not come to pass for them that night, nor would it the next day, when we were busy outside and in the forest. They could explore their surroundings and make good their escape if they wanted to, but I admit that without shoes, it would have been difficult. That evening, when we came home, they were still there.

Uncle Franz returned from the village with the news the shoes could not be repaired and it was a skilled job to measure for new ones. All he could do was to buy rough clogs. The cobbler said he would call by one day. The women were grateful for the clogs, a little bit.

"You're Russian," Rosina challenged us, "Russian peasants." She spoke in Russian, but it was unlike any Russian we'd heard.

Albert nodded. "We're farmers."

"We were farmers," corrected Franz.

"That's true," agreed Albert. "There was famine following famine. If we had stayed, we'd have starved. The barns held nothing. The

45

fields yielded nothing. There was nothing to put away for winter. Before it was too late and the snow set in, we left."

"Because it was such a terrible decision we tarried too long. Some of us didn't agree to go. Mostly it was the old ones who wouldn't leave." Uncle Franz shook his head as if he was trying to rid himself of the memory.

There was a long silence. Uncle Albert had tears in his eyes. I'd never heard this part of our story before and I'd never seen Uncle Franz take his brother in his arms. Albert sobbed.

They parted. "I'm sorry." Albert wiped his eyes. "Our parents stayed behind. You see, it wasn't until we'd been on the road for some days we discovered they'd put the food we left for them back onto our wagon."

Franz was crying openly now and he hugged his brother.

"They starved themselves for you?" asked Rosina.

"Oh, yes. Oh, dear God, yes!" Albert choked and wiped his face with the back of his hand. "Or they froze to death when winter came."

In the silence no one even Anna, who was always active, moved.

Rosina hugged the two men and then looked at me. She didn't hug me, although I had tears on my face. I could remember my parents, but I could not remember my grandparents.

"When was this?" she asked.

"Years ago. We've been walking for years," Franz answered.

"We seek to better ourselves, or one day, we'll die like the others," added Albert.

"One day, you'll die like the others anyway." Rosina scratched her head. "You just don't want to die like rats in this forest."

"There're only the three of us left." Franz's eyes stared blankly at the flames leaping in the hearth. "The boy doesn't even know what a home is. His parents were killed by bandits. Now we've an opportunity." He turned to face Rosina, "But we can't take it because we can't read. We want to become artisans and make locks to sell to the gentry."

Rosina shook her head. "You'll need to learn more than how to read. You'll need to speak German properly if that's what you want to do. You must also learn manners, courtesy, bookkeeping and many things besides if you want to sell to the gentry."

"We must learn so that we can prosper," Albert confirmed.

"Then you must be careful because you speak bad German and that's worse than speaking none. You'd be better off to speak in French." She thought, holding her hands to the fire, as the winter wind hissed under the door. "When did you come here? I mean, do you live here?"

"No," I answered trying to take part in the conversation. "We only arrived here two months ago, maybe a little longer."

"We'll stay here for the winter," Franz added.

"Then where?"

Albert opened his arms and shrugged. "West."

"Why not go now?" she asked.

Albert shook his head. "No, this is no time to travel. It will snow soon and then no one travels. People perish in the snow and it's already late. We must wait until spring now. There won't even be coaches and we couldn't afford a place anyway."

Rosina thought for some time and then smiled. "We come from Moscow and I lived near the Kremlin." Even in her worn-out clothes she had a presence: a quality about her and she made the most of her hauteur.

"I'll teach you what I know." She counted off on her fingers as she spoke: "Russian and French, both reading and writing—some German as well, but not the language you speak. You speak the language of the farmyard. I speak the language of the Court." We changed between German and Russian as we spoke. But Rosina corrected us in both languages.

"Are you a member of the Court?" I asked, wide-eyed.

Rosina smiled. It was very attractive. "Should I say, 'Yes, of course,' or should I be truthful? My father is a secretary to a member of the Court. I will not tell you his name, because I am bound not to, but he is a close advisor to the Tsar. I've seen the Tsar. I did not speak with him or him to me, but I've seen him. We lived in part of a great palace and we had a position so elevated that there were servants who waited on us."

As you can imagine, we were agape at these revelations.

"Our patron often had meetings with the Tsar and many foreign dignitaries used to come to our palace. My father frequently took messages to the Kremlin and sometimes he would let me go with him as a special treat. Occasionally, the children were asked to sing for the dignitaries and so we saw how they dressed and behaved. If they spoke to us, we had to answer with proper respect and so we were taught manners."

We knew nothing of the Court or its language, so we didn't know whether to believe her or not. It seemed sensible to believe her and so we accepted her.

"And why are you here and where are you going, Rosina?" Franz asked when she had finished her story.

The questions seemed to annoy her and there was a flash of exasperation on her countenance.

"I was told to accompany my uncle on a journey as a companion for Anna. Our journey must take us south, but not yet. It seems we are to be trapped by winter."

"You're free to go whenever you want to go." Albert was absolutely sincere. There could be no doubting him. "But it's too late in the year to travel. As I said, we've been lucky. It hasn't snowed yet. It's overdue."

"Yes. When it comes, it'll be heavy," Franz elaborated, "because it's so late."

"Then it's not a sensible time to be on the road," she conceded.

"No. Every sensible person will have come to the same conclusion. It's just too dangerous," Franz added.

"Bandits?"

"Well, yes. But the cold itself will kill, along with the lack of food and shelter." He shrugged to emphasize his point. "No. Travel now is impossible except for the desperate or the rich. But I agree with Albert. You're not prisoners. We'll give you board and lodging in exchange for lessons. When you want to go, go in peace. But not before winter has run her course."

Rosina nodded and scratched her head again. Whatever was in her mind, she kept it there and the conversation turned to general topics.

Every day we prepared for winter. Albert worried because there were adequate supplies of fodder and fuel wood. We couldn't understand why the huts had been abandoned.

It was me who answered the question when I found two graves in the forest. Were these the people who had lived in the huts? We could think of no other explanation. What had they died of? Starvation? Probably not: disease or attack seemed to be the only alternatives and the only way to answer the question was to ask the dead.

My uncles knew enough about gathering food to support life and Rosina knew enough for us to learn.

Chapter Two: The Very Finest English Duplicity

The Englishman's papers proved something of a challenge. But he had a lexicon that gave the German meanings of the technical words which helped. Rosina found a use for his coat by wrapping herself up in it as she taught us. At night she used it as an extra blanket on the bed she shared with Anna.

We learned, as the roads turned from churned mud to frozen furrows and then to silent white ribbons, in the starched-winter forest. The snow came late. And when it came, lots of it came and it stayed for a very long time.

But as winter deepened, both Rosina and Anna became ill. They were exhausted. For months, or possibly years, they had lived on the charity of others who would have had little enough to share. They had become so weakened by continual hunger that they had come close to their deaths. Possibly, the portions we cooked were too big, or our food was not to their taste. Or possibly they had come with disease already in their bodies. We were sorely afraid the sickness that killed the people who lived in the huts before us might have returned.

We cared for them, more accurately, we cared and I learned. The men knew about women from the experience of their wives, long since dead. I was a fifteen-year-old boy and I didn't know. You can't keep the secrets of your being from someone washing you with warm vinegar water and changing your bed straw while you remain in it. They were delirious for some days and cold sweat soaked them. Albert carried them close to the fire and wrapped them in the quilt. I was instructed never to let the flames die down.

Uncle Franz had ridden into town to speak with the apothecary only to return with a tub of honey and a despondent air. We mixed the honey into hot water for them and gave them gruel from our stew. Later, they took bread when we had it. They recovered slowly. After that Rosina insisted on doing her own laundry.

"I'm sorry if I've done it wrong," I said to her.

"It's not that. You wouldn't understand."

"Well I won't, if you don't tell me."

Rosina changed the subject by holding the hem of her dress to my eyes. "There was something in here. Where is it?"

"Yes," I replied. "There were some brown stones. They were tearing the dress, so I took them out."

"Where are they?" Rosina spoke quietly, but her eyes were fierce.

Everything I did was criticized, so I replied, "Who knows? They were only weight."

"No, they weren't."

"You want them back?"

"Don't play games with me."

"Then don't play them with me, Rosina."

She drew a deep breath and let it hiss out between her teeth. "Paul, do you know where the stones are?"

I nodded.

"Then can I have them back, please?"

"They are hidden—"

I was about to say where when she burst out furiously: "Paul! Tell me where the stones are!" She moved towards the cupboard where their possessions were and I remembered the blade.

"They're behind the box beside the fire."

Rosina didn't say a word, but went to the fire. She returned with four dirty crystals.

"There were five," she stated bleakly.

"Then there are five there. If there were four, there are four there. I have not stolen from you."

I remembered hearing something clatter against the wooden chest when I took the dress away to wash. I'd removed the crystals because they'd made a hole in the cloth and I reasoned that one might have fallen out. Rosina walked away muttering like a witch and slumped down on her bed facing away from me. I entered their room without asking.

Rosina did not look around.

I knelt on the floor to search under the box and stretched my arm into the space until it was nearly stuck and felt about. I touched the missing crystal.

"Here. I told you there was a hole in the dress."

Rosina turned and I saw she'd been crying. She held out her hands and I dropped the last piece into them. She closed her hands tightly and began to cry again.

I've done many difficult things in my life, but getting Rosina to explain what she means remains the hardest.

Later, she came out and was all friendly, but she never spoke about the crystals. When we were not working, we played games and mimicked each other. She strode about teaching me how to walk and how not to. I found it quite hard to change the way I walked and sometimes I teased her by walking like her. Rosina took her revenge and slipped her other dress over my head. She laughed at my bright-red face.

"Now try to walk like me," she suggested.

It wasn't so easy, but I tried and we laughed. Our games stopped when Anna saw us from the door. "He's prettier than you, Rosina," she said.

The next day I went hunting with the men and in the evening we resumed our studies. The women recovered their health fully, but it took a long time—as did winter.

We explored our surroundings. We were in a state called Thuringia near the town of Sömmerda. At this time, in early 1806, many changes had taken place. The French despised us and levied huge taxes against everyone who lost against them in battle. After the taxes they stole. The French contempt for us was only matched by their fear and hatred of the English.

The French armies took everything they wanted and we were unable to protest. Prices rose and there were shortages. My uncles didn't think that, even with the Englishman's money, we could buy a farm the size of the one we had abandoned all those years before. Also, there was the problem of finding someone who would accept English banknotes. But as some opportunities were denied, others became apparent. We became ground rabbits. That is to say, we worked for a craftsman in Sömmerda making parts for his products. The first money we earned was spent on new shoes for the women and having our boots replaced.

The guilds controlling the production of artefacts were breaking down as industrialization spread. We couldn't suppress our happiness when we heard of a local locksmith, von Dreyse, who had lock parts that required finishing work. We became regular visitors to his workshop delivering completed components and hoping for more. With the Englishman's pictures we could see the differences between von Dreyse's work and that of the Englishman, whose name had been Winchester, we thought.

We became friends with the locksmith's son, Nicolaus. He was fascinated by our muskets and always wanted to come shooting with us. He questioned us about everything to do with hunting and it wasn't long before he could set up a musket like an expert.

As the days became warmer and the forest a wonderland of blooms and scents, Rosina and Franz took to walking into town together. The track, that in winter was a stinking muddy trap, now stretched out like a green carpet covered in woodland flowers that basked in dappled light. Butterflies would dart in and out of the flickering sunlight that penetrated the forest. In the evening, Rosina often regaled us with tales of seeing fawn close to the track or of piglets jumping as they met each other. It was almost like dancing, she said.

The priest had agreed to improve Rosina's German comprehension and to teach her the English he knew in exchange for her instructing him in the French language. She was a ready student: particularly in the matter of accents and idioms acceptable to the educated classes and those that were not. Until Rosina met with the priest, we had no idea of English pronunciation and we had great difficulty with it. It sounded very peculiar.

I heard their voices as they returned from Sömmerda and came out of the barn to greet them.

"Look at me." Rosina stood in front of the hut. She stood with her arms slightly apart from her body. She spoke to Franz, not me. "Not like that," she said, giggling.

"You're a fine-looking woman, Rosina."

"And you're a fine man, Franz. But you make my proposition for me. We cannot travel alone on these roads. Two women by themselves! It's not to be thought of."

"So you'll stay?" I asked hopefully, stepping forward.

"Paul, Anna and I have our own lives and our own goals. We must go our own way. The point I'm making is that we cannot travel alone. The priest says that there are no travellers going south, which is the direction we want to go."

"But why do you want to go there?"

"That's their business, not ours," Uncle Franz answered.

"Yes, of course. I beg your pardon," I said.

"You've certainly learned manners," Franz observed.

"Then may I ask why no one is travelling south?"

Rosina answered me. "The priest says there are many travellers coming from there. They all speak of lawlessness and upheaval. A large force of French soldiers has assembled there, so it's a place to avoid. No one is travelling to the east, either. They only go north or west." Rosina smiled at me. "To answer your question, Paul, yes, we will stay a little longer. We'll stay until we find a group we can travel with."

"I hope you never do."

"That's very selfish of you, Paul."

"Must I beg your pardon again?"

Rosina smiled at me. "No, I don't think so."

There was an awkward silence. Franz started a new topic. "We were followed today. He was not a robber. He never came close and we weren't attacked. It was almost as though he didn't want us to see him."

There was nothing much we could do, but we became more alert.

The year wore on and still there were no travellers going south. If there were, they would not accept the responsibility of two women alone. By that time, we were able to read and write quite well and that ability separated us from the country folk who couldn't. There were many published tracts—old, it's true—but through them we learned of our surroundings and of the revolution in France and the terrible executions. We learned about the English Industrial Revolution and the war the French made on us. We read about the rebellion in America and the new country the colonists had founded there. It was a long way away, but it sounded exciting and brave.

But here, in the German-speaking states, the French had swept all before them. The Prussian armies, so feared by everyone in the 1750s, had been destroyed. Everywhere the French ruled. They defeated us and they dictated to us. The northern states tried to be big, like fish in a shoal, but fish can dart about. States sit still like apples and the French ate us all, one by one.

In the following months, as summer wore on, most of our work was on musket locks and we visited von Dreyse frequently. Franz worried because he saw the man who had followed him many times. Each time it was as if he'd been waiting. Franz noticed he had been joined by others and they seemed to be working together. They watched my uncle and followed him a little way. But they did nothing. They never said anything and never approached.

We had planned to stay in the forest for the whole of that year. For the women it was a time to rest and recover, although Rosina fretted at her inability to continue her mysterious journey south. For us it was a time to learn and work and to accumulate some money. We intended to become locksmiths in our own right and to move west where there was greater prosperity and so there would be a demand for locks.

On a late summer's day—a beautiful day, a day when you know there is a God and all the sounds in the forest are of contentment—I walked from behind the barn to see Rosina and Anna together. Rosina's hair shone as though a wave of night had escaped. She stood behind Anna, brushing her chestnut hair in turn. It glowed with heat in its colour.

"Am I allowed to watch?" I asked.

"Certainly not." It was Anna who turned to me and I realized just how blue her eyes were. I think they must have been watering because they sparkled, but it might have been that she was looking into the sun.

"Will you brush mine?" I asked Rosina.

"Certainly not."

"Unfair," I replied. Anna moved her head against Rosina's brushing and made the movements of a woman, not a girl. With a level of surprise, that almost had a physical impact, I saw Anna as someone other than the child she'd always been. I needed time to adjust my mind, so I mumbled, "Unfair," again and strolled off.

A man rode by on a smart horse. He was in no hurry. The horse walked calmly and he rode casually. By that time, I was standing next to Uncle Franz at the saw pit. He watched the man intently. The rider studied everything, but he didn't stare. It was obvious to me that he was looking at everything, but he didn't appear to be doing so. After he'd passed us, he just rode on. He didn't hurry and he didn't look back.

I helped my uncle collect sawdust and shavings for smoking meat.

"That's the man who follows us in Sömmerda." Uncle Franz was pensive. "We must take care now."

About a week later, when we'd gathered to eat in the evening, there was a sudden beating on the door. Three men stood there. One was the man on the horse. The other two were well-dressed gentlemen. I had never seen such elegance and finery so close. They were clean and smelled sweet, not of horses and work, like us. They didn't introduce themselves but smiled politely.

One of the gentlemen asked, "What's your name?"

"Rosina, sir."

"And the little girl?"

"Anna, sir."

"I'm not little. I'm fourteen," protested Anna indignantly.

The man smiled. "Anna, do you have a cloak?"

"No, sir."

"For a cloak, you need cloth. Isn't that so?"

"Yes, sir."

"And you, Rosina, do you have a cloak?"

Rosina shook her head. "But we have shawls, sir."

"Put them on. I'll not keep you outside for longer than necessary." He turned to the man who had ridden the horse, and said, "Martin, help us, please."

He led the way outside. "Anna, show Martin where you keep the firewood. We'll need a great deal tonight because we shall prepare a feast, but don't stray far. There's little moon. Rosina, will you help me bring supplies from the horses?"

The gentleman who remained in the cabin looked at the three of us. "Have no fear. We're not French, but we have questions for you and I hope you'll answer honestly." He spoke in German, but it was not his usual tongue. Of that I was certain.

"Naturally, eminence," confirmed Albert.

The man smiled a particular, little smile. "What happened to the Englishman?"

"What Englishman?"

The gentleman snorted. "You said you would answer me honestly! The Englishman whose coat you wear when you go into town." He indicated Franz with his elegant, clean hand. "If there were ever a clear signal that you wanted to contact another Englishman, it would be to wear an English coat. So I ask again and remind you that you've claimed you would answer me honestly. I take it that the Englishman is dead and that you killed him."

All three of us denied the accusation. The man held up his hand and smiled. "I didn't really think so. Now tell me the truth."

So we told him the truth, but we ran out of words when it came to the coach and horses.

"So you sold his coach?" he asked.

We denied it.

He looked relieved and rose. "Show me." I led him out into the darkness and to the barn at the same moment Rosina and the others returned. I carried a lantern. The coach stood there just as we had left it: covered in mud—and blood, too, if you knew where to look.

"Hold the lantern higher," he commanded. The man opened the door and pulled back the panel below the seat.

Of course we'd looked there. Everyone knows about that hiding place in a coach.

"Shine the light here."

I held the lantern so the light flickered into the dark space. The panel at the back was also false. There was a secret room inside a secret room. The man pushed and pulled for a while and the board came away. He reached inside and pulled out a large leather bag. It was the sort a dispatch rider might carry. He opened it and looked at the papers inside. I couldn't see what they were, but the man looked relieved and happy. He put them back in the pouch and tucked it under his arm.

"Tell me, Paul. The two men—do they love France?"

61

"No, sir. They invaded us and they robbed us. We're from the east, sir, and we seek to better ourselves. But it's difficult when the French take what they please."

"Did you know the English King, George III, speaks German as we are doing, even now?"

"No, sir."

"And that he comes from Hannover and his wife from Mecklenburg-Strelitz? The heir to the British throne has married Princess Caroline of Brunswick-Wolfenbüttel and his brother, the Duke of York, has married princess Frederica of Prussia. So you see, England and the peoples who speak German are very close friends."

I nodded, not really understanding, as we walked back to our hut. He took the other gentleman away from the fire and spoke quietly with him. They came back to the fireside and the Englishman asked us all to step away for a moment. They spoke quietly together, but we could hear. I listened intently because it was the first time I'd heard English spoken naturally and I wanted to learn.

The man who had come with me to the coach took a paper from the pouch and, having read it, passed it to the other gentleman. He also read it.

"Robert, I cannot tell you how I am relieved to hold this document. For over a year, I have fretted myself to sleep for conjecture of where it was and who might peruse it."

"Graeme, read it and consign it to the flames."

The man called Graeme did as he was bidden.

The first man, Robert, stared into the fire. "My heart leaps with relief even as the flames rise."

"Robert, do you consider that the letters have remained undetected?"

The first man, who had come with me to the coach smiled, then ran his fingers delicately across his mouth. "We know how the French have been searching for poor Anstruther. And we know why. However, I now conclude they did not succeed in finding him." He smiled again, this time broadly. "And I further conclude their sticky hands and prying eyes have not been over these letters." With that he handed another letter to Graeme, for that was the name of the second man, who read it and let it flutter into the flames. This went on for some time.

"Robert, we should learn from this. Anstruther was carrying far too much information and it would have been catastrophic had it fallen into French hands." He fed another letter to the fire and repeated, "Catastrophic!"

At last the pouch was empty. Robert stared into the inferno as he spoke watching it consume all those secrets. Naturally, we had no idea what they were. "We have tonight prevented a great disaster befalling English policy. It has taken a year to achieve and we must take greater precaution in future. But now I am considering another matter."

"What, Robert?"

Robert looked at the other gentleman before turning his gaze back to the flames. The light flickered and the shadows danced transforming his face from benign to satanic. "I think we should oblige those people with sticky hands and prying eyes. Because if we do not, they will go unsatisfied and they are searching so hard for evidence of Anstruther and his message bag."

Graeme smiled and licked his lips. "What are you up to?"

Robert leaned back and laughed dispelling the chill that had settled on me. "I think we should place a letter in the pouch and ensure the French find it."

"Where do you have in mind?"

"In Anstruther's coach, of course."

"But the French never found it."

"No, and out here they never will." Robert's eyes narrowed. "But consider this: what if our friends, in whose home we now stand, decided to sell the coach to the French?"

"Then they would find it."

"They certainly would the moment they discovered it was an English coach."

The two men stood looking at each other for a while. They were smiling slightly and as they considered, their smiles grew. Eventually it was Robert who spoke, "Graeme, I need time to think. I don't require your further presence here. Why don't you return to the inn?"

"You're not going to sleep here, are you, Robert?"

"Not unless it becomes necessary. I must distil my plan. I will join you at the inn as soon as I can and we can start for the coast. Possibly tomorrow."

"What'll you do?"

"With luck, I shall not be far behind you tonight. With James Fox dead and Yarmouth recalled, there'll be changes in London and I should be shaping them."

"Do you think that news was correct?"

Robert snorted and turned to face the fire again. "When travelling, one is always at the mercy of rumour and falsehood, but I think what they said at the attorney's office was true."

"Let's hope so. The government of all talents and master of none was hopeless."

"Fox was an admirer of Napoleon—did you know that?"

"It's quite extraordinary how it occurs that the French are able to influence the decision-forming forums of the English government for their benefit and advantage. Where exactly does their influence derive?"

"Perhaps Talleyrand can answer you, Graeme."

"What do you propose?"

"I shall fulfil my destiny."

"Robert, if you're speaking about the ghost in the Blue Room, please remember the prediction that your brilliant career would be followed by a violent death. I beg of you not to tempt fate or believe in the sayings of ghosts."

Robert smiled at his friend but said nothing.

Graeme continued, "What do you propose to do?"

"I shall write a letter."

"A letter the French will find?"

"Oh, yes."

With that, both Martin and Graeme left. Only Robert remained. He stood stirring the fire with his boot and staring into the flames, but possibly making sure that every scrap of paper had burned entirely.

He smiled at Rosina. "Please help yourselves to the food. It's for you all, but if I may, I would like to be private for a while. When I have completed my business, I shall eat with you and pass a little time here if you permit. By the by, my name is Robert Stewart."

Naturally, Franz and his brother agreed with Rosina.

The Englishman dallied beside the fire. It seemed to me that he was making his mind up about something until I realized it was about us that he was making up his mind. All the time he continued general conversation, but I was convinced he was following a plan.

He went into the women's room to be private. It was a room only because the canvas screen separated it. I must admit there was a particular place where you could sit by the fire and see something of what happened in the room the women used and, from time to time, I had been known to sit there. That night I sat and watched and was fascinated. But I gave my secret away to Rosina. She saw that I could look into her room from where I sat. She said nothing, but she looked at me in just such a way, with one eyebrow raised. I blushed terribly. My red face made her smile.

From his saddlebag, the Englishman withdrew an elaborate leather pouch, containing a small wooden box like a tabletop. He opened it and inside lay paper, pens and inks of different colours. The papers were of several types. He selected two similar sheets having held several up to the poor light. He laid one out, and with a cylindrical ruler, drew a margin very carefully down the left and right sides. He wrote his letter between the margins. He changed both pen and ink to make notes in the margin to the right and then again, with a different pen and ink, made marks on the text and notes in the margin on the left.

Eventually he was satisfied and I watched him search through some papers to find a signature. Robert Stewart studied it very carefully and copied it. He folded the letter so the end of the paper was in the middle of the blank side.

I was amazed. He tore a piece out of a perfectly good handkerchief, spat on it, and stuck it over the middle of the join. He rose and came to the fireside where he held the letter to the flames, turning it many times exposing different faces to the heat. The letter became dull and wrinkled. He peeled off the cloth and where it had been, the paper remained white. He poured hot sealing wax onto this area and fixed it with an elaborate seal from his desk. When it had cooled, he wrote an address on the front and left it to dry. He rejoined us and I only just had enough time to pretend to be feeding the fire. But I couldn't look at Rosina.

He had that little smile about his mouth as he glanced in my direction. It was as though he knew. We ate well that night—such a feast—and we had wine. Eventually he said to Franz, "I want you to sell the Englishman's coach to the French. Can you do that?"

"But they won't pay."

"If they don't, I'll pay what they owe. But you must go to Hannover for the money. I'll give you an address there. All you need do is tell them that Mr. Brown of the Board of Control said they would reimburse you for the cost of a coach. You must tell the man you meet your name is Brandt."

I should inform you now that this was the moment we came by our family name. We'd never had a name before. It may sound odd to you, but we were only known by the area we came from.

"We intend to travel west, sir, so your requirement is not a burden."

Albert agreed. But I knew the Englishman was drawing us on.

"What do we say if the French ask why we're selling the coach?"

Mr. Robert Stewart or Mr. Brown, or whoever he was, looked at me with that little smile. "You tell the truth of course. You want to head west and a coach is not suitable for your needs. You need a wagon for your belongings."

We looked at each other and I asked, "And if the French ask us how we came by the coach?"

"You tell the truth of course."

"And if the French ask about you?"

He looked at me solemnly for a moment.

"You tell the truth of course. You have neither seen nor heard of me and nobody ever came here." His look now was calm, but serious. There was no little smile playing around his lips, but then it came back. I understood. We all understood.

The Englishman took a lantern and the pouch with his letter already inside and stepped into the scuttling night. I followed, ostensibly to stable his horse. But, first I ran around the back of the barn where we had buried the Englishman and stood on the mound of his grave. From there I could peer inside through the gaps in the planks. In the lantern glow, I saw the Englishman replace the saddlebag behind its secret panel. Then he did something quite extraordinary. He took a gold coin and placed it alongside. He closed the panels so the secret within a secret was as it had been. Only the letter in the bag was different and now there was a gold coin in there.

Mr. Stewart, for I think that was really his name, snoozed in the chair beside the fire and in the morning, rose early to leave. After I had brought his horse and saddled it, he took my chin in his hand quite gently. "Paul, I have a nephew about your age in Ireland. You remind me of him wonderfully. I know what boys are so I'll tell you this. Don't interfere with my plans for your own. If you follow me carefully and thoughtfully, you will prosper."

"I don't understand you, sir," I answered.

"Don't steal the gold coin."

I swallowed. He and Rosina knew all my secrets. I blushed again. The Englishman smiled.

"Take care and always think." He let me go, handing me the address in Hannover and a silver piece. "I'll answer your thoughts and give you information that'll make you take very great care, young Paul Brandt."

There was no smile, but a serious, sardonic look came over his face. He placed his gloved hand gently but firmly on my shoulder. "The letter in the saddlebag confirms English government support for the Tsar of Russia's planned army of one million men to fight against Bonaparte. It asks how many cannon and muskets will be required initially. It also asks some questions about how such an army might be supplied and fed and how the Royal Navy might help solve these questions. Such an army would be ten times the size of Bonaparte's. If you told anyone this information your life would be in great danger. It represents a terrible threat to the French."

I asked, "But are you Mr. Brown or Mr. Stewart?"

That little smile came again and he answered me, "For the purpose of the address in Hannover, I am Mr. Brown. But do not make any assumptions should we meet again, Paul Brandt."

I knelt on one knee so he could use the other as a mounting block. He was in his saddle before I realized what he'd done. "But you have to tell the French."

He patted his horse's neck. "That's your task. Sell the coach. You need the money for a cart."

After Mr. Stewart had taken his leave, Franz walked into Sömmerda to return lock parts and hopefully to collect more. We were happy. The Englishman had left many things behind in the way of food and even some delicacies. He had also left a bolt of cloth: what luxury! There was enough for both the women to make cloaks. We also had Anstruther's coat, if we could ever get it back from Rosina and also his coachman's cloak. Now we knew his name had been Anstruther and not Winchester.

Franz returned that night with more lock parts and the news he had tried to sell the Englishman's coach to some French officers. They had not agreed to buy it, but they would possibly come to see it, so he had told them where we lived.

Two days later, when I was with the women alone and carrying wood to stack by the hut, six Frenchmen arrived on horseback. An officer and a man in elegant black civilian clothes rode in front of an escort of four cavalrymen. The sunlight flickered and flashed on their brass armour. The officer scoffed when I asked if he'd come to buy the coach. The civilian looked at him disapprovingly.

"Is this the right place?" the civilian asked looking around in distaste. "We would see the coach before we agree to buy."

They dismounted while I stacked the wood. One soldier held the horses while the others followed me to the barn. I hoped the women would stay out of sight.

"Ah, yes. An English coach to be sure. There can be no doubt. We'll examine it before we agree to a price." The officer then said something in French that I didn't understand.

One of the soldiers grabbed me and pushed me out of the barn. "Leave them to their work. We require hot food."

There was no refusing any French demand, so I took him to the hut to give him our supper. Once inside he looked around for things to steal and found the women in their hiding place. He dragged them out and started to wrestle with Rosina tearing at her clothes. Anna and I rushed to defend her, but he drew a knife and held it under Rosina's chin. "Go to the other room and keep quiet, or I'll cut her."

We did as we were told. We kept our Brown Bess muskets in the other room. Franz and Albert were hunting with two, but the others were there. Our muskets were old, but von Dreyse's son Nicolaus was already an expert at setting up weapons and they were in good order. Anna and I loaded all three. A terrible moan came from behind the curtain. It was followed by the noise of something falling. We rushed back.

When Rosina was ill, I'd seen her without clothes because we'd washed her and changed her bedding. But today was different. Her dress was torn open, it was true, but she wore a look of such fury I'd never seen before. She held her needle-thin dagger in a bloody hand: on the floor lay the Frenchman. But I couldn't see a wound on his body.

Rosina and I looked at each other, eye to eye, as she pulled her clothing around her. "The other soldiers?" she asked.

I nodded and took two loaded muskets outside to lean against the back of the hut. Collecting the third, I made my way to the barn. I saw the cavalryman walking their horses on the far side of the track. He was talking to them quietly as I might. He ignored me. He had names for them and he stroked their noses speaking all the time like a father to sleepy children. He paid me no heed. His world was horses. By itself, it was a peaceful forest scene: a soldier caring for horses on a bright day. All was calm— even the wind murmured, hardly bothering to disturb the branches. But as I walked, I heard noise.

An incredible sight met my eyes in the barn. They were reducing the last bits of the coach to splinters. There was nothing left. Even the wheels had been destroyed. The soldiers had farriers' axes and they had chopped it to bits.

"What have you done? You must pay," I shouted, rushing in.

"We do not wish to pay. We find your coach is rather broken." The officer waved his hand dismissively.

"But it's you who broke it."

"I think it was like this when we arrived."

"You must pay. We must have money to buy a wagon."

"You'll have to sell something else." The officer turned to the civilian and asked, "Do you have what you came for, Gaston?"

Gaston, the civilian, looked pensively at me. I saw him turn a gold piece in his fingers and I also saw the pouch tied to his pommel.

"I must ride to the Emperor immediately." He called to me, "You, boy! When did you find the coach?"

"A year ago, at the beginning of last winter. But you must pay."

The officer said something to one of the soldiers who put down his axe and approached me. I ran out of the barn and back towards our hut. Two cavalrymen followed and called to the man walking the horses. I watched them mount.

"Where's the other man?" the officer demanded as he stood at the barn door.

"In the hut."

The officer called out in French to the mounted soldiers who sidled their horses towards me. They padded the hard ground, turned, and took positions apart from each other. Suddenly both reared and the soldiers drew cutlasses. They charged at me from only a few yards.

I shot one. I took a musket from behind the hut and shot the other. I was trembling at what I'd done, but I'd been well taught. As the echo rattled back from the pines, I breathed in a waft of gun smoke that hurt my throat. Even as the second cavalryman toppled from his saddle, I tapped the butt twice and poured a new charge. I tapped the musket again and spat in a ball. I was about to ram it when the officer's horse reared up and the rider drew his sword. I took the last Brown Bess from behind the wall and shot him in the chest. I rammed the ball home in the musket I had been loading and primed the pan.

73

There was only the civilian and the soldier who'd been walking the horses left. The civilian ran to his horse and mounted as I cocked the lock.

"Don't leave, sir, or I'll shoot your horse." I tried to make my boy's voice threatening.

He took his chance and spurred the animal. So I shot it. It was a clean shot and the beast just dropped, trapping the rider by his leg.

I reloaded all three weapons. The civilian could hear me, but he couldn't see me. I walked around the back of the dead horse carrying a musket. "Is your leg broken?"

"I don't know. Get me out."

"Why? You'll only try to shoot me or run away without paying for the coach."

"I agree we should've paid for the coach."

"And you should not have attacked me."

"No, obviously."

"Are you going to attack me now?" I asked.

"No, of course not. I'm not a soldier."

"But you have a pistol."

"It's in my saddlebag."

I walked around him to see both his hands and reasoned he wouldn't try to hurt me until he was free and on another horse. The remaining soldier had gathered the horses and was trying to calm them. He had no interest in anything except horses. Killing the civilian's mount would make me his enemy forever. I told him to collect rope from the barn while I loosened the girth of the dead beast's saddle. We tied the rope around its hooves and used the other horses to drag the carcass from the civilian.

"Can you get up, Monsieur Gaston?" I asked.

"My name is Dumarque, peasant. You will address me as 'Sir' and certainly never use my given name." The man kicked himself free of his saddle and struggled to stand. He brushed his hand over his clothes angrily.

"Leave the saddle and the bags. Stand away," I demanded.

He looked askance, but obeyed.

"Will you pay me for the coach, or will I shoot you and sell another horse?"

"I have but little money."

"You're a liar. I saw you with a gold coin."

"I found that in the coach."

"Now I know you're a liar. We searched the coach many times and never found any gold coin."

"Our circumstances may appear to you to have changed, peasant. But in reality they have not. Do not dare call me a liar. I am a high official and you are," he waved his hand in exasperation trying to find the most insulting word, "of no consequence. You do not exist as a human being. It is not for you to question me and never dare insult me." We looked at each other. He was as calm as I was angry. I fingered the lock of the Brown Bess.

He smiled. "Just so. It is necessary for us to talk and not to fight, so I will tell you this: I found only one coin. But I must offer you some compensation, must I not?" He looked at me in just such a way as though he had made an important conclusion.

"If you have no money what can you offer?"

"I'll offer you great wealth. I'll give you a letter to a friend of mine. He's appointed head of Customs at Cuxhaven. The Emperor Bonaparte has prohibited all trade with the English. The trade between England and the German peoples used to be very large."

He watched me intently as I lowered the frizzen onto the pan gently to avoid a spark. He smiled slightly realizing he was winning the war of words.

"Now all trade is forbidden and smuggling has flourished. It's not without risk. Only a few people can work the magic. I will give you the letter in exchange for my life, a horse naturally and my freedom. It will give you great wealth. Wealth you never dreamed of. But you must share it with my friend in Customs and he, in turn, will share it with me. You may understand."

"Write the letter. I'm not a soldier. I kill only in defence or for food. But what about the soldier with the horses?"

"I think his name is Bernard. Do what you will with him."

"I told you I'm not a killer for killing's sake. I live in the forest and I live by its rules. If I break those rules, the forest will kill me, so take Bernard with you."

"Very well. It's of no matter."

"And in which direction will you travel?"

"What is your meaning?" asked the Frenchman, surprised at the question.

"If you go towards Sömmerda, I'll shoot you."

He nodded. "That's clear and it's sensible. In my saddlebags is my writing set. If you don't mind, I'll retrieve it."

I heard a man cough behind me and turned to see the officer dragging himself on one elbow across the dirt to our hut. There was blood on his face as well as his chest. To be honest, I thought I'd killed him outright. Perhaps the powder was poor or I had not used enough.

We had walked passed the two troopers. They were dead.

The civilian looked dispassionately at the heaving officer, propped up against the wall of our hut beside the scythe and some fence posts. He lay, with his head drooping, in a patch of celandine. "De Launcy, I have questions for you," he announced, stooping over the injured man. I thought, how suddenly fortunes change. The little yellow flowers were, at that moment, more dangerous than the French cavalry officer.

The officer looked up and coughed blood. He was dying.

"Do you carry a letter on your person, de Launcy? Answer me if you can. Yield your secrets and die at peace with your Emperor. Are you a member of the Philadelphi? Do you carry a letter to Colonel Oudet, possibly the Philopoemen himself and would it propose the Sequanese Republic? Such a letter would prove you are a traitor—a traitor to the Emperor Bonaparte, to the Revolution and to France itself. Do you carry such a letter? Tell me the truth now and redeem yourself. Spare your family."

Blood bubbled around de Launcy's mouth as his head sank and he tried to speak.

"I'm no traitor," he rasped. "I have only one letter, for Antoinette. I pray you, give it to my wife." He coughed and gasped for air. He looked up, but his head hardly moved. His body heaved. He coughed again and sprayed the ground bright red. Slowly, he lost balance and strength and slid to lie on his side in a patch of yellow flowers.

The civilian neither said a prayer for him nor bid him adieu. He just studied him for a moment, his lips pursed in distaste. "Possibly, I was wrong." He stooped to pluck a letter from the other man's inside pocket. Fortunately, it was not the side on which I had shot him. "Possibly," he repeated and walked to the door.

Inside, Dumarque was confronted by the body of the other soldier. He looked at it with exasperation more than revulsion and used his boot to roll it over. Seeing no wound on either front or back, he studied Rosina through narrowed eyes. He bent down to raise the hair at the nape and found the tiny cut that had killed him. He rose and scrutinized Rosina again. "Who taught you to kill like that? Answer me, woman."

Rosina said nothing but pursed her lips.

"I said answer me! This is the method of killing used by the *Tayny Prikaz*. You are not a member. So answer me! Are you Russian?"

Eventually, Rosina spoke, "Yes."

"Do you know someone who is a member?"

"My uncle."

The Frenchman nodded. "He's dead now?"

"Yes."

The Frenchman snorted and walked outside to pace about in the dust, but avoiding de Launcy. He returned to stare at Rosina and pointed at her. "And you? You have been appointed a Determined Servant?"

I must tell you, but I didn't know it at the time, a "Determined Servant" is a person who's been chosen or determined for a certain task. He or she must continue with that task until it's done. But if the task is not completed when the Servant's death is near, the Servant must appoint another to continue with it after his or her death. There is no choice for the Determined Servant. The tasks and the Determined Servants are ordered by the *Tayny Prikaz*, which is the office dealing with confidential matters in the Kremlin. That is the palace of the Tsar himself in Moscow.

Rosina stood still. The Frenchman raised his palms to indicate there was no conflict or contest between them.

"And you killed the soldier because he raped you?"

"No sir, I killed the soldier because he tried to rape me."

Again the palms upraised. "I must write a letter of introduction."

He made a great show of flicking his coat tails when he sat where the Englishman had sat just a few nights before.

"What were you looking for?" I asked him.

Dumarque turned to face me. "What do you mean?"

"You were looking for a letter on the man you called de Launcy. Suppose I found such a letter. What would you want me to do with it?"

"But you will not find such a letter because I asked for it and he didn't yield it. A dying man would go to his God with a clear conscience. I don't think he had one."

I wondered if he meant a letter or a clear conscience.

"You haven't searched the other soldiers. If I had a secret letter, it would not be me who carried it. I would make someone else carry it and they wouldn't know what it was or where it was hidden."

The civilian looked at me, thinking and tapping his fingers on the desktop. "You are possibly right," he answered at length, "and you have time to make such a search that I do not." He considered and then leaned forward to speak conspiratorially. "If you find papers on any of those men bring them to this address in Cuxhaven for a reward. And a grand reward you shall have."

He handed me a note with the address of the senior French Customs official in Cuxhaven. With that he rose, packed away his writing box and stepped outside. The wind had risen quite suddenly and the sky had become a dark grey with black patches. "Bernard, or whatever your name is, come here," he ordered the last soldier.

Bernard dismounted and approached. He saluted in a most unmilitary way, standing with his mouth agape. The civilian shook his head in disapproval and unbuckled the girth of de Launcy's saddle. He just pushed it off the horse's back and let it fall, saddlebags and all.

"Get my saddle," Dumarque ordered.

Bernard mumbled "Monsieur," or "Milord," and ambled across the track to the dead horse. He picked up Dumarque's saddle and staggered back with it.

"Well, don't just stand there. Put it on this wretched beast."

Bernard saddled the horse after he had rubbed down its back.

"We haven't time for all that. We're on important business. Give me your hands." Bernard made a cup with his hands for Dumarque to use as a step.

He looked at his dead horse and then at me. "You shot a thoroughbred, peasant. That's a capital offence."

I didn't answer. Two loaded muskets leaned against the wall and I held the third. There was no need for speech. I watched as the dusty and bad-tempered civilian checked that the pouch he had stolen from the coach was firmly tied to his pommel.

He re-established his authority by ordering Bernard to gather the remaining horses. "They are the property of the Emperor."

Dumarque roughly turned de Launcy's horse and rode in the opposite direction to Sömmerda. Bernard followed with a string of his children. As they disappeared from sight Rosina emerged from the hut looking up at the darkening sky.

"There's little time and a great deal to do." She frowned as she looked at the bodies.

I turned to face her. "*Tayny Prikaz?*" It was my turn to raise my eyebrows.

Rosina smiled, but just a little.

"Do you know, Rosina, that the letter the Englishman wrote and put in the coach was addressed to—" I had to think to get it right, "To the Special Emissary of his Excellency, His Britannic Majesty's Ambassador to His Imperial Majesty the Tsar of all the

Russias, at Berlin and it was from someone called the Lord Mulgrave?"

"How do you know that?"

"I went to look, of course."

"And the address was in German?"

"Yes."

Rosina smiled broadly. "Boys," she exclaimed raising her hands as though to weigh something and added slowly. "I think the Englishman is a very dangerous person and I don't think his name is Lord Mulgrave." She looked at me pensively. "And I think you should be careful of him."

Rosina did not elaborate, even though I pressed her. It was another example of my most difficult thing: finding out what Rosina meant.

We set to work. I don't like to think of that afternoon. Rosina butchered the horse while I stripped the soldiers of their boots and uniforms and searched them for papers.

"Look at this, Rosina." I had found a collection of papers and drawings under the lining of one of their hats. We didn't have time to study them, so I hid them behind the mantelpiece with the other papers. I stuffed their uniforms under sacking in the barn where the coach had stood and collected de Launcy's cutlass and saddle. Like his boots, those were expensive. Certainly, they were not to be left out in the rain. I took a quick look in his saddlebags and saw a mass of papers including a map. They would have to wait.

"What should we do with them?" I asked looking at the bodies.

Rosina looked up, her hands bloody with the horsemeat. "We haven't time to bury them. Can you drag them into the forest?"

So, I tied a rope around the ankles of the first man and dragged him across the track into the bracken. It was as though he resisted me. His arms tangled with fallen branches as if he held them. He stared at me. I heaved, pulled and stumbled into the forest dragging my burden. Eventually I came to the hollow. It was just an overgrown dip. Possibly it had been a quarry once and I tried to roll him over the edge with my boot. But bodies don't roll like that. Even with my hands I couldn't tip him over. He just flopped. Holding the rope, I clambered over the rocky lip of the hollow and pulled him down after me. We tumbled to the bottom in a terrible parody of wrestling.

With the next body, I allowed more rope and, when he rolled over the edge, I stood aside.

By the fourth I was exhausted and turned to study my handiwork. It was a mistake. They lay sprawled close by each other. Three of them looked at me—accusing me and daring me to join them. The one who looked away lay as though in sleep. I heard the first drops of rain.

I had never tried to drag a dead horse before and I found that it was impossible. Between us we managed to get it to the far side of the track and into the bracken. I dug an offal pit and Rosina eviscerated the beast. With so much less weight, we could drag the carcass to the hollow and we were about to pull it over the edge when we heard horsemen.

Rosina peered through the trees. "Get rid of the horse, Paul." She made her way stealthily back to our hut as I pulled and tugged the animal over the edge. The rain increased.

As it rolled over, the beast's legs flailed and one of its hooves hit me on the head as it tumbled by.

I staggered and slipped falling into the bracken with the dead. I must have lost consciousness. Later, I remembered only that my head hurt as though burning. I held my hand to it and it came away bloody. I struggled up the bank feeling faint and sick. There would be scenes of savagery when the wolves smelled their quarry. Tonight, they would howl and the boars would grunt and squeal.

As I scrabbled up the damp earth my joints began to throb with pain. First, my knees wanted to fail me and then my shoulders and elbows. The pain seemed to be bursting from every joint, crippling me and trying to trap me in this terrible bowl for the dead. I could hardly move without pain and climbing to the top seemed impossible. I panted with my face pressed against the tangy earth. I reached up but slipped, banging my knees on the stones and roots as I slithered all the way down. To touch my joints was agony. To hit myself against the ground was unbearable. I was drawn into an abyss.

I lay there panting, even as the rain beat down. I listened to a bird singing and breathed deeply. Breathing deeply is the first step to recovery of mind over matter. I didn't have a limb free of pain, but I couldn't stay there. Neither wolves nor boars care if their food is breathing when they tear at their meal.

Like some crippled spider, I made my way to the lip of the hollow and lifted myself half over. I lay there heaving for breath and in such pain as I had never experienced. Before I slipped again, I forced myself over the lip and rolled away. For some reason my backbone didn't hurt. I relished that area of calm, but I couldn't stay there. Using a tree trunk, I stood and, with blurred vision, began to make my way home. Every step hurt. Every movement of every joint stabbed pain into my brain. I cannot describe how it hurt. In every movement, it was as though I was being prised apart against the joint.

I sweated and became faint, shivering terribly. I remember trembling at the terrible things I'd done and shouted for forgiveness.

I lost my way and my senses. My joints swelled and the pain burned. I could only shuffle from one tree to the next. With a sweaty body, blurred vision, and a stomach that threatened to vomit, I selected my next objective: another tree and fell towards it. I became delirious and finally unconscious.

I woke, covered in rough animal bedding, mostly bracken and lay still to listen to every noise. My sanctuary turned out to be a barn deep in the woods and a long way from our hut. I knew it. We sometimes took shelter there.

Remembering the events of the previous afternoon—or possibly, the day before—made me feel physically sick. But all I could do was retch. My joints still throbbed, but it was subsiding as the swelling had done. Outside it teemed with rain driven on a wind that hissed through the branches making them touch and rattle. It was an unnatural clattering noise. A mythical demon bent on slaughter?

A wooden pole came to my rescue. I used it to lean forward on and to take some of my weight on every step. My ankles hurt so much that any movement was carefully planned. The torrent soaked me, but it also chilled me. To anyone who saw, an extraordinary three-legged monster must have appeared limping in the rain along a deserted forest track. Finally, the monster limped into our clearing. I heard our hut door hitting its post. It opened again as though a ghost had entered to slam behind him. The barn door groaned as it swung. Painfully, I made my way across the streaming mud and closed it. The barn was empty. The horses were gone. I made for our hut, but I felt it: history repeating itself like foreboding. Our home would be deserted. As deserted as the day we had found it. Was my family dead like the soldiers I had killed? Or like the people who had died here before us?

Inside there was no one: neither Rosina nor Anna nor Uncle Franz nor Uncle Albert. The fire was out and the ashes dead.

I stood, soaked and trembling with cold and fright. My knees throbbed with pain that threatened to regrow. Panic flapped in my head like a trapped bat, so I could make no sense of the world. I stood before the dead fireplace, with its draughty chimney chilling me. Behind me stood our dim hut, still and empty. I found the Englishman's papers, the address in Hannover and also the one in Cuxhaven. All were in their place. There were also the papers I had found in the hat.

I panted in tiny gasps. I swallowed, dry and painful to make myself breathe calmly through my nose. After three or four deep breaths I re-established myself and regained control of my mind. The feeling of panic subsided. There was no one in the hut, alive or dead. I stepped out into the slashing rain to search all the outbuildings. I found no one. I hobbled to the stream and saw no one. I scoured the whole area and found no one.

I gathered an armful of logs. My family, the only people I knew in all the world, were not here. But I concluded they were alive.

I did that because the alternative was too terrible to contemplate.

I made a kindling fire and struck a flint over a little powder to light the tinder. The tiny flames took and lit the dried pine needles. I built up the fire, rushing the process with little twigs and then sticks and logs and made a blaze to heat stew—and me.

My clothes were drenched, so I peeled them off and wrung them out before hanging them on poles over the fire. I actually laughed when I thought, this is the moment Rosina walks in.

As the warmth penetrated my being, the swelling in my joints slowly reduced. I drank from the kettle and when the stew pot bubbled, ate and thought. I squatted on a stool crouched over the grate absorbing every bit of warmth the fire would yield. I turned my boots all the time. You can ruin a pair of boots by drying them too fast and these had been expensive once, even if the coachman's feet had been a bit bigger than mine.

I concluded the others had left involuntarily because the papers were still in place and so were their clothes. Had they decided to ride off without me, everything would be gone. So, they had been taken prisoner. I spent some time trying to think of any alternative, but none came to mind.

If they were prisoners, then whose? The French obviously.

The sounds of wild boar squealing carried on the wind. They were tearing at their feast. Later, wolves would howl.

I crouched closer to the fire. There were some rude drawings on the papers in the hat. They were on a card with a pinhole in the middle. The hole had been worked and the paper strengthened many times with layers of cloth, waxed and glued into place. So the piece of paper spun around. Why?

After several attempts I discovered that, with another piece of paper with a slot cut in it, the rude figures appeared to move when you spun it. There were other papers that made no sense, but they obviously had a purpose. I worked for a long time, drying out bit by bit, while trying to arrange them together to glean a meaning. It was not until late in the evening and by lantern light that any sense emerged. It looked like coincidence initially but, as sections came into place, the letter became clear.

It was a warning that there was an informer in an organization called the Illuminati, who worked for Bonaparte's Imperial Police. But the letter was all written as questions, so it was possible to interpret it as saying that the Illuminati had the informer in the Imperial Police and it was them who were being spied on.

Quite clever: the courier could be an ally with whomsoever he came in contact. Only when he met the intended recipient would the true meaning become clear. In the meantime, the courier carried insurance. I thought the rude pictures just made him more ordinary, less serious—quite clever. But I needed more.

I also thought about Dumarque. Too many facts must be rolling about in his head for him to rest. He knew Rosina was a member of the *Tayny Prikaz*, the Kremlin's office dealing with secret matters and that she had been appointed a Determined Servant. The question he had not asked, but which must have been teasing him, was what the nature of her task was? Dumarque had also recovered a letter from the English government concerning the Tsar's army. Surely, he would try to link the two in his interrogations and he would never accept a denial.

I had to free my family from terrible danger.

Another question occurred to me: What was Rosina's task, if indeed she had one? And did it concern her mysterious journey south? Yes, I concluded. Of course, it must. I also concluded that the man in the coach was Mr. Anstruther: a man in whom the French had interested themselves. Dumarque had not asked about him, but he would when he had time to think. Yes, the danger was certain and it was grave.

I took the lantern and, wearing my boots but nothing else because my clothes were still wet, hobbled to the barn through a night of cold rain borne on a winter wind. There, shivering mightily, I recovered the lieutenant's sword and saddlebags and limped back to the hut, gratefully fastening the door behind me. Truly thankful that my night-time naked capering was over I crouched over the flames again. It was October and I trembled, chilled to the bone and dripping wet. I stoked up the fire and returned my boots to their privileged position on the hearth. I needed information from the saddlebags and eventually I found it in the form of one name: an officer called Le Foy who was posted at Sömmerda.

Once dry and warm, sleep became irresistible and I rolled myself up in the feather quilt we had taken from the Englishman: the one that Rosina and Anna shared. As sleep came a plan formed and grew like dough in the night.

The next day was bright, but cold and windy. I woke late but with my health more restored though I felt sore and bruised. My plan, like bread, was ready by morning. My boots would have to do, but my clothes were dry enough.

Slinging de Launcy's saddlebags over one shoulder and his sword over the other, I donned the coachman's old green cloak to hide them.

The forest fell silent as it watched me trudge along the track to town where I made my way to the livery stables and left the saddlebags there. It is normal to leave things at the livery stables for collection later and no one remarked on me doing it. After loitering around the town I decided on my approach. The depot was just one of a number of outposts of French authority in unconquered territory. But they stood unchallenged, just as the French garrisons went unchallenged. French power was accepted. There was no alternative.

By mid-afternoon, with my courage victorious over common-sense, I made my way to the guardhouse. Spirited complaining about the incompetence of officers and remarks about how they should never be let out of the sight of a sergeant followed my presentation of the sword. But a boy returning a sword was considered to be of no significance and I was directed to a large house guarded by cavalrymen standing either side of the front door. They wore shiny breastplates with great brass helmets and each rested a sabre on his shoulder. These troops were altogether smarter and their uniforms a different colour from the men who had tried to kill me and rape Rosina. Their enormous shiny boots came halfway up their thighs. The guards didn't stop me, so I made my way to the front door and stepped inside, carefully closing it behind me.

I looked around a barren entrance room stripped of all its furnishings save a desk at the far side, a small fire and a few chairs. Behind the desk sat a functionary. I approached quietly. "May I speak with Monsieur Le Foy, please? Is he at this depot?"

The scruffy clerk behind the ink-spattered desk did not look up but stopped writing and shuffled some papers. When he spoke he was brusque. "Possibly you mean Chef d'Escadron Le Foy?"

"Yes, please."

"He is here, but what is your business with him? He is a busy and important officer. So, if you state your business, I will determine if he has any time for you."

"I think it must be for him to answer that question because it might be a secret."

That rather stopped the clerk who looked up into what I hoped was my most innocent expression. He coughed and ran his hand over his mouth, unable to continue his interrogation. He shuffled more papers across his messy desk and fidgeted. After making some deprecatory noises, he moved the candle aside and pulled a more or less clean square of paper forward leaving a smudgy thumbprint on it before he even started to write. He took up a quill and having dipped it in the inkwell, wiped the nib on the side, spilling a drop onto the desktop.

"I will send a message," he mumbled grumpily. He looked at the quill and wiped the dripping nib. I watched him write inexpertly, blotting the paper copiously. I could write better than that!

"Sit over there. If you have a weapon, leave it on the chair beside you." He used the feather to point to the empty chairs by the window: as far from the inadequate fire as it was possible to sit. As I unbuckled the sword, the man rang a bell and a messenger arrived. The clerk handed over the inky note, warning the messenger not to slam the door on his way out. He left it open instead. But when the front door opened again, as it did almost instantly, the wind slammed the door shut with such a mighty crash that the clerk jumped, blotted his paper, swore, screwed up the note and threw it on the floor behind him to join what appeared to be quite a pile of previous failures. Two men in thick capes now stood before the clerk and an urgent conversation in undertones took place. The clerk's tone was of adamant refusal. The new arrivals' was of supplication tinged with wheedling. Slowly the two tones became similar and brisk. Something crossed the desk. The two cloaked men turned to sit and smiled briefly in my direction. The clerk wrote a note, rang his bell and a messenger arrived to receive the note and depart, this time he closed the door. Convinced that I had just witnessed bribery, I was considering just how corrupt Bonaparte's system must be. To gain access to an official required inducement and I supposed the more the applicant supplicated for the business he wanted the higher the price rose. I was considering this when the inner door opened to admit a sous-lieutenant looking as self-important as he could manage. The clerk put down his quill and, standing to attention, spoke to the ceiling rather than to the officer. He certainly never looked at him directly. The officer glanced in my direction and decided, with evident distaste, to approach. I stood and took off my cloak.

"You wish to speak with Le Chef d'Escadron?" he asked as though degrading himself.

"Monsieur Le Foy, yes please."

"You will have to tell me why."

I looked at him full in the face and said, "It depends if he is a member of the Philadelphi."

"For heaven's sake!" The officer exclaimed in horror. He turned to see if the desk clerk had heard, but he showed no sign of having done so. "Come with me." The officer picked up the sword. "Is this yours?"

"No, but I brought it with me."

The officer looked at it and then me. He strode off through doors and I followed, leaving it open, just for fun. We hurried along a dim corridor.

"Wait here." He pointed to a spot beside the door. The officer knocked and immediately entered.

Moments later I heard the internal door slam again and I was still smiling when the sous- lieutenant ushered me into a large salon. It was a forlorn room, depressed at its lowered status as an office. The centre of attention sat behind an ornate desk, dressed in a most embellished uniform of green cloth with silver lace. Before him lay de Launcy's sword.

"I am Chef d'Escadron Charles Le Foy. Are you armed?" asked the man in the splendid uniform.

"No."

"Brodeur, search him."

Brodeur patted me all over trying to feel for a weapon. The search was so cursory I could have hidden a cannon. "He is unarmed, Chef," he confirmed.

"You asked to see me?" asked Le Foy.

"Yes sir, as you know one of your officers, de Launcy, is dead. To prove it I bring you his sword."

"I have been informed of his death."

"By Monsieur Dumarque?"

"As you ask, yes."

"Do you know where he is, sir?" I asked.

"Monsieur Dumarque does not inform me of his plans."

"He has ridden to see his Emperor," Brodeur announced haughtily.

The look on Le Foy's face could only be read to mean "And how did you know that?"

Le Foy nodded for me to continue.

"De Launcy was speaking with Monsieur Dumarque who had accused him of being a member of the Philadelphi and suspected he carried a letter for Colonel Oudet. He said, if that was the case,

Lieutenant de Launcy would be a traitor to the Emperor, the Revolution and to France."

"How do you know all this?" It was the curious junior officer who asked. I ignored him and continued, "De Launcy did carry such papers, as you know Monsieur Le Foy, because one of them mentions you by name. There are also other papers that the civilian did not know about. But I think you do, sir."

The junior officer looked at his superior slyly, I thought. But he burst out, "How dare you?"

"Be silent Brodeur and think. Get the boy a chair." Le Foy shook his head in frustration and to my surprise laughed.

The Chef d'Escadron rose and walked around his desk to rest on its edge facing me. I sat still. "De Launcy is not one of my officers. I barely know him." He rubbed his fingers together and regarded me speculatively. "And now de Launcy is dead. Do you know it was inevitable? And Dumarque suspects he was a Philadelphi. And you come here and attempt to associate me with this group. You obviously hold information that brings you to this conclusion just as you have a purpose in coming here." He smiled and looked at the ceiling, bit his lip and chuckled. "It just remains for me to discover what that purpose is. But you are in great danger. I could order Brodeur to shoot you. And I ask this: Why do I not?"

"Because you must recover all the papers de Launcy carried that identify you as a member of the Philadelphi."

"Why not kill you and take them?"

"Because I don't carry them."

Le Foy smiled. "Oh, how I am enjoying this. Of course you don't. But what do you carry?"

94

"De Launcy's sword."

"We call it a sabre. That is to prove that de Launcy is dead, I presume. And that being the case, I am happier with you disarmed."

I shrugged.

"Yes, you make me think I've made an assumption and, of course, you are right to do so." He stood and leaned forward. "Let us come to the bargaining table. What is it you seek?"

"I think you have arrested two men and two women—well, one woman and one girl—in the forest. They are my family and I want them free. We have committed no crimes."

"And in exchange I get all the papers you found on de Launcy's body and that Dumarque did not find?"

"I confirm he found nothing. But he tasked me with looking for them and informing him. I am to receive a reward."

Le Foy faced his aide, "You see Brodeur, all our problems are about to disappear like morning fog in the sunlight." He smiled at me. "Young man, I'll deal with you and I will also thank you, for I have not had such fun in a long time. Furthermore, I suspect—although I don't know why—that we shall see each other again one day." He laughed. "At least I hope so." He waved his arm. "No, no, let me correct myself. I hope I am happy to hope so. You are remarkable—an original."

He turned back to Brodeur, "Now find the four prisoners he speaks of and bring them here."

"Now, sir?"

"Yes and hurry."

95

When he had left, Le Foy asked quietly, "Tell me: the letters. Do you have them here or do I have to go running about the countryside to collect them?"

I looked at him and smiled.

Le Foy chuckled. "Stay where I can see you. I have some papers to finish. We'll talk when Brodeur brings your friends."

I waited a long time. Le Foy worked through his papers, occasionally looking up and smiling at me, or in my direction. I did not detect a threat and believed he would do as he said.

Outside it was already turning dark when the door opened and a sergeant entered. "Sir, I need a signed order to release the four prisoners the sous-lieutenant asks for. They are held by the order of the Imperial Police and I cannot release them without their permission."

Le Foy rubbed his face. "Sergeant, you are in a difficult position. Which prisoners are you speaking of?"

"The four arrested in the forest, Chef."

"How many others do you hold?"

"Twenty in all."

"And are the others held on the orders of the Imperial Police?"

"No, sir. They are held by military authorities."

"I am giving a general amnesty to all prisoners to celebrate the Festival of the Blessed Saint Cyprian of Toulon, whom I am sure you study and revere." Le Foy raised his eyebrows the better to see confirmation on the sergeant's face. "And whose feast day is upon us," he added.

96

"Yes, yes, sir. Surely, as any true Catholic."

Le Foy smiled. "Quite so. And a little generosity never goes amiss, I say." Again the eyebrows.

"Yes, sir. Most laudable. Whenever it's possible."

"Quite."

"I see no reason why certain prisoners should be excluded from the amnesty. Do you?"

"No, sir."

"Good. Then release them with all the others."

"Alas, I am unable to do so without an order from the Imperial Police."

Le Foy smiled slightly. "So be it. Release the others."

The sergeant saluted and left.

Chef Le Foy stared at the closed door for several moments before he turned his attention to me. "Alas, you are no better off, but I have demonstrated my goodwill to you."

"Where are they?" I asked.

"Your friends? With all the other prisoners. Come here. I'll show you."

He rose, making his boots click on the parquet floor. At the window he turned the handle and pulled the two panes open to expose the cold gloom of the early evening. "You see this next building?" He indicated, as a ballet dancer might (not that I knew it at the time), a one-storey farmhouse. It was of no great significance: just an old, dilapidated, rubble-built dwelling.

The reflection of fire in Le Foy's grate showed in the windowpane as he opened it, giving the appearance of the farmhouse ablaze. I almost spoke before I realized it was a *trompe d'oeil.*

Le Foy shut the window and once again the flames' reflection spread across the farmhouse. He rubbed his hands against the cold. "That building is now used as the local office of the Imperial Police." He turned and smiled conspiratorially. "They do not like it. It is not suitable for their elevated position. They will find bigger and grander premises. It is certain." He turned his gaze back to the building, but it was so dark outside by that time that all I could see was his reflection.

It looked too humble to be suitable for any purpose. Its back door stood ajar and without a guard.

"Dumarque and his cronies toil there making their plans and schemes," Le Foy continued.

"But it's not even guarded!" I exclaimed.

"Naturally not: they are adequately protected by a thick layer of arrogance. Besides, they are in the middle of the camp and they feel no one is likely to stray near them." He chuckled and added, "Most people spend their days trying to avoid them. So you can see, they believe there is no need for guards."

"And the jail?"

"It's at the end of the building in the old animal pens. Perhaps they like to keep their sport close by. What do you think? There is a jailer: you saw him. He's one of ours and a decent fellow, too. He can't ride anymore, so now he looks after prisoners."

The jail was just a continuation of the next building: a rubble-built one-storey construction, but it had no windows unlike the end built as the farmhouse. The difference was that the prison had a wooden scaffold at the far end.

"Are they repairing it?" I asked.

"Yes. The roof leaks."

I saw the canvas spread over part of the tiling and studied the scene. I peered through the glass and watched the leaves teased by an evening wind. It would soon be totally dark and I was nowhere near releasing my family.

Even at that moment, the sergeant came into sight, limping across the courtyard. I watched him and concluded that was why he could no longer ride. He disappeared from my view. If ever there was a moment for action, it was now. But I had no idea what to do.

For no reason my new name, Brandt, came to mind and with it a list of words: *brand, feu, fire* and the Russian word for fire—*ogon.*

Without knowing how my plan would develop, if indeed it did, I put the first steps into action. "Monsieur, you have done your best. Now I must try to recover my family. I'm sure that in my place you would do the same."

"What's on your mind?"

"I must go to the Imperial Police."

Le Foy was alarmed. "To do what?"

"To ask for their mercy."

"You make an assumption, young man." He nodded to Brodeur. "Show him out."

Just before I left he asked, "Where are the papers?"

"I'll see you at the livery stables. I have de Launcy's saddlebags," I replied.

He nodded.

Brodeur walked me by the inky clerk who still scratched away on scraps of paper. I collected my cloak, thanked Brodeur and ran down the steps into the cold night. The two guards were no longer on duty.

I ran around the building and crossed to the next where I slipped through the open backdoor of the farmhouse to stand in the space occupied by Napoleon's Imperial Police. It was a dim lobby with a crude wooden stairway to some sort of loft. There were coats and a wooden chest with a mirror and a lantern. A pile of papers wrapped in blue ribbon stood in the corner on a quantity of packing boxes. I pulled papers from the bundle and pushed them between the boxes and the wood panelling.

I took the candle from the lantern and set the tiny flame to the papers and stood back, mesmerized as the flame took hold. They grew and flicked the papers into the air. They would waft about for a moment and settle on something else to burn. I felt the heat and thought about what I had started and how easily I had started it. The draught from the open door urged the flames to greater excess. I gawped as a blazing page made its way up the staircase. It was followed by another. The packing boxes started to smoke until flame burst from them as though they had been filled with it. They contained wood shavings. Almost as good!

Reluctant to leave the heat and the enthralling glow, I made my way to the door and slunk outside to stand against the wall. In the darkness the firelight flickered on the doorstep.

I moved to the end wall and peered around it until I could see the scaffold.

I hoped the sergeant was busy releasing his prisoners. I will admit that justification for my action was generated after the event rather than planned before it. But in the event of a fire, he would surely get his prisoners away? But I had to make sure.

I made my way up the wooden poles until I reached the roof: my eyrie, my refuge. It was dark up here. I pulled the canvas aside.

"Brand, Brand! Feu! Feu!" Came the cries as the sky burst into colour and a signal tower of orange flame lit the heavens.

"Ogon!" I whispered. As the flames blasted above the prison roof I knew no one would extinguish the blaze. I basted in heat. The Imperial Police offices would burn to the ground and I felt happy at serving Dumarque such a turn. After all I had aided him in his search for better premises.

I saw Brodeur run from the side of the main block to the jail while I clambered through the hole in the roof to stand on the rafters. I could see smoke wreathing through a partition and dropped, sweating and fearful.

On either side there were doors and I tried one after another. They were flimsy and not what you would expect for cells. Three were locked, but the remainder not so. If this had been a stable, these should have been storerooms. I concluded that a stable would not have a cellar.

I put my shoulder to a locked door and split it open.

On the floor lay two sets of shackles but the room was empty of prisoners. I tried another door. I could hear the fire roar behind the partition wall now and I could feel heat. The smoke curled in. Through the gaps in the tiles, I could see the flames leaping from the farmhouse. I could smell smouldering varnish, feel the heat and knew the fear of being burned alive.

I saw sparks and glowing smuts float into the corridor. There must be an open door somewhere. The prison filled with smoke.

I barged into a locked door and eventually broke it to find another empty room.

There was one last locked door on the attic gallery. I leaned my ear against it to hear voices, but I felt heat. I stood back and ran my hand over the wood. It was hot. I kicked the door, but it wouldn't yield. I began to panic and charged it. It burst and I fell into a world of flame that billowed out to envelop me. The air seared my lungs.

There was no one in the room for which I thanked God. I retreated from the writhing fire, towards the hole in the roof, gasping and hurting. Flames licked out of the rooms as though searching for me. A serpent of flame writhed from an open doorway and made for the hole I had entered through.

The blasts of heat were becoming unbearable and the air burned in my lungs again. I stood below the rafters and jumped, scrabbling for a hold. I hauled myself up and scrambled onto the roof before another tongue licked at me.

I made it to the scaffold before stopping to breathe in the night air. It was like gulping stream water. At the very edge of the glow, I saw movement. It was a woman's white dress. She was walking away and in seconds was gone.

I scampered down the scaffold, even the stone wall was hot, and ran in the direction of the dress. It was also the direction of the livery stables. I ran heaving and sweaty.

I leaned on the doorpost and peered into the barn gathering my breath. My family stood facing away, but I could see the shackles on Anna's wrists. Brodeur was speaking to the ostler as I felt a hand on my shoulder, like the devil's tap, that made me start out of my skin.

I turned to see Le Foy in the shadow with a pistol in his hand. He placed his free hand over his mouth to indicate I should be silent.

Brodeur spoke, "A boy brought some saddlebags here this afternoon. Give them to me."

"But I should only give them to the boy," the old ostler replied.

"If you do not give them to me, I will report the matter to the Imperial Police and that will go very hard for you."

I heard the click of a pistol lock. Le Foy stepped into the light. "Oh Brodeur, so, you are a nark for Dumarque! After all the kindness and support I have shown you? Do you betray all your fellow officers or only me?"

"I do not betray anyone who is a loyal servant of the Emperor. I do my duty to him and to the Republic."

Le Foy stepped up to his subordinate. "And these prisoners?"

"They will be kept safe for Monsieur Dumarque."

"But they will hardly be safe in his hands, will they?" Le Foy almost purred.

"If they are criminals, they will be punished for their offences."

"And me?"

"It is not my decision," Brodeur replied.

"I see. But you know the answer?"

Brodeur said nothing.

"Prepare to meet your fate, Brodeur. You are a traitor to all that is decent in France and deserve to die."

Brodeur's eyes opened wide, he blustered. "You would not dare."

There was the crash of a pistol and the sous-lieutenant just dropped to the straw.

"Stupid man." Le Foy stepped over the body of the informer and pulled the ring of keys from his hand. He undid Uncle Franz's wrists and handed him the ring. I took the saddlebags from the ostler and passed them to Le Foy, who stood very close to the ostler and whispered, "When you are asked, you will say you returned after the fire and found him here, dead. You do not know who killed him or why. Is that agreed?"

The ostler nodded.

"There is no one here who will gainsay you."

"Uncle Franz, Uncle Albert!" I called.

"What happened to you?" It was Rosina.

"I was hit and became unconscious."

"What by?"

"A horse's hoof."

Rosina nodded. "And what happened to your eyebrows?"

"I got a bit too close to the flames."

Rosina regarded me with mock admonishment.

Le Foy held his pistol behind his back and turned to me. He glanced at Rosina appreciatively. She raised her chin and looked arch. It just made her more attractive. Le Foy smiled and turned to me. "Does trouble always follow you, young man?"

"Me, sir? Never. It's always peaceful wherever I go."

He laughed. "This fire?"

"Was all I could think of."

He shook his head in disbelief.

Uncle Franz had unlocked the women and was freeing Uncle Albert by that time. Rosina held Anna to her. She looked upset and her face was tear streaked. Rosina smiled, but she betrayed signs of the challenge. Standing tall in his body was Uncle Franz. You could see his defiance. But he held dear Albert by the arm and it was as though my giant uncle, who was always so kind, had shrunk. He had a defeated and cowering posture. How he must have hated being chained up.

Le Foy looked at me. "Your family, I presume." I nodded. "You must flee," he continued. "Dumarque will be back and all his prejudices will have been excited by your capering tonight."

"But they stole our horses," Rosina protested.

Le Foy turned to the ostler and asked, "Have you anything to sell they can ride on?"

"There's Barnabas' bullock cart. That's still for sale."

"But we have no money," admitted Uncle Franz.

Le Foy looked at me and then the saddlebags. "I will pay for the bullock cart, Ostler. I will pay you tomorrow for, like these folk, I have no money on me."

"Very good, sir."

"Go and assemble it."

The ostler took up a rope halter and left for the bullock pens at the other end of the livery stables.

Le Foy turned to us and spoke urgently, "You were arrested on the orders of the Imperial Police. You have made powerful enemies. Only the Emperor himself scatters terror more widely." He looked at each of us in turn. "You must depart, while you can do so in peace. Make careful plans to leave and make them quickly. As I have said, you have made powerful enemies and they are vengeful."

"Thank you, Monsieur. I hope we meet again," said Uncle Franz.

The Frenchman left patting the saddlebags slung over his shoulder. "I have another fire to light tonight."

We fell to talking at once and hugging each other and confirming we were hale. That was why we didn't hear the bullock cart approach. The two oxen were snorting and grunting as they do at the outset of a journey.

"It's time for you to depart," said Martin, the man who had ridden by us and who had been at the hut with Robert Stewart only a few nights before.

He turned the wagon in the open space before the stables and clambered down. "It's too late to start your journey tonight, but you must leave as early as you can tomorrow. The Imperial Police will not agree to your release. They'll come back to re-arrest you. I leave you with this thought. They'll be on horseback. They'll travel in one hour the same distance this bullock cart can travel in one day. You might consider starting in the opposite direction to your intended course for a week or so." He smiled, almost a smirk and added, "Go with God, but go quickly."

With that, Martin walked into the darkness.

There wasn't much to discuss. The man's warning was the same as Le Foy's and none of us doubted it was genuine.

We drove the bullock cart home by such moonlight as there was and loaded it with everything we possessed before we rested. First light saw the Brandt family already on the road and some considerable distance off.

Chapter Three: An Apparition! An Angel Appears at the Battle of Jena—1806

We had set off under a chilly, cloud-shrouded, moon in the opposite direction to Cuxhaven, our stated goal and headed southeast towards Apolda. It was our intention to pass through the tiny village of Buttelsted, while the population still slept, and skirt the base of the massive Ettersberg until we reached the road running south. If we continued on the road eastwards to Apolda we'd have to cross the River Ilm. The Ilm isn't much of a river unless you're driving a heavily laden bullock cart and we could not risk damage to either the beasts or the cartwheels, so we would not cross it. Our chosen route took us over the only bridge crossing a tributary of the Ilm and southwards.

I thought of the coach all broken to pieces and our horses. I supposed they had been stolen by the troopers who came to arrest us. I had left the second home I had ever known and I was convinced I had left it forever.

"I was terribly worried when you didn't come back," Rosina scolded me.

"I'm sorry, Rosina. I fell ill. My joints ached and swelled up. I don't know why, but it hurt so much I passed out." I moved a sack aside to make a chair shape out of the canvas screen and sat in it. That was more comfortable. "When did the soldiers come?"

"That night. The horses we heard were the advance guard."

"That was quick. I wonder how Dumarque got back so fast."

"Dumarque?" asked Rosina.

"That's the French civilian's name. He's member of Bonaparte's Imperial Police. At least, that's what he said."

By now Rosina was moving bundles about to make herself a chair. I rose to help her, which was the signal for Anna to steal mine. She is such a pest! Eventually, we had three comfortable places to sit in the back of the wagon, while my uncles rode on the perch. If it can be called that on a bullock cart.

Our way south would take us over the main Weimar-to-Jena road and on to Mellingen before finally turning west.

Martin was right about the weather, too. The days started cold and foggy as one might expect in October. It was only late in the morning that the sun's slight strength warmed us, but it hung low in the sky and shone right into our eyes.

Once you've overcome your impatience, travelling by bullock cart has a certain majesty about it. Its speed is not variable, but its progress is assured. We settled down to our relentless but gentle journey.

Towards the end of the squeaking, rattling and snorting second day, we rumbled over the wooden bridge and turned south. To our right stood the glowering bulk of the Ettersberg with the sun setting behind it and to our left, across the river, we could see campfires around Apolda. Ahead we saw the place where the side of the Ettersberg came close to the road. My uncles agreed it would be as well to have that obstacle behind us before we stopped. Hillsides and woodland are good places to hide in—or to lie in wait, if that's your purpose.

An hour or so further on, we stopped in open meadow with a stream nearby. Albert unhitched the bullocks and led them to drink. He checked them carefully to make sure the heavy yoke had not worn at their hides. He stroked them and spoke to them quietly as they drank.

Rosina prayed to give thanks. She was on her mysterious journey again and heading south.

Other than campfires on the far bank of the river we could hear shouting and singing. But there were no sounds near us and no other fires, so we lit ours to cook and keep warm by. During an October night, a fire is an absolute necessity. We felt secure where we had pitched for the night. There were people at a safe distance, but not too close and somehow crossing the bridge was like passing a boundary marking our increased safety.

I heard it first and sat up—my mouth open to hear better. Franz looked at me and became quiet straining to catch any sound on the breeze. Anna started to talk. Irritating girl! Rosina slipped her hand over the child's mouth. Albert raised his head. We heard the hoof beats. Someone was galloping in the twilight—a very dangerous thing to do. We heard him cross the wooden bridge. The sound became constant and louder. There was only one horse: a rider alone galloping in the darkness. We heard his pace slow and then slow again. We heard him pat his horse's neck and talk to it, but we couldn't make out the words.

He turned his horse off the road and walked it towards us. We became defensive. Rosina had taken her hand from Anna's mouth. It was incredible. Anna had bitten her and drawn blood. Rosina said nothing but led Anna to the stream.

"May I share your fire on a cold night?" asked the rider. We recognized Martin's voice.

"Welcome." Albert rose and held his horse's bridle.

"I'm glad to find you. But, I have news, and it's not good. The Frenchman who told you he was going to Bonaparte?" We nodded. "Do you know his name?" Martin asked.

"He said it was Dumarque," I answered.

"I can tell you it is Dumarque and he's a member of Bonaparte's Imperial Police. They're extremely powerful. Bonaparte is near here, which he must have discovered on the road, so he returned to the depot where upbraided the jailer for releasing you and sent troopers to arrest you again. They returned empty-handed, of course, but I regret they reported they had burned your house to the ground but they had found nothing. Dumarque apparently said it was of no matter because he knew you were going to Cuxhaven. How did he know that?"

We crouched by the fire. I was glad we had brought de Launcy's saddle and boots. Now they were hidden on the back of the wagon. We had brought them to sell, naturally, so we had left nothing for the soldiers to find—even the uniforms. It was another of life's trades. All that work making the huts weatherproof just for the soldiers to burn them. But we were here and we had a bullock cart.

We told Martin about Dumarque's letter to the head of Customs. Martin thought about it as he warmed himself. The wood smoke whisked about us in the breeze, making our eyes water. I stoked the fire, making it blaze a little and sending a spray of sparks into the night.

"You won't go there, will you? It's obviously a trap," Martin warmed the backs of his hands. "He wants to arrest you and he knows you're going there. He'll tell the Customs office in Cuxhaven to report your arrival. Yes, it's obvious he'll do that. You mustn't go."

"It's a pity because he offered us great wealth," I admitted.

"To make sure you would go. The reward is no more than bait on a hook. There's one other thing: remember the name Claude Fougas. He works for Dumarque and he's used for unpleasant tasks. Fougas has been told to find you."

"For what purpose?" asked Albert.

"Ah, yes. I did not say. To end your lives as speedily as possible. He's also to burn all your possessions. At least now I know why."

"Why?" I asked.

"To destroy the letter with Dumarque's name on it, naturally. May I see it?"

I retrieved the letter from its hiding place as Rosina and Anna returned. Rosina's face was grim. She had bandaged her hand, but it obviously hurt where Anna had bitten her. Anna looked terrified and quite rightly. Rosina always indulged and protected her. Now she had literally bitten the hand that fed her. The look on her face meant she knew her world was about to change and not before time.

The man read the letter. "Look at the end. It's Dumarque's signature. There can be no doubt and it shows he's corrupt. I can understand why he wants this letter burned."

Franz asked, "Tell me Martin: We have two men whom we hardly know, Monsieur Dumarque and Monsieur Fougas and both are bent on killing us. Am I correct?"

Martin nodded.

"Then we'd better kill them first."

112

"But where are they?" I asked.

"Dumarque is hereabouts. He's taking a letter to Bonaparte, so he's looking for his Emperor. Fougas, the little assassin, is on his way to Cuxhaven but he'll realize he's on the wrong trail in a day or so and turn back."

A light supper of warmed-over horsemeat and the news that two people are intent on killing you were not the best ingredients for a good night's sleep. At least my hand wasn't throbbing from Anna's bite. I wondered if it was poisonous, like a snake and that thought amused me as I closed my eyes. My worry was that it would be Rosina who'd be poisoned. Rosina was like an elder sister and she was fun. Just as Anna was a nuisance, always interrupting people.

Farmers wake early and so do bullocks. But at eight o'clock the next morning, just as it was becoming light, we heard gunfire. It was not just the putter of muskets although that could be heard. There was also a flat thud, much louder than the muskets. The sound came again and again.

"That's cannon," our visitor remarked. "Lots of cannon."

The noise came from some distance ahead and on the other side of the river. Rosina said nothing, but Anna wanted to turn back. That would be dangerous, because we didn't know how close Fougas might be. We had to press ahead and do so immediately. Bullocks don't run, but they might stampede and destroy our cart.

Our night visitor left promptly to head home.

The bullocks snorted and blew steam from their nostrils as we started off with Anna complaining she wanted to go back. As the morning progressed and we drew nearer the noise, the weak sun began to penetrate. It was then that it all went wrong. Rosina said she had to go to the woods, to relieve herself, presumably. Well, if you have to go, there can be no argument. We stopped the cart while she made her way amongst the trees. The noise from the other side of the river was incredible. By that time, we could smell burnt powder and the concussion of the guns impacted on our ears.

Anna started to cry.

Franz and Albert speculated about the nature of the battle that must be reaching its peak over the river, but they knew nothing and some of their theories were incredible compared to the truth once we knew it. Rosina returned and clambered up onto the wagon. We were about to start again when she asked, "Where's Anna?"

She wasn't there. We looked everywhere. It was Franz who saw her. She was running across the meadow towards the shelter of the Ettersberg and already a long way off.

Rosina jumped down to run after her.

There was no choice. It was Franz who reluctantly offered, "I'll go." As he jumped he made the cart creak and rock. He took the musket and powder horn I handed over the side and trotted off after the women. It was a disaster. We had divided our party and could not progress. It would have been the right thing to do to abandon the girl, but of course, we couldn't.

We were stopped in a lane with sparse trees and the river to our left. To our right lay a meadow and beyond it stood the wooded hillside of the Ettersberg. Albert drove the cart onto the left verge and we waited. We knew we would wait for a long time.

The battle was nothing to do with us. Our threats came from behind, we hoped, and we were alone. Across the river, the guns roared, the shot shrieked and the drifting smoke choked us.

A while later a soldier broke our solitude. He erupted from the trees onto the lane some way ahead. He looked both ways but ignored us. He threw down his musket and his tall shako, took off his white cross-belts and just dropped them. He ran in the direction Anna had taken. He was just gone.

Soldiers followed him. They grew into a stampede. They burst from the trees beside us. The more we watched the more the litter of abandoned equipment grew. The gunfire lessened.

Very close by we heard a scream. There are screams people make only once: when they die. That scream was his, whoever he was. I loaded all our muskets: pour in the charge, tap-tap the butt on the floor of the wagon. Albert turned and nodded his approval. He was no use with a musket anymore because his eyesight had deteriorated so much. He could only make things out that were some distance from him. He went to comfort the bullocks. Pour in the charge, tap-tap. Tamp the charge, spit in the ball and tamp it. Cock the lock and prime the pan.

I stood on a box in the back of the wagon. From that vantage point I could see the river with its shallow banks through the trees. I was nearly sick. I saw a French dragoon chasing a Prussian—actually a Saxon infantryman as I learned later— fleeing for his life. The dragoon leaned forward in his saddle and just spitted the soldier with his sabre. The Prussian squealed and fell into the water. His white waistcoat and trousers suddenly sprayed scarlet with his blood. The dragoon spurred his horse around looking for another quarry. There were lots of them all running to the safety of the river. The dragoons killed for sport.

I marked a guilty dragoon and shot him. It was a shot to be proud of. His head exploded, leaving the shiny brass helmet rolling on the ground. I poured powder, tap-tapped and tamped it as I watched the riverbank. They had heard me and now they saw me. The dragoons wheeled about and another raised his sabre to slash at a running Prussian. I shot that dragoon too. It was a classically easy shot. Pour the powder, tap-tap. Because of the effect of the wooden floorboards, the tap-tap of the musket butt was as good as any drum. They heard.

A lancer appeared over the horizon, leaning forward to aim at a running soldier's back. The soldier looked around in terror and stumbled. His life was over if I missed. But I didn't. The Prussian cowering on the ground watched the lancer's body explode. The lance dipped and buried its point in the earth.

Tap-tap.

Other dragoons wheeled about, but they didn't raise their weapons any more. The soldiers splashed through the shallow water to sanctuary, they hoped, on this side. The French no longer rode to the water's edge.

A ball passed me making the noise of a hornet. I looked for the shooter. It was a dragoon in all his brass plate, hiding behind a tree, as he thought. He was reloading his carbine and preparing for another shot. I jumped down carrying a Brown Bess and ran along the track until I could see him clearly. Someone shouted something in French and he looked up. It took him a moment to see me standing in the lane. He hadn't finished reloading and it was no time to learn about speed.

If you fire a Brown Bess from the hip you have to know what you're doing. You must fix the target with your eyes and continue to look at it until the ball strikes. Waver and you miss. I did not waver. I ran back checking the scene in the river and on the far bank. At the wagon I took my high perch with its excellent view, but of course, I could be seen and I had not expected their musket fire. I'd been lucky.

Tap-tap.

There had been a French officer on his horse a way off amongst the trees. He held no weapon and as he was not slaughtering the fleeing soldiers, I'd ignored him. In truth, it would have been a difficult shot. He'd just watched, but now he talked with another on horseback.

The lane was crowded with soldiers. They had splashed through the shallow river and fleeing across the pasture to the sanctuary of the Ettersberg. They dropped their hats and cross-belts, some their swords, and others their muskets and powder horns. The lane was strewn with, what would be, essential equipment in a fighting force. For them it was just weight, so they dropped it. Up and down the lane they fled, more and more.

Bursting onto the track ahead rode three French dragoons. They ignored the fleeing soldiers but not me.

Tap-tap.

They were waiting for something, possibly a signal. I looked behind me. They waited for three more dragoons who trotted up the bank and onto the lane behind us. I studied the river. Somewhere down there would be a third group preparing to attack straight up the bank at the side of our wagon. On a signal the dragoons in front of the bullock cart charged.

Tap-tap.

The ones behind us waited a moment, so I turned to face the assault from in front. The middle rider was leading. I shot his horse. It fell and somersaulted onto its rider bringing down the horse next to it with its flailing legs. I changed muskets and target, but the remaining rider reined his mount in and turned to protect his fellows from fleeing Prussians who closed in for revenge. I treated the attack from the rear with the same plan except the middle horse didn't bring down its neighbour. I shot the more aggressive of the remaining two riders and the third milled his horse.

Tap-tap.

There they were: the main French assault on a boy standing on a wagon trying to protect soldiers fleeing from a battlefield. Six dragoons led by an officer in truly magnificent braid. I wondered if it was Le Foy and hoped it was not. They spurred up through the trees from the riverbank. Even animals know to spread out. I regret it, but I deliberately shot the officer's horse in the mouth. It reared and whinnied in the most terrible way, spraying blood. It plunged and lunged. I shot the rider at the back who was trying to make his way around the mêlée.

I took up another Brown Bess, stood on the box and watched. One man was dead in the saddle with his horse plunging to rid itself of the corpse. The horse in the middle of the front rank was rearing and flailing its hooves in agony. It had cannoned the next horse into a sapling, leaving its rider hopelessly entangled. There were three left: two at the rear, who were making no serious attempt to come to the fore and one in the front who was making a serious attempt to get to the rear. I waited until the bleeding beast was up on its back legs and shot it in the head. There was silence, wonderful drifting silence. Except for one sound:

Tap-tap.

"*Retraite!*" the officer called from the top of the far bank. He was no longer alone. The Prussians fled on either side of the French but they made no move to stop or kill them. I watched as nine of

118

the original party of twelve dragoons crossed back to the other bank: three of them on foot, two leading lame horses and the others with as much dignity as they could assemble.

I made no move to kill them and I made no move to take cover. The officer in the middle of the standing group raised his hat. When he did that, the others followed his example. I made a simple wave and jumped down from the box into the body of the wagon and out of sight.

The lane was full of fleeing Prussian soldiers. I sat on the box and to my horror felt the joints in my hands swell. "Why?" I called. "Why?" I sobbed, fearing but also knowing, what was to come.

Suddenly the pain was there in every joint: my knees, elbows and shoulders. All were as though doused with hot lead. Then my nightmare came. For some reason the pain in my hips was worst of all. It was more than I could bear.

Just before I lost reason I heard Albert shout, "Here are the women." As they clambered up he whipped the bullocks into their steady movement. Franz walked beside the cart passing up good muskets and powder horns. They're expensive. We crunched over the rest.

Eventually I became delirious and passed out of consciousness.

I heard voices.

"So this is the Angel of Jena." I opened my eyes to see a face I didn't know. I looked around. I saw no one I knew. I tried to rise, but it hurt terribly. I fell back. Another face loomed over me. It was an intelligent face and he spoke the German that Rosina had been at pains to teach us. There were about six of them in magnificent uniforms. Naturally, I knew none of them and I was frightened. A hand rested on my shoulder. "Do you know you're an angel?" one asked.

"No," I whispered.

"But you are. The French say so. It was not Ney himself, but one of his commanders who saw you. He ordered the French to allow fleeing Prussians quarter. He said the Prussians have an angel at the Ilm River. The angel allows Prussians to flee but he will kill every Frenchman who attacks them. The French told our soldiers there was an angel waiting at the river and they were safe when they reached it. Now all Prussian soldiers believe they have an angel to protect them and those who saw you are sought out for their narrative."

The face retreated and another voice took over, but initially I couldn't see his face. Then he leaned forward so I could see him and his uniform with its braid and his medals. He was much older. "When there is nothing good to hear, there will always be the story of the Angel of Jena who saved so many. Good night, young man—Angel of Jena." The man leaned forward and kissed me on the forehead very lightly.

Another lifted my head and gave me a draught to drink. "This is laudanum. You will fall into a deep sleep that will herald the end of your pain."

I woke—I don't know how much later, in charge of my faculties and with the swelling gone, but thirsty. The wagon rumbled on. There were no men with medals. Perhaps I had dreamed it.

Rosina lent over me. She smiled. "Now it's my turn to bathe you with vinegar water."

Gently she wiped the cloth over me. I felt we were walking on the edge of something unknown. I wanted to jump in, but Rosina didn't. I slept again and when I woke, at last prepared to face the world, it was chilling at the end of day. Rosina's face just showed over a blanket as she slept beside me in the back of the wagon. Anna sat between the two men as we jolted along. The sunset was to our right.

"We haven't changed direction?" I asked.

They made room for me on the perch.

"The gentlemen left this for you, Paul." Albert handed me a scroll sealed with a ribbon.

"True," confirmed Franz. "Rosina has begged us to continue south to Saalfeld. It is about thirty kilometres from here and she says the end of her quest and her servitude might lie there."

"Did she say what she meant?"

"Not so we could understand. But it refers to young Anna here."

"Sorry." Anna hung her head. I put my arm around her and we felt the warmth of the sun's rays in the evening.

Chapter Four: Prussia Is Lost; We Seek Sanctuary— 1806

I tucked the parchment away for later. I had not imagined the men in gold braid after all and I tried to fix those intelligent faces in my mind. But the sad truth was that we had witnessed the Battles of Jena-Auerstedt and the total defeat of the Prussian forces resisting the French invader. The complete destruction of Prussia followed. Bonaparte just dismembered it in the same way as he had dismembered the Prussian army. Of one hundred two thousand men in the Prussian force the French killed, maimed, or captured over thirty thousand. I thought of all those families and all those farms where crops would fail and wild nature win over. But we also heard of the Prussian cavalry officers who had honed their swords on the steps of the French embassy in Berlin. We heard how they were going to give the Corsican upstart a lesson and how arrogant they had been.

It was a terrible defeat. Napoleon didn't negotiate surrender terms. He dictated them. Prussia and its king became trivial: to be ignored and derided.

At every night's rest, we heard the same tales of defeat and woe: of pillage and rape. But to restore some balance and to give a little hope, someone would tell the story of the Angel of Jena. The stories had become fantastic, so I listened but said nothing. Once we were identified at an inn by the river north of Schwarza. A soldier beside the fire had told the story with all its exaggerations. Then a man wearing a blanket over his clothes who also stood near the flames folded back the blanket so we could see he'd been a Saxon infantry sergeant. "You weren't there," he said. It wasn't a question.

"No I wasn't, but I've told what I heard," replied the storyteller.

"I was there. I crossed the Ilm River and I saw the Angel. I saw him shoot dragoons who were killing our soldiers and I saw him allow those not involved in the killing to live."

He stirred the logs with his boot and looked into his ale mug. He put it down and stared at it as though to wish it full again. He returned his gaze to the fire. "And because I was there, I can tell you one other thing, old soldier. We're in the presence of the Angel. I can't see him from where I stand, but I know their bullock cart and it's in the stables here. He's here. So be careful what stories you tell."

"Why do they call him the Angel? Answer me that."

"It's difficult to explain. We were running for our lives and there he was on the other bank. He had golden hair and a pale clear face." He shrugged. "Perhaps a face you don't see on a woman often. He wore a white shirt and pale breeches. He stood on a box in the back of a wooden bullock cart. Fog and gun smoke swirled around. The Angel looked towards the southeast and the sun was on his face. It made him shine. He never missed, certainly never that I saw. And after each shot he reloaded. Always he tapped the butt on the floor of his wagon."

He stamped twice on the floor of the inn.

"Just so. His were the only shots nearby. So there was silence afterwards and everyone looked around. He just stood there reloading with the French milling about trying to understand what was happening. Whenever a dragoon tried to run one of us down with his sabre, there would be a crash. The Angel would fire another musket and down came the dragoon." He ran his hand over his mouth. "The French understood the Angel had the power of life and death over each of them and they understood his terms. What more would you want from an angel?"

I sat with the hood of my dark-green cloak forward looking across the table at Rosina. She looked back, smiling slightly and I wondered if she was mocking me. I rubbed my wrists as they began to throb, but it faded. A gentleman had sat at the empty table behind Rosina. He studied my face then smiled. He rose and walked around to look at Rosina. He left the room without saying a word. But he knew. I was sure he knew. I didn't think it was Fougas. I certainly hoped he wasn't.

The next day we left before dawn.

Our magnificent bullocks pulled us along a few miles every day. We had enough for our needs and we were content to continue with Rosina's plan. We learned as we travelled and wondered at what we saw. We stopped at Saalfeld, hopefully for some time.

Rosina took Franz with her for company and protection, while the rest of us stayed with the cart. Whatever Rosina's quest was; it took all day. At day's end they returned tired and despondent. It was Franz who told us the news. "Rosina is looking for the seat of the noble family of Saxe-Coburg-Saalfeld, but they've moved and gone further south to Coburg. It is nearly a hundred kilometres further."

Exhausted and in despair, Rosina slept in the back of the wagon as my uncles discussed what was to be done. There was very little choice and the next day we rumbled off further south to find the city of Coburg before the roads became too bad for travel. It took us a week to make the journey and the bullocks had obviously given of their best just as the weather was about to give of its worst. On the journey we were able to enjoy that wonderful display the trees give that rivals anything the birds can display. The colours of autumn are unlike any other. Even spring is dull by comparison.

Whatever we may have wanted to do, we were going to stay in Coburg that winter. Franz and Rosina set out to discover the seat of the noble family. They returned at the end of day exhausted and with Rosina in tears. A year before the family had decamped again and moved to a castle called Rosenau at Rödental.

The next day we discovered that Rosenau was but seven kilometres away. We also heard the family was in residence.

Although Rosina was in high spirits as her quest came to its close, she would not take us into her confidence until I asked her. "This is about being a Determined Servant, isn't it?"

"Yes. You heard, didn't you? Yes, yes—it is." She was pensive and paced about with her hands clasped in front of her. She looked up at me. "Now I must approach the family, but most of the evidence I was entrusted with is gone. I lost it before I met you all." She stopped and smiling in mock severity added, "And you captured us and held us prisoners." She held up her hand to stop my righteous protest. She smiled to mollify my indignation and returned to her narrative. "It isn't my fault," she added. "We were ambushed and I was lucky to escape with Anna."

"Anna's your charge?" I asked.

"Yes." She nodded.

"All you can do is tell the truth and ask for guidance."

Finally, four of us agreed that Anna was to stay with my uncles, while Rosina and I, as the Angel of Jena, were to ride to the castle on rented horses. First though, we were to trade de Launcy's saddle for some respectable clothes. We couldn't afford to be turned away at the gate.

Two days later we set out.

"This is most uncomfortable," Rosina announced.

I looked back. Rosina rode sidesaddle elegantly, but it certainly looked uncomfortable. "I'm glad I don't have to do that."

The livery stables had been efficient in every detail and our saddlery was as well presented as our horses. Mine was a fine stallion while Rosina rode a shiny chestnut.

In the early afternoon of a cool, blustery day, we came to the vicinity of the castle, where the farmland was more particularly cared for. The field walls were in good repair and the hedges showed only one year's growth. As we came closer, we could see some attempt had been made to repair the roadway with broken stone. We passed a group of workmen rehanging a gate onto a new post. They stopped work to watch us ride by. We bade them good day and they doffed their caps in response.

Rosina was and is an attractive looking woman and she wore her new blue cloak. She had made it herself from the Englishman's cloth and the colour of the hood made a perfect frame for her face. The workmen needed no other excuse to study us.

They watched us for some distance, while we looked at the fields already ploughed for winter. The trees stood in properly husbanded woodland with logs stacked for the carter to collect.

We turned into an avenue towards the castle itself and saw the building for the first time. It was an extraordinary confection of bits that don't belong together. There was a tower, and if you have a tower like that, you have four. There was a roof, naturally, but there was lots of roof and there wasn't enough wall height to go with it. Overall the castle was bulky without being big and it wasn't very attractive. Possibly to hide its imperfections, it had hidden behind some trees. Maybe its owner had planted them. That might make the castle cold in summer and wet in winter.

"It's not welcoming, Paul, do you think?" observed Rosina.

"No, but it makes me curious."

I rang the bell on the outpost to announce our arrival and we walked the horses into the grounds and up the drive. The ostlers heard the bell and came to see who had arrived. Their reaction would set the tone for our welcome.

We were not gentry because we were not in a carriage. We were not itinerant because we had no baggage. We were not peasants because we were on horseback, but we were of some consequence because the lady rode sidesaddle.

We were met by one ostler who led our mounts to the stables. The main door was opened and we were bidden to enter. We had not been directed to the servants' entrance.

We were neither expected nor welcomed, save for the rather frosty civility of formality. We were bidden to wait in a small anteroom and I was asked my business. I looked at Rosina, but the lackey looked at me so I answered.

"We have business with the Duke or one of his secretaries. It is a delicate matter that concerns this lady and it requires that confidences are kept."

The lackey left. I looked at the empty grate. We knew we would be kept waiting and I wondered if we would be kept waiting in the cold. It was almost as though they thought it would be good for us. We lowered our hoods but kept our cloaks wrapped around us.

I looked around this barren space with its high windows and bare walls. There were a few chairs, so we sat. I wondered if it would be pointed if we moved the chairs near the empty fireplace. I was considering this when the door opened and the bark of a laugh followed.

The source of the laugh called back through the door. "Christian, inform His Grace the Duke that an angel awaits an audience with him: an angel who has come all the way from Jena. For the protection of his divine soul, he should not keep this angel waiting, perhaps."

It was the gentleman who had sat opposite us at the inn at Schwarza. As he turned back to me, I saw him clearly and had the opportunity to study his face. In truth, it was not a face that required study because he compelled attention. He possessed an attractive smile and keen, intelligent eyes, that neither questioned nor criticized with hostile glares, but welcomed with lurking humour. The telltale lines of responsibility and authority conscientiously administered were clear to see. I studied his wavy hair swept back over his ears. He did not wear a peruke, but his natural hair was turning silver. Here was a fair man with a strong persona. A man with a smile set in an alert face.

"I knew I would see you again, Angel. I regret I crossed at the Ilm River too, but I did have my horse. It was a terrible rout and you, young man, are the only soothing subject in that whole battle. I salute you." He strode over to us. "My name is Jerome Rickard and I am His Grace's factor. Tell me, what is it that brings you to us today?"

We shook hands and I indicated Rosina who rose and stepped forward. Suddenly her face looked delicate and vulnerable and it took a moment for her to speak, "I must only talk with the Duke. Please tell me, how should I address him?"

"Your Highness will be correct for you, until he directs otherwise. But do you not trust me?"

"Sir, it is not that I trust you or do not trust you. It is the terms of my vow that direct who I may speak with and who I may not."

"Terms?" asked Jerome.

At that moment the door at the back of the room was flung open and an elegantly dressed older man entered. He was followed by a priest and two monks. The older man spoke, "Where is this angel who summons me, Jerome?"

"He's here, Your Grace." Jerome indicated me.

I bowed as the Duke approached. He did not hold out his hand for me to kiss, but as Rosina curtsied and I stood straight again, he held out his arms and hugged me to him. "I'm glad in my heart to have this opportunity to thank you and to hold you to me." He stood back and studied me. "What is it that brings you here?"

"Sir, Your Highness, I apologize. It is not I but Rosina who would speak with you."

The Duke smiled. "I shall not be disappointed. Now you are here, we will talk later." He turned to Rosina. His look becoming a little more stern, perhaps fixed. "Speak."

"Your Highness, I am a Determined Servant."

There was a sharp intake of breath from the priest and the two monks crossed themselves.

Rosina continued, "I don't know why your clerics protect themselves. I'm no witch. I did not ask for this task. My uncle was made a Determined Servant by the *Tayny Prikaz* in Moscow. As he lay dying, he inflicted his task on me. For more than three years now I have tried to fulfil it."

A resigned look had spread across the Duke's face. "Tell me."

129

"My uncle was bringing a child out of Russia. She is illegitimate and she is claimed to be the daughter of either Princess Marie Louise or Princess Juliane Henriette according to the information I was given."

"And you were charged to do what?"

"To bring her to the safety of her family. To protect her with my life and virtue and to see no harm came to her."

The Duke nodded and suddenly before my eyes looked older. He became tired. "What evidence do you have?"

"All that is left after the attack that killed my uncle are five crystals. I think they are magic because I was told that in the right hands they could provide for Anna. There were papers and also some gold, but the robbers took everything. I know I have failed to uphold the terms of my vow, but I have done the best I could with the resources I had."

"And the girl, where is she? Did you bring her?"

"Sir, no. We thought bringing her here might give rise to expectations that could be difficult to reduce."

"Very wise." He smiled. "I'm impressed." He turned to Jerome and asked, "Do we have any food for angels? Do angels like warm rooms to wait in? Arrange all that is necessary because I must think. And for that I need time."

He turned to Rosina and asked, "Tell me, do you have the crystals?"

"Yes, sir." She held out her hand with the crystals I had found in her skirt hem.

The Duke looked at them. He handled one and studied it before crossing the room to the window. I watched curiously as the Duke scratched a line on the glass with the crystal. He nodded to himself and returned it to Rosina's palm. "Keep them safe."

He smiled briefly and swept out of the room with his entourage. The monks followed, while the priest seemed curiously reluctant to take his eyes from an angel.

Jerome led us to another room, a warm welcoming room, with a bright fire burning. He then left us and after a while, we heard the Duke speaking, "No, no. It's my prerogative to conclude the woman is genuine. Whether she's right or not is a different question. The question. Ha! The issue is whose issue the issue is! There is a riddle for the monks to fathom. Indeed, it is. One could wish, as we attempt to position ourselves for a secure future, that the loins of my family were not so obviously fecund. I think I must write to Moscow to determine the guilty parents' identity. And I must wait for them to answer and then I must interpret their answer. In all, it will take six months, I presume."

"Winter is coming, Your Grace."

"Find a house for them on the estate that is comfortable and properly appointed. Tell them I will send for them in summer to inform them of my deliberations."

"Very good, Your Grace."

"Now I wish to be diverted by speaking with an angel. Bring him before me and ensure that we have all we could desire."

"And the woman, sir?"

"Oh dear. Well, yes; all right. But the priest can stay to talk with the woman. Let us properly serve him a dish of his own self-righteousness."

Chapter Five: A Life Storm—1807

We were treated with great kindness wherever we went on the estate. We entered a long and sublime period in our lives, that lasted several years. I hope everyone has a chance to enjoy such conditions in their own lifetime. The house the estate manager found, on instructions from Jerome, was capacious, but it had not been lived in for a while and needed work. But it was habitable.

Our neighbours helped us over the initial period by supplying us with necessities and the carter delivered us firewood.

Smoke plumed from the chimneys as we heated and dried out the house. It was on two storeys and we had the novel experience of climbing upstairs to our bedchambers.

We had planned to further our lives as locksmiths and makers of small brass pieces, but no sooner had Uncle Albert shown Uncle Franz the overgrown vegetable plot outside the back door (for there were two doors to the property) than they were farmers again. They worked every daylight hour to bring the land to where it should be for that time of year and I was pressed to help by mending the hen coop and chicken run.

At the weekly market, we bought hens and feed together with winter plants for spring harvesting. Rosina worked her way through the house with Anna following along behind, except when it was time to feed the chickens. That task Anna took for her own. But they were off-lay.

"Well now, Anna, we can't go on feeding hens that don't lay eggs. Maybe it's time to put them in the pot. What do you think, Franz?" Albert asked.

Franz looked at his brother and detected a smile lurking behind that great beard.

"No, no, you can't. I won't let you." Anna jumped up, protesting.

"I think we should ask Rosina." Franz deferred to her more and more. We all noticed it.

Thereafter Anna would talk to the hens when she fed them and warn them a terrible fate awaited if they didn't lay eggs. But it made no difference. However, the birds were destined to die of old age. It was inevitable once they had names.

It was then that Franz bought Chanticleer. Our mornings became raucous with the cockerel's calling and cackling. He strutted around the pen like a fop, picking up his feet as though he did not wish to get his claws dirty. But the hens were not moved and still they did not lay.

When I was allotted a particular task, I mentioned we might not be there in spring, but my words did not bear fruit. My uncles' attitude was to make the best of what was available.

We learned where we stood in the eyes of those we lived amongst. There were farmers and there were tenant farmers. The men would talk business, but their wives would not talk across that gap in rank. There were tradespeople and labourers, who were more serfs than free men, and even when they were in the same line of business they had nothing in common, except work, to speak of. There were guildsmen and other professionals and they spoke only for business. There was also the aristocracy. They may talk to us, but we didn't talk to them—and if they spoke with us for any reason, we would stand with our cap in our hand. Some of the young noblemen were assiduous at retaining their privileges and would assault anyone from a lower order who wore a feather in his hat or who carried a sword.

I was the Angel of Jena, so I had fame in my own right and those with me had, I like to think, a better time because of it. But Franz, Albert and Rosina earned the respect of others. We'd been lent lodgings for the winter and we'd cared for and improved them.

Anna and I received instructions from Jerome. We discovered that, as the Duke's factor, his word was all but law. We were bidden to attend school, so each day, we would walk to a neighbour's house where lessons were given.

We had a lot to learn and over the ensuing years, I sat before what would turn out to be a long list of tutors, some of whom were to be regarded by history as eminent thinkers.

Life around the castle had a pattern. As people grew older, they wore down the barriers to seniority in the guild that represented their chosen work. They would rise at the appointed time to fill a vacancy caused by an older person's death, illness, or retirement. Naturally, plague and battles—to say nothing of the French—could cause more rapid promotion, but haste was frowned upon.

There were certain barriers it was impossible to jump. It was impossible to become a member of the aristocracy. There were rich merchants and skilled craftsmen who actually had money of their own to keep, but they were not aristocracy. The aristocrats kept themselves apart.

Between the richer tradespeople and the aristocracy there existed a number of people, who lived in the castle or on the estate, entirely without money it seemed to me.

It took me a long time to realize how they survived. Their needs were met because they were permitted, from time to time, to purchase what they needed by giving the name of someone who had an account with a supplier. Woe betide those who charged any matter to any account without permission. It was impossible for such people ever to repay because they had no reliable access to money. They risked being turned out of their employment, which was some genteel activity, like being a librarian or a housekeeper with responsibility for embroidery. They also risked being turned out of their home. They had nowhere else to go and no other support. It was not a line they crossed—ever.

For day-to-day needs, they bartered or received supplies delivered as tithes to the castle. Everyone's needs were met however small. That is not to say their appetites were assuaged, because they were not—needs, yes. Those were met. The reconciliation of all these credits and debits was finally balanced by Jerome each quarter day.

I had two unfortunate encounters with these unmoneyed employees. One was with the priest, who wanted to know if I could sing. He asked me to meet him at the chapel. We sat beside each other as he talked and I tried to sing, but I couldn't. As I now know my voice was about to break. It did not stop the priest from emphasizing the point he was trying to make by resting his hand on my leg. Not at the knee, you must understand, but entirely higher.

I will admit the sensation was difficult to define—new and perhaps a little thrilling. The problem the priest faced as he allowed his hand to linger and then to wander was to introduce the ideas he had in mind in the context of the lessons he had volunteered or been instructed to give me. He held me tightly to him with his other arm around my shoulders and his face very close to my cheek. I could feel his breath. "You have nothing to fear." He squeezed me a little. "Brotherly love is an outpouring of natural affection and greatly to be encouraged. I'm sure you feel a great surge of affection rising up that you want to share."

"I fear for my mortal soul," I informed him bleakly.

The priest pursed his lips and a look of caution crossed his face. "It is your immortal soul that should be of concern to you."

"I'm sorry. I didn't mean that I feared for my immortal soul because of brotherly love. I fear for it because I've been killing people and their horses." I paused and added as an afterthought, "I regret killing horses."

The priest coughed slightly and swallowed. His arm let go of my shoulder and he withdrew his hand from my thigh. We looked at each other and he twitched me a small smile. In hindsight, I think at that moment he determined not to explore virgin territory that day but to direct his attentions to other opportunities he had turned to previously.

The clock struck and I realized I had dallied with the priest for too long. I had been bidden to attend a seamstress. From her I learned how society worked for the mutual good. The rich did not discard old clothes but passed them into the hands of others. To avoid someone from the lower orders parading in the finery of the elite, the clothes would pass through the hands of the dressmaker who was charged with altering them for the new wearer. In that process the decoration and finery was, to a greater or lesser extent, removed.

However, that day was to be more centred on my body than I could possibly have anticipated. I left the priest with an idea of what he had in mind, and as a young man, I was free to consider or reject it. Because of my remark about killing people, I had more time for consideration than the priest had planned. I will admit to a feeling of resentment towards him and his approach, because through speed he was trying to overwhelm me and prevent me making my own decisions.

I knocked on the dressmaker's door still with these thoughts swirling in my mind and was asked to enter. The room had slender windows designed to let in a lot of light, as they would have done, had I been on time and earlier in the afternoon.

I paid attention to the woman, whose name was Frederica Storch, because she represented a contradiction. She wore a dark-blue dress that fitted as it would a young woman. But her hair, greying slightly, was piled high as though to get it out of her way and her face was lined with disappointment or a lack of appreciation, not age. The impression she radiated was of a fading maiden spoiled by a brooding, disapproving countenance.

Her house had once been quite comfortable, even grand in a modest sort of way, but now it was filled with piles of material. All sorts of clothes and coats—men's, women's and children's— hung on pegs and rails, or just in piles on tables. There was hardly room to move. In the corner stood a cheval mirror and she asked me to stand before it.

"You're late and the light's poor now. We must hurry. Take off your clothes."

"I apologize. I was delayed by the priest."

She snorted in contempt as she shut the creaking door firmly. "Hurry, now." She studied me carefully and rummaged in a pile of shirts.

I stood by the mirror and slowly disrobed, nervously pulling my flax chemise over my head. With a branch of candles in one hand and a pile of shirts over her other arm, Frederica Storch approached. There would be a house fire one day of that I was certain. She looked at me.

"It's so unfair," she muttered.

I looked at her but she was not addressing me: she was talking to herself. "Look at his eyelashes. Have you ever seen them so long? What a waste on a boy. And that complexion!"

She muttered so quietly that I could hardly decipher her words as she ran her fingers over my shoulders and down my arms. "So slender, so slender."

She felt the back of my arms. Her hands drifted across my chest. "So firm, so flat."

I didn't know what to make of these words. I just thought it was some part of her routine. Her hand drifted across my stomach making me flinch.

"So firm, so flat, so unjust. So unfair. Such a waste to give it all to a boy."

Then louder, "Your breeches: How can I measure you with them on?"

I did what I was told, but I felt some anxiety.

"So slender, so firm."

Her hands ran over every inch of the back of my body as it became exposed. All the time, she muttered, her hands on the backs of my thighs, just as the priest's had been on the front.

"So slim, so slender, so smooth."

I should say that a woman's touch caused an entirely different response in my being to that of the priest. I am not saying it was any response I chose and if I might be inclined towards the obvious, it could be said to have caused an outstanding result: in a small sort of way. I'm looking back in time, you must understand. As she turned me to face her, she saw and suddenly erupted into uncontrollable rage. She slapped me wherever she could and shouted the most horrible accusations of my base beastliness and being filled with foul lust.

I overflowed with humiliation, shame, frustration, guilt and a flood of emotions I could not categorize. My self-confidence ebbed in a way I had never experienced and I was deluged with self-doubt. I begged to apologize for my terrible offence.

She continued to shout and slap, so I grabbed my clothes, pulling them together and fled the house running in the cold evening back to our temporary home.

As I approached, the pain in my joints started to roar again and by the time I reached our front door, it was raging in every inch of my body. I staggered in and made my way passed an astonished Rosina and a gaping Anna. I stumbled up the stairs though every step was like fire. I fell onto my bed in agony and misery and wept.

I know these attacks and dread them. They start bad and become infinitely worse. They plateau trying to linger before eventually subsiding. In all they usually take three days and nights.

Rosina had been my saviour before and she came to my rescue again, wiping me with cloths soaked in vinegar water. Anna helped her. As usual I became delirious. Rosina poured the last of the laudanum into my mouth and I slept like the dead.

Much later, when I had fully recovered Anna told me what happened next. When they had washed me, they had seen the red slap marks all over me. Rosina had held her hand over one and seen they were made by a woman. In my delirium I must have told Rosina what she wanted to know.

"She stormed off to Frederica Storch's house and I followed."
Anna's eyes were alight with mischief as she told the tale.

I could just imagine it: Anna ready for anything especially
trouble and not wanting to miss a moment.

"Rosina opened Frederica's door without pulling the bell chain
and went straight up to her and slapped her face. My God, but it
was a hit! She fell down with Rosina screaming at her. 'How dare
you do that? How dare you? To a boy? How dare you?'

"Storch got up and Rosina hit her again. Down to the floor she
went and that time she stayed there. Rosina became quiet and
we both know how dangerous that is."

I nodded. We were both well aware of Rosina's temper.

Anna continued, "They started to talk, or Rosina did and Storch
listened. It was then I saw another person in the room. One of
the noble ladies had come to visit. I saw her, but Rosina hadn't.
The lady looked at me and held a finger to her lips to signal me
to be quiet."

"That would have been difficult for you, Anna," I remarked.

"Beast! I shall tell you no more and next bit's the best bit."

"All right, Anna. What's the next bit?" I knew she would tell
because she had to. She could never keep a secret even if her life
depended on it.

"Rosina said that Storch had better make amends to you in fitting
form. Storch asked what she meant by fitting form and Rosina
said something so quietly that I couldn't hear. Storch went as red
as this blanket. Just before we left, Rosina turned to her and
announced furiously, 'You've become a sour old woman before

your time. Your spittle would kill grass. It's not for the boy to reform. It's for you.'"

I'm glad Anna had not heard what Rosina said and she never repeated it.

I didn't recover from my inflammation (because that's what it's called today) for two more days. It was only on the day of the Duke's Assembly, for which Frederica Storch was dressing me, that I was fully recovered. Rosina sent me out early in the afternoon even though I was not due to be in the Duke's presence until the evening.

"Who knows what alterations have to be made?" Rosina had told me.

I should add one more fact. I had called out, "Is anyone there?" when I had woken.

Rosina had asked, "Who's that?"

"It's me, Paul."

"Paul?"

"Yes."

Rosina laughed. "Your voice has broken. I didn't recognize you." She smiled. "Hello, young man. You're quite dangerous now, I think."

"I hope not."

"Let's wait and see." She laughed. "Dress yourself and go to Frederica Storch. She has clothes for you for this evening." She laughed again.

Chapter Six: I Am a Young Man at Large with a Reputation—1808

I arrived late at the Duke's Assembly, elegantly attired and in a state of euphoria. I looked around the great receiving room. Shoals of men moved about. They stopped, talked with each other and moved on. Each shoal contained a principal who wore a coloured robe, usually red and usually with a fur collar. These principals each wore a gold chain of great complexity and many were accompanied by an assistant dressed in a black robe who carried a staff with an emblem at the tip. One was a sheaf of corn and another a cape. All shone like gold. There was a strong smell of lavender that, only just, overpowered the smell of a large number of people. The noise was like many cooking cauldrons bubbling. Uncle Albert's cooking smelled better.

One of the ladies standing aside detached herself from her fellows and came to speak with me. It was a noble gesture because, once she'd demonstrated I was acceptable, others might follow her example.

"May I beg you to inform me the purpose of this gathering, please?" I asked her.

The lady inclined her head. "Very well, you see here the guilds and the associations that encompass all commerce in this region. Each association has an area of responsibility and each makes rules to ensure proper order."

"But they're all men," I observed.

"I'm not."

I looked at her. She smiled. Her eyes were bright and questioning. Her mouth was most expressive and was hardly still as her thoughts showed themselves on her lips.

"I meant that all the people in the main hall are men," I explained.

"They're the local guildsmen, so of course they're all men. We, the ladies of the castle, are here out of mutual courtesy."

"I see," I said, not really seeing at all. "What's happening?"

"Between them, the guilds decide the terms for business during the coming year and where the authority of the church will hold sway. It's all discussed here. Where there's a gap in authority, a body will be appointed to fill it and where there are two authorities regulating an activity, one will lose its influence, but it'll be by agreement."

She smiled and studied my face, I thought. "Did you spend an enjoyable afternoon?" she asked.

That made me blush, but I had the presence of mind to answer, "I learned a great deal, my lady."

"There have been many travellers such as you, although perhaps not with your looks and magnetism. No, don't blush. Accept the compliment for what it's worth. By the way, I heard what Rosina—that's her name, isn't it?"

I nodded.

"I heard what she suggested to Frederica Storch. As a mere unreformed widow and music teacher, I would venture to suggest the experience would have been beneficial for you both." She chuckled.

"I would offer you one suggestion," she continued. "It is this: should you find the experience has whetted your appetite for more, you should not return to Frederica Storch to sate it, but possibly you should look to higher planes."

I could hear blood pumping in my ears. "My lady is too kind."

"For what? I have given and offered nothing."

"For the advice alone, my lady."

"I was about to inform you of the problems posed by travellers, but possibly His Grace can inform you on that subject."

I looked where the lady's gaze had fallen and saw a group, headed by the Duke himself, approach.

The lady spoke quickly and quietly, "This is where, young Paul Brandt, you'll learn the value of every word you utter. And remember this: silence can be just as revealing as speech. We have a dictum: speech is silver, but silence is golden."

She curtsied and I bowed as the gaggle arrived.

"Susannah, you're monopolizing our hero. He's a national treasure at this dark time in our history." The Duke's mild rebuke was belayed by his smile.

"I had no such intention, Your Grace. He is yours for the taking."

"Now, I want to introduce you to Mr. Talbot from Canada and, with him, Mr. Smythe from the United States of America."

I already had in mind the lady's advice: that words and silence were equally expressive. So I smiled. "I'm no hero, sir. I did what I should do."

I looked into the eyes of Mr. Talbot, or Mr. Stewart, or possibly Mr. Brown of the Board of Control and remembered his words not to make any assumptions. "It's an honour to meet you, sir."

"The honour is mine, sir." He smiled that little smile he had. "Do you aid our deliberations today? Do you, sir?"

"Mr. Talbot, I can add little that is original. Only what I've been taught: that the divine right of kings has been swept into history by the age of enlightenment. But now we have conflict. The French have codified rights in their Declaration of the Rights of Man and imposed them. Therefore, Human Rights are no doorway for free men to pass through but a barrier."

That little smile flickered. "And what do you conclude from that, young man?" he asked.

"Rights are the refuge of the voiceless, sir: subjects. They represent only a first step on the road to citizenship, a status offering freedom with responsibility. But with rights imposed as a barrier, it would appear that the Code Napoleon is preparing us for a future of subordination."

Mr. Smythe, so suddenly transformed into an American having been so very English in the forest, asked, "I long to know who teaches you, young man. He's done magnificent work. He's planted a garden in your mind that'll give you great pleasure for all of your life." He moved his hand to prevent my interruption. "And I have a suggestion, which is that you should consider becoming an American. A new democratic republic exists with all the freshness of idealism and none of the expedience of privation to pollute it."

"Sir, to answer your question, I am most fortunate at the moment to be a pupil of Georg Hegel and you can see him over there." I pointed to my instructor who stood almost pressed against the wall by an admiring crowd.

"And I thank you for your advice about America and its democracy because the recent French victory will leave no understanding for democracy here, even though the word is as vague as fog."

The Duke held his hands up in horror. "We'd lose a great deal that might have been possible. But to answer your earlier question, Mr. Smythe, I have indeed been most fortunate to secure the teaching services of Georg Hegel. A man whose thinking is so elevated that I hesitated to put him before such young ones. But I see to my delight that he's transformed Master Brandt here into a young man with a future of contribution to the human condition. My regret is that Hegel can only be with us for a short time before he resumes his journey southwards. My blandishments have only induced him to delay his departure rather than to postpone it."

Mr. Talbot smiled. "It would appear that Hegel has found fertile ground." He turned to the Duke and became serious, "The French will exact a price for their victory, perhaps?"

"It is certainly the case," the Duke confirmed. "One hundred eighty million thalers have been levied on Prussia and a loss of lands besides. The state is nearly bankrupt, and it looks everywhere for revenue."

"And wherever it looks, it finds the French have been and the cupboard is already bare."

The Duke nodded sadly.

"So, young man, you hide here and that is why we cannot find you," said a voice behind me.

I turned to face the voice and must have paled. I looked at Monsieur Gaston Dumarque, the French civilian who had been with the soldiers I'd shot in the forest last year. I breathed in deeply. It helps the brain and yields a little time.

"I'm not hiding, sir. We are involved in business here."

"And what business would that be?"

"Hopefully, Monsieur will accept it is family business and therefore of a private nature."

He bowed slightly. "You did not go to Cuxhaven?"

"We have been delayed a full year, sir. Next spring, sir. It is probable that we shall go there at that time."

"When your family business is concluded?"

"You're correct, sir."

He studied me showing disapproval in his demeanour. "Have your lodgings changed as considerably as your raiment?"

"I have indeed been very fortunate. Do you object, sir?"

"Not in the least." Monsieur Dumarque shrugged, turned and strode off across the room to join a different conversation.

He had neither offered his respects to the Duke nor asked to be introduced to the others present. His Grace sighed and said quietly, "I think I have been shown a foretaste of the treatment we must expect at the hands of our new masters." He looked at me, suddenly very sad. "Do you know him?"

"Your Grace, he's a member of Bonaparte's Imperial Police. He's a liar. He's unprincipled and his name is Dumarque."

Those remarks made everyone shift their feet, cough, or put a hand to their mouth.

"But he's on the winning side and we must do what is necessary to oblige him," the Duke replied.

"You'll never oblige him because he isn't his own master. He has no appetite except for the immediate gratification of Bonaparte's bidding. I should have shot him and not his horse. I do regret shooting horses."

Talbot sniggered. "Pray, do tell."

Now it was my turn to think. A most eminent group waited on my words. I knew Mr. Talbot and Mr. Smythe were of the English government. There was the Duke, who I had come to adore and who now watched his world fade like twilight: and Susannah, who listened attentively. But Susannah was never quite still and the slightest of her movements captivated my eyes, enslaved my heart and paralyzed my mind.

I faced the Duke to help me concentrate. "Sir, if anyone hears of a Frenchman called Fougas, I would be glad to know of it."

"Who is Fougas?"

"Claude Fougas is an assassin, Your Grace. He works for Dumarque and now he knows I am here, Fougas will follow."

"Bent on your murder?" asked the Duke.

"Those were his instructions the last time we heard of him. But, with God's help and yours, Your Grace, I shall thwart him."

"How did you meet them?" It was Susannah who asked.

"When we were in the forest we had a coach to sell." I didn't look at the Englishmen, but I needed to inform Mr. Smythe of the progress of his plot and this was the opportunity. "We tried to sell it to Monsieur Dumarque. He arrived with an officer and some troopers and said he wanted to inspect the coach before buying it. But his troopers chopped it to pieces. Later, I saw Dumarque with a gold coin." I glanced at Mr. Smythe who stared back so blandly I knew he had understood the importance of my reference. "Dumarque said he'd found the coin in the coach but I didn't believe him and said so, because we'd searched it many times before. Dumarque then said he had to ride to the Emperor Bonaparte immediately because he had a letter to deliver. And he instructed the officer to kill us all."

"How did you escape?" Susannah held her delicate hand across her breast as her eyes studied me in anticipation. I glanced at her as she moved again and yet again.

I looked back to the Duke. "Because I shot them, apart from one, someone else killed him. I shot Dumarque's horse when he tried to flee. He still wouldn't pay for the coach but told me to go to Cuxhaven for payment. "Later, I heard about Fougas who had been told that Cuxhaven was our destination. As you see Your Grace, my life may be short and therefore my education wasted. But that aside Monsieur Dumarque is not to be trusted."

"It appears to me that your education is being put to excellent interpretation and you have friends." Mr. Talbot smiled and Mr. Smythe grinned broadly. Mr. Talbot's remark had very nearly been a question.

"I hope so," I replied.

"Young Brandt, I will ensure you know of this man Fougas's arrival the instant I hear of it. And I'll do what's necessary to ensure I'm informed," the Duke announced.

149

I bowed. "Your Grace is most considerate."

The Duke nodded. "I know." He agreed and, nodding to himself, shuffled off into the throng perplexed at the ways of the new world. I turned to see Talbot leading Smythe away by the sleeve. They spoke quietly, but they were smiling and I knew why. I was alone with Susannah again.

"How exciting." I felt her hand, or possibly her fan, glide across my backside. "Did you enjoy your first visit to Frederica's house?" She patted me twice lightly to remind me.

"No, I did not."

Her hand rested on my forearm. "Then you should not fall into a liaison with Beatrice either. Unless you wish to learn how to repair ancient tapestries." Susannah rocked her head at the improbability of her suggestion. It was another of her movements, such as very slightly pushing one shoulder forward and back and then the other. It left an impact on a young man.

"Who's she?"

"Suffice it to say that she's dressed in brown with a cream bodice. No, don't look around. She'll think you're interested, because everybody knows."

I started to blush and Susannah laughed. "Your blush makes you look so vulnerable, but you're obviously not. I think you should stay close by me. You would be safer and I neither bite nor slap."

"I'm yours to command, my lady."

"Oh, good."

Chapter Seven: Suborned and Conscripted—1809

My lessons continued over the next years as I studied under various tutors after Georg Hegel continued his journey south. I also studied extensively with Susannah and, very occasionally, Beatrice. However, my instruction had been interrupted by two events: the arrival of Fougas and the messenger from Moscow. Consider my surprise when they turned out to be the same man. It was a clear manifestation of the long reach enjoyed by Bonaparte's Imperial Police.

The messenger had become seriously overdue and the Duke had remarked on it by speculating on the ramifications. In His Grace's mind delay equalled diversion.

The message's arrival occurred one spring afternoon and I will admit to snoozing when I should have been revising. I lay stretched out on my stomach on the padded window seat and basked as the sun's rays cooked me through the glass. My Latin primer lay open at its tables of tenses, but abandoned on the floor and I had dozed off. I was jumped awake by a hefty slap on my backside. I sat up sharply to see the grinning face of Beatrice. What is it about German women and my backside? So far as I'm concerned, it's mine and it's for sitting on.

"What is it that you interrupt me so, Beatrice?"

"You are required in the great hall. A Monsieur Fougas awaits you."

My blood ran cold and drained from my face. Beatrice saw me and exclaimed, "Are you unwell?"

"Is he armed?"

"Armed?"

"That's what I asked. He is tasked with my death."

"I didn't know." She shook her head in bewilderment. "He says he's a messenger. I didn't see any weapon."

"His superior is a liar, so I don't see any reason to believe any better of the servant."

I asked Beatrice if she could find a weapon, anything for self-defence, while I made myself presentable.

She slipped out of the room in a rustle of flowing lavender silk to return moments later carrying a beautiful polished wooden box. It contained two short pistols with compartments for ammunition. I loaded both weapons and hid one in the pocket of my coat, which I draped over the hand that held the other pistol. I followed a sombre Beatrice downstairs to the main hall. As I followed her, I concluded that Beatrice was an attractive woman: attractive, but dangerous—not as dangerous as Fougas though.

Standing in the doorway, I surveyed the great hall. Its walls festooned with antlers, spears and boars' heads in such profusion it was as though they had grown there. The sparse furniture had been pushed to the sides leaving the stone floor as a massive empty space. It was all so irrelevant. The giant fire blazed, but the room never warmed. A few people spoke quietly in groups discussing some matter or other that had brought them here. Jerome broke away from the nearest conversation and beckoned me. A thin man I didn't know stood at the hearth.

I had not seen Jerome since he had admonished me for treating the castle as my own, for being bumptious and for interrupting others who were busy about their duties. I had been summoned to his cluttered office, which contained everything from a plough, the subject of a dispute, to a barrel of molasses. I was chastened and apologetic. I was also guilty. I begged forgiveness.

Jerome had smiled very slightly. "It is not my forgiveness you should seek, but that of His Grace."

I felt terrible. I stood aghast. I had come to adore the Duke and to offend him was more than I could bear.

"What can I do to make amends?" I had asked.

Jerome had replied, "Behave!"

He had returned his attention to the papers before him and without looking up had added, "You are dismissed."

I had been taught a lesson I did not want to have repeated. I had upset the Duke and made a barrier between myself and Jerome, the one person who guided me into the polite world I struggled to enter.

His face today was as sombre as it had been then. It showed all the warning signs.

"Ah, Paul, this is Monsieur Fougas who has come to see you." He indicated the thin man who was not warming himself by the fireside but studying me.

"Well, if it's only to see me, I'm glad to see him."

I approached Fougas whose eyes never left my face for a second. "But do you not have business with His Grace, the Duke?"

Fougas bowed slightly. His eyes never wavered. "I come in peace, Monsieur. I can conduct my business with His Grace only when I've concluded my business with you." The man by the fireplace stood away. "And you? Have you come in peace? I should add that I can only discharge my business with His Grace if I'm alive to deliver my messages." He looked at my coat.

"I have to go out afterwards."

"I see."

"You have business with me?" I asked.

"To make peace between us."

"There is no quarrel or dispute between us that I know of. We never met before today."

"Then we have made peace?"

"That depends on your employer's instructions to you."

"My employer?"

A log crackled loudly and spat an ember that flew onto the stone floor between us. Fougas and I were fixed on each other's faces, so I heard the crack before I saw the ember. I breathed in sharply and my hand twitched. My body rocked a little. Fougas blew through his mouth. His gaze, like a cat's, never deflected, but he had noticed my hand and he flicked a smile briefly.

I swallowed and spoke slowly, "Monsieur Dumarque."

Fougas replied equally slowly, "Why, he wishes peace between us also."

"When you speak of 'us,' are you speaking of yourself and Monsieur Dumarque, or yourself and myself, or of Monsieur Dumarque and me?"

Fougas smiled easily and spread his hands, opening his coat. It allowed me a glimpse of a weapon in his waistcoat pocket. "All of us. We are at peace, are we not?"

"Monsieur Brandt is a credit to us all. You should be impressed at his caution, Fougas."

I knew that voice. Dumarque and a man I didn't know rose from a sofa that faced away from us. The two of them strolled slowly to the fire.

"I confirm I want peace and that Fougas here has no instruction to harm or injure you or yours. In fact, his role is now to protect you from all dangers. Is that not so, Fougas?" Dumarque asked.

Fougas smiled at me. A knowing smile, a confident smile, but not friendly, I thought. "Those are my instructions," he answered.

"But those instructions might change?" I suggested.

The man I did not know spoke, "Indeed they may. I present myself to you, Monsieur Brandt. My name is Henri Du Vallois. It is I, who instruct Fougas in his new task, and Dumarque can countermand me to his heart's desire. It will not avail him. My instructions are those of the Emperor Bonaparte. It is not you who exists under the threat of death but Fougas."

Fougas smiled and added, "My lot in life is hardly improved. I'm certain that I'm so close to receiving fire from Monsieur Brandt that the threat of death at the hand of the Emperor, although just as certain, differs only in that it is a little more distant."

"Possibly, Fougas. But remember, I am the Emperor's proxy," Du Vallois remarked.

"As I said, my lot in life is not improved."

Du Vallois smiled. "Poor Fougas! Every day you eat and drink and every day you live. Every day people look after you and every day you want more."

"Living from one day to the next is an existence. It is not a life."

Du Vallois smiled and asked me. "What do you know of the two men Dumarque saw you speaking with at the Assembly?"

I frowned, as though remembering them. "One claimed to be American and the other Canadian. I've never met anyone from either of those lands before, but to me, they appeared friendly."

"But you've never met them before?"

I shook my head. "Not that I'm aware of. I think I would remember," I lied glibly. "But please bear in mind that, in the last year or so, I've met many people and many new experiences."

"Including shooting Frenchmen?" It was Dumarque.

"Sir, I shot only in self-defence. I do not kill for sport but only for food or self-preservation."

Du Vallois inclined his head. "It would be as well if you refrained from killing my countrymen whenever you can accomplish it. If you are armed now, as Fougas is convinced, I would prefer it if you laid your weapon down and accepted our parole. I have instructions for you and you need to concentrate on them fully."

I laid my coat over the chair I stood beside and closed the frizzen on the pistol I held before lowering the flint gently onto it. I placed the pistol on a small revolving bookcase that stood beside the chair. Fougas smiled and took the pistol from his waistcoat. He placed his weapon next to mine.

"Dumarque, Fougas, wait here. Brandt, come with me." With that Henri Du Vallois strode across the room to a sofa turned to face the window. The studs in his soles clicked on the stone floor. We sat and he looked at me for a long time while he ran his hand up and down his thigh. It was a movement designed to soothe pain, I thought. It had no sensuality in it and certainly none directed at me. That made for change.

"Paul—I will call you Paul, because you are but a boy. Your youth attracts me in the task I have for you, but your lack of experience also warns me. So I will tell you this: at the drop of my handkerchief you will be arrested and executed for the murder of two French troopers and an officer of the cavalry. You will have no defence because there will be no trial and if there was a trial the lawyers would say what they are instructed to say."

I understood the threat but could not gauge its proximity, only its magnitude. I also considered that he had not connected me to the battle of Jena-Auerstedt. He did not know I was the angel.

He looked at me. There was no malice in his regard, but there was no interest either and certainly no compassion or humanity. "We understand each other."

It was not a question.

"Now listen intently. Fougas is to be your manservant. I will establish you financially and you will work for me as I direct. You do not have a choice. You will follow instructions as they are delivered to you and you will report to me through Fougas who will come to me as I require. You will remain here and continue your studies. You will also use your position to discuss the measures we, the French government, introduce."

He let that penetrate my mind by remaining silent. He rose to stare through the window. It had started to rain. He turned to face me. I felt uncomfortable sitting. It was deliberate.

"Make no mistake. In time you will not be able to tell the difference between the northern German states and France, except by the food and the language. Both countries will be run according to the scheme the Emperor has devised. This is a delicate and complex undertaking requiring strategic thinking and devoted attention for a lifetime. The Roman Empire lasted for over four hundred years. Bonaparte's Empire is designed to last forever and to encompass all Europe. To play your part, you must remain alert. I have no doubts about your ability, only your diligence. You must also report any plans you may hear for the rearming of Prussia or any other state against us."

I stood beside him and asked, "I am to be a spy for France?"

Du Vallois studied me for a moment and then stared through the glass again. "France now governs. Prussians are subjects of the Republic. You are a servant of the Republic." He turned and faced me smiling. It was an engaging smile that made you trust, or at least made him appear trustworthy. Du Vallois was dangerous and I was in danger. That was clear.

"You must understand there is a great deal of advantage to be had in that position." Du Vallois continued, "I will give you one caution. You may be tempted to overreach your remit. Resist it."

He returned his gaze to the view for a moment. He appeared to be struck by a thought. "The two North Americans interest both me and the government of France. What they say and do might have a bearing on events. If you see them again and if they confide in you, confide in me. Both of them could be instrumental in the Emperor's plan for the defeat of the English."

"Sir, I would ask one question."

"And what is that?"

"Everyone who has seen us will know that I am to spy for France. They will exclude me from their confidences, surely?"

"Let's sit." We did so and he rubbed his leg again. "Our experience is the opposite. You will be plied with information exactly because people know it will come to me."

I was left with this interpretation to consider.

"Why did you invade us, sir?" I asked at length.

"You mean Prussia? There are justifications. There are always justifications and if there was none one may be created. Why do you ask?"

"I do not understand why."

"Possibly you mean what was the policy? Consider our position. The revolution left the French government without its head, literally. The new government was weak, untried and bankrupt. It fell to the strongest force, also naturally. Napoleon Bonaparte is that force and he faced certain problems. Most of those problems were resolved during the Terror. During that time, many competitors for the leadership of France died one way or the other."

Du Vallois stroked his leg as he considered that part of his country's history. Maybe that was when he received his injury.

"France had no money, no internal order and many unemployed young men. Thus, we invaded our neighbours and removed every possible threat. We occupied our young men and the spoils of victory filled our coffers. But that was just the beginning. A great plan now unfolds. It is too vast in scope and time for ordinary mortals to comprehend. It is Napoleon's plan. It is the master plan worthy of God himself. It is a plan in which each person will play his or her part for the glory of France. And France will repay with peace and stability throughout the conquered lands."

I shook my head as though trying to clear enough space in it to absorb the scope of what I was being told.

"The Grande Armée directly employs well over two hundred thousand men and indirectly at least twice that number. And all of them are best removed from France and idleness. Under the Code Napoleon, we have money, stability, employment and internal order. Now, as you see, that order spreads across the continent."

He yawned delicately tapping the backs of his first two fingers against his teeth.

"I see," I answered, although I didn't, not entirely. "What will happen now?"

"Fougas is now your manservant."

"But not my assassin?"

"But not your assassin. However, Paul, if Bonaparte wants either of us dead, that is what we shall be."

"Will Fougas be a good manservant?"

"No, but he'll do his best. He'll steal from you as he steals from me. Tolerate it but control it. He'll find lodgings and either you'll approve of them or you won't. Move forward from that."

"And Anna?" I asked.

"I believe His Grace will find space for her in his household, but she will not have exalted status."

"It will release Rosina from her vow," I concluded.

"Ah yes, Rosina. Not a spy for the Tsar, but she has the right pedigree for the task."

"I don't think she has the appetite."

"I do hope not. Do you know her plans?"

"I think they involve my Uncle Franz. I think they have come to love each other. Rosina could not have fallen in love with a kinder man. Our problem is Uncle Albert's sight is failing."

"Franz and Rosina postpone their lives for those in their care?" He regarded the backs of his hands as he considered the proposition. He yawned, "Such people are to be revered, I think."

"If His Grace accepts Anna and now that you have taken me into your employ, that leaves only Albert. If you permit, he could live with me. Could Fougas look after him also?"

"I approve," concluded Du Vallois. "I will instruct Dumarque to make the arrangements."

"I thought it was Fougas?"

"You don't expect me to deal with him, do you? Your manservant? Certainly not. You have a great deal to learn."

"Will the Duke approve?"

"The Duke will do what is suggested to him by me."

"Ah."

Chapter Eight: Crosscurrents Expose a Secret— 1810

As the years passed, changes occurred in government and our household that were as dramatic as anything as the turning seasons bestowed.

I treated Fougas as a spy. He was a willing enough manservant and learned his new trade well. I was thankful, yet again, to Jerome for teaching me the responsibilities of being a master. I tried not to be easygoing and to keep Fougas busy. The Duke hired many tutors and even though none matched Hegel's lofty heights, my learning continued and broadened. When I was not studying I loitered in the Duke's entourage. It has to be said as fodder for Susannah and Beatrice, both of whom lay in ambush for me, when it suited them.

I was easily caught and vanquished.

There were times when Susannah's inner fire left her. One evening, as the sun set through the trees, marked such an instance. Susannah stood beside the window staring at the fading light.

"What are you thinking of?" I asked recklessly.

"My husband."

"I thought—"

"You thought he was dead." She turned and her wistful expression evaporated to become harder, "Yes, he is. Bonaparte created twenty thousand widows that day. All of us had our lives blighted by that little man and when I think of Marcel, I cry."

I stood behind her and put my arms around her.

"No don't."

"I'm sorry." I stood away.

She turned and asked, "Am I not allowed to mourn him? And when I do, I want to think of him." She rubbed her hands together favouring the finger on which her wedding band remained. She looked away misty-eyed. "If you touch me, young Paul Brandt, I think of other things."

"So long as I don't make you sad."

"On the contrary, you keep sorrow at bay."

Beatrice was not a widow—at least not a war widow. She said her husband lived in Berlin. I concluded he took refuge there, because the passions that burned in Beatrice showed as a raw urgency. Imagine my surprise when I discovered, at one critical moment, that the delicate slippers she often wore had tiny spurs. I will not dwell on the incident except to inform you that sitting afterwards was painful for several days and everyone laughed at me because they knew or, if they had not known already, Susannah had told them.

I retreated to my new lodgings for a while. Amongst my scant possessions was the parchment given me after the battle of Jena-Auerstedt at the Ilm River. It had remained forgotten and unopened for all those years.

Lying, face down, on my bed I read it. I still have the paper, so I can repeat it word for word.

The defeat of Prussia is so severe that our countrymen will be vassals of the French for years to come. We, the army's

163

commanders, must bear the blame for the defeat as our country suffers its shame.

We must plan our recovery. It will be slow and difficult.

During the recovery our people have only one image of hope. It is of a boy who stopped the French slaughter of our men by holding his ground and keeping his nerve. Your resolve, as well as your skill with a musket, are to be admired and emulated by all men who would free us from the invader. The story of the Angel of Jena will spread across the land and live in every true heart. Wherever you rally them, our men will assemble.

You have demonstrated both willingness and ability to serve your people and they will call on you again.

The signatures that followed were von Blücher, von Clausewitz, von Gneisenau, von Scharnhorst and von Boyen.

The paper remains my most treasured possession.

You cannot imagine how I felt. I was immersed in the sensation of being overwhelmed.

I needed time and quiet to think and made my way to the estate's chapel. I hoped the priest was out on his rounds spreading guilt and misery to the residents he called his flock. I really had no desire to see him and certainly not alone. I entered the dark, tomb-cold hall and smelled the lingering incense.

Kneeling and gazing at the cross, it occurred to me what utter hell Jesus Christ's death must have been: His inability to move and the misery inflicted by just one buzzing, biting insect. The pain He suffered and the pointless sadism He endured. The contempt for life His punishment represented. I felt tears in my eyes again. I also felt a hand on my shoulder.

"Do not be alarmed, young Brandt."

I looked around and saw the benign, lined face of His Grace. He saw my eyes and smiled a little. "You carry a heavy weight for one so young."

"And you, sir? You, too, carry heavy weights."

He smiled. "But I'm used to them and you're not. That's the difference. Perhaps, if you told me your worries, you might find I could advise you."

Again I was overwhelmed. I showed the Duke my paper. He sat beside me and read it out loud.

"Scharnhorst, Gneisenau and Clausewitz, also Blücher, whom I know well. I think it's ungracious of them. The time was difficult to be sure, but they should have expressed their admiration for you and offered you their thanks. I shall write and inform them of my criticism. It cannot hurt. But that letter, however ungracious, is not the cause of your sorrow. Nor possibly is the death of Jesus Christ, although I'm glad to see a fellow human being exposing his emotions as honestly as you are doing."

I wiped my face. "Sir, did I tell you the story of the Englishman who came to us in the forest?"

"The man who hid the letter expressing English support for the Tsar's army of a million men?" he asked, smiling.

I looked at the Duke and saw amused interest. "Yes, sir," I continued. "You see, the American and the Canadian I met at your Assembly are the same two people who said they were English in the forest. It was Mr. Talbot who left the letter in the coach. In the forest he called himself Robert Stewart."

The Duke chuckled quietly and stood. He looked around the empty chapel, studied the figure of Our Lord and crossed himself.

"I can tell you about the Englishman—the one who pretended to be the Canadian, Mr. Talbot. Robert Stewart is his real name. But he also has a title. He is the Viscount Castlereagh and he is at the very heart of English foreign policy."

The Duke sat down close to me, speaking quietly, "Castlereagh runs huge personal risks coming here, but he is bold and adventurous. The story of the Tsar's army of a million men fascinates me because France and Russia have signed a peace treaty. An army of one million men is possible for Russia alone. No other country could raise such a force."

The Duke's voice reduced to a whisper, "Bonaparte must react to that threat, peace treaty or no. The questions are: How will he do it and when will he do it?"

He placed his hand on my shoulder and squeezed slightly. "Young Paul Brandt, you'll have to be clever and adroit to survive the coming years; for one so young, it will be difficult. They will set traps for you that you cannot imagine." He thought as he leaned back on the creaking chair and speaking normally, added, "I will see to it we dine alone once each month; more if necessary. We will dine in the hearing of no one and in the knowledge of no one. So don't tell anyone. I will send word by one person I trust."

With that the Duke rose, crossed himself and was about to leave when he turned back.

"Something I must tell you." He came to sit beside me again. "I've had a meeting with Rosina at my request because I received an answer from a second messenger I sent to Moscow. I was not satisfied with Fougas's information, so I sent another request."

I looked at him, waiting for him to continue. He was thinking.

"I have relieved Rosina of her task. She can claim, should she ever be asked by the *Tayny Prikaz*—of whom she lives in fear, I may say—that she discharged her obligation to me regarding Anna and I accepted it.

"The other thing you should know," the Duke went on slowly, "is that Anna is no relative of mine. The two princesses, who are of my blood, are not involved. The message from Fougas implied one of them was Anna's mother. But neither has any part in her history."

The Duke looked at my face, searching it. "There is a terrible story to tell though. It is possible—. No, that's not right. It is probable that Anna is the illegitimate daughter of the Tsar Alexander himself with his first love, a woman called, or who calls herself, Catherine de Brunswick. No one knows if Catherine survived, but there were plots to kill both Anna and her mother. Now Anna is safe and where she might pass unnoticed. Rosina thinks the truth might lie in the papers—"

"That were stolen?"

"Yes, but without them there is no proof."

"I understand."

"I'm glad you do because the rumour must not spread, for Anna's sake. Rosina will guard her tongue. No one has told Anna, so she doesn't know. Rosina doesn't think she can keep confidences."

"That's true," I interrupted again.

167

"The problem is made worse. The Tsar had admitted to his advisers that he wanted to marry Catherine. That he didn't was because members of his Court told him she had died. But her death is not certain." The Duke squeezed my shoulders and shook me gently to make sure I was fully alert and listening. He looked into my eyes. "But should the current Tsarina die—and she's childless—and should Catherine live, as rumour suggests, and if she and the Tsar did marry—" The Duke breathed out noisily and looked at me to see if I would make the connection, but I kept quiet. "Then Anna would be legitimized. There are people who will go to great lengths to prevent that. Anna's line must remain a secret."

"Do the French know, do you think?"

"Paul, they may suspect, because the information Fougas brought was unclear and suggested Julianne was her mother. That was not true." He took my chin in his hand. "I'm sure I don't need to tell you to keep this to yourself." He released me.

"No, sir," I whispered.

The Duke rose, bowed to the cross and left as quietly as he'd come. I turned to face the crucifix. Christ's agony had not abated, but mine had.

"She'll have to be told one day," I said and turned to the Duke. But he'd already gone.

Chapter Nine: Conflicting Demands on My Future— 1811

Various predictions came to pass over the following months. The Duke accepted Anna into his household and under his protection and both she and Rosina moved to live in the castle. The Duke shared the crystals between Rosina and himself as trustees for Anna, taking two pieces each. Rosina was awarded the fifth. She was astounded when he told her they were uncut diamonds and of value. Amsterdam was the city she should travel to if ever she intended to sell them.

Rosina accepted Franz's offer of marriage. From that moment all her energies were devoted to her wedding preparations. It left a void in my life because Rosina had been a true friend, and now she had other priorities.

Albert was happy to move in with me. His eyes were failing, and he needed a well-ordered household, which was something the dreadful Fougas could achieve. Albert spent as much time as he could outside. He would walk in the forest or tend the garden of the house where Franz would live alone until his marriage.

The person most upset by the changes was Anna. It was not that she was ungrateful to the Duke. How could she be? The report from Moscow that Fougas had delivered was hardly satisfactory from her point of view. Anna was, the report confirmed, illegitimate and while neither of the Duke's nieces admitted to being her mother, it was supposed that one of them, in fact, was. There was a carefully worded passage that implied her real mother might have died.

Anna would stare into the distance and wonder about the truth of her life and dream of what might have been. But she was, occasionally, a realist and her memory remained full of those terrible days and nights on the winter roads coming west. She knew how lucky she'd been to escape, to say nothing of having Rosina to care for her. But Rosina was occupied with her own life and no clear plan for Anna's future had emerged. She began to speak of those days of disaster and privation as though they were about to return.

Anna drifted into a depressive, combative state of mind.

She concluded that everyone's plans deliberately excluded her and that was their intention. It was hardly fair to the Duke, but Anna's state prevented her from being impartial. She had been cast adrift by part of her family and the remainder of it was planning leave her.

I visited our old house. Only Franz lived there now and Rosina spent her days looking after her husband to be and making plans with him for their future. Most of our chattels had been moved out by that time and Rosina worked to clear the rooms one by one before we returned the house to the estate.

I found her in the kitchen speaking with Frederica Storch. Our encounter had never been repeated or even referred to.

The seamstress looked at me aloof.

"Good afternoon, Miss Storch," I greeted her, smiling.

Frederica did not respond, but looked at Rosina frowning, and said, "Perhaps this young man can provide an answer to your problem, Rosina, for I do not know what to suggest."

"Naturally, I'll do anything I can to help." I walked around Rosina and took a saucepan off the hob, catching it just as it boiled over.

"I must return to my workshop." Frederica looked at me. "That reminds me I have a suit for you. I trust it will fit."

"May I come to collect it?"

"I will certainly not deliver it."

"Miss Storch, peace I beg of you. May I come later today?"

"Very well." She relented and left.

Rosina smiled thinly. "What do you expect?" She chuckled, but then became serious and, placing her hand on my arm, said, "Paul, I require your help. Please bring Anna to her senses. She has stormed off and she's making our lives a misery."

"She feels no one loves her," I offered.

"Well, they don't," she studied me quizzically, "Unless you do."

I pulled back a chair and sat heavily. Rosina leaned on the table.

"As a sister?" I asked.

"She will want more."

I nodded.

"You know the story?" Rosina asked me.

"Yes, but—"

"Yes, but what?"

"I need to think," I added lamely.

Rosina turned to adjust the damper on the stove and replaced her saucepan on the heat. "She's not a child, you know."

"I know."

"And she's quite pretty."

"Rosina, she's actually very pretty but I have thought of her only as a sister, just as I have thought of you." I held my hands up to fend off any rebuttal. "Even though I know you're not."

"Don't play with her. She's not a Susannah or a Beatrice."

"Rosina, I've never done so."

Rosina wiped her hands on a cloth and added, "And now you are condemned for it."

I rose. "Rosina, I'll do what I can. Where is the little wretch?"

"I don't know. As I said, she stormed off ranting about injustice and the end of her family. I think she went to the lake. She feeds the ducks there, sometimes."

Whatever Rosina was cooking smelled good, but the aroma was all I would enjoy of it. I stepped outside into the late afternoon. The sun was warm, the breeze light and the sky filled with puffy clouds. All should have been at peace. Instead, I had to deal with two women who blamed me. Talk about injustice!

I made my way to the lake through the side of the orchard. The apple trees bowed, laden with fruit busy ripening. The hedgerow sagged under a tangle of blackberries and sloes. I stopped to pick blackberries and sample that essence of summer.

As I tarried I felt a premonition. Franz always taught me to respect such feelings and never to ignore them. I hurried on to the lake and entered the meadow in which it stood.

There was a jetty to which a rowing boat had been tethered, but the boat had become waterlogged and the jetty rotten. The local boys had played there until Jerome forbade it. The water was choked with weed and if someone fell in, they would not be able to extract theirself even if they could swim and no one I knew could do that. I decided there and then that I would find someone to teach me.

Anna knelt at the far end of the jetty staring into the water. I called out and she ran to me crying. She flung her arms around me and held me tightly. Sobbing, she asked, "Is this how Susannah holds you?"

"Anna!" I recovered my composure and buried my self-righteousness, putting my arms around her. "No, but there's no need to move. This is fine."

She wriggled closer.

"That's enough, Anna. What are you up to? Rosina is worried about you."

"Do you like it when I hold you?"

"As you ask, yes, but beware."

"I shall not beware. I want you to promise to marry me."

"But I'm too young to marry and Anna, so are you."

"No, I'm sixteen. But when the time comes, will you promise?" She looked up at me.

"What would happen if you wanted to marry someone else?"

"I shall not, but if I did, I would release you."

"And what if I wanted to marry someone else?"

She didn't hesitate but answered immediately, "I will throw myself into the river and be swept out to sea with the mermaids."

"In that case, I promise."

"Then kiss me."

There followed a moment that has never really been equalled throughout my life. Anna, who was proving she was no child, kissed me using every advantage she had to the full. She pressed herself so close and her arms were so tight about my body that I could feel the warmth of hers and her kiss was passionate, if not desperate. When eventually we parted, I needed some time for my body to leave me alone. I never thought of Anna as anyone other than a woman after that.

"Tell me, Anna. What has brought on this passion? Have you just discovered you love me?"

"I've always loved you, Paul and you've never noticed me. So I had to do something, or I would be quite alone forever."

"What do you mean?"

"Rosina and Franz are talking of going to Höxter when they're married. They'll take a ship for America and I shall never see them again. And Albert will stay with you. And I shall live in the castle and I don't know anyone. I shall be alone. But now I know you'll marry me."

"Anna, you are unprincipled."

"No. I will have what I want. I've spent enough of my life on its very edge."

"And you bit the person who protected you."

"Oh, Paul!" She took my lapels in her hands and looked up at me. Her eyes had become clear blue pools of light. "There's not a day I do not kiss Rosina and beg her forgiveness."

"If I were Rosina, I wouldn't give it."

"Not everyone is as vengeful as you. I hope that is how you will protect me," Anna observed.

I was looking down onto a quite pretty face—actually a very pretty face—and it was becoming difficult to think rationally. "I hope we shall live in a country where you need no protection," I mumbled.

"And which country will that be? Because with the French stealing all we have, it cannot be this one."

"Yet! Anna, I have a meeting, so I must hurry." I tried to break away.

"With Susannah?" she asked urgently, pulling me back to her.

"No, of course not."

"With Frederica Storch?"

"Certainly not in that way, but actually, yes. I have to see her to collect some clothes. And Anna, it's not your concern. Don't be jealous already."

"I am not good enough?"

"Anna, you are certainly good enough, just as you are certainly too young. Now, go back to Rosina and tell her you have everything you wanted."

"No. Kiss me."

I did, but I remembered Rosina's demand that I did not play with Anna.

We parted. "I must go."

I didn't wait, but turned and walked towards the castle and my dinner. No one must know. The Duke was emphatic and Anna couldn't keep secrets. It was this conclusion that kept me from telling her about her true identity, but it couldn't last for long.

After a few moments walking towards the orchard I turned to see if Anna had made up her mind. She was skipping home like an innocent child: a posture nothing short of deceit.

I picked an apple, dislodging another, which I gathered as a present for Frederica. My boots swished through the grass. The sheep hadn't grazed this side of the orchard. I could see them loitering in the deepening shade of the hedge on the far side. Everything was well on a warm evening.

"Now you wish to play Adam and Eve with me?" Frederica asked archly as I offered her the apple at her front door.

There is no answering such remarks. I collected my clothes and begged to change there and then. Frederica consented rather than agreed and thus I made up time. Even her examination of my appearance was cursory.

I thanked her and left hoping that an improvement in our relationship might follow.

I hurried to the castle and ran up the spiral steps to the Duke's private quarters and entered, closing the door as quietly as I could. I turned to see him standing in the middle of the room. He wasn't there when I had opened the door and I had not heard him arrive. It was as though he'd just appeared. I glanced at his shoes to see he wore a wonderful pair of bright-red Turkish slippers with curly toes. The room was warm and I glanced at the fireplace surprised to see it set and lit.

"You're late," he observed.

"I apologize, Your Grace, but I've just had an extraordinary encounter."

"And what was that?" He led me to a small table. He picked up a decanter and poured wine for himself and mixed wine with water for me.

"I've just had marriage proposed to me."

"And you accepted?" the Duke enquired with a smile over his mischievous face.

"With Anna, it's difficult to do otherwise."

The Duke chuckled and indicated the sideboard. "Here you see before you a smorgasbord, though today, the word 'buffet' is often used."

I looked at the display of food. There was pickled red cabbage and herring, a whole roasted trout and a goose, also roasted. There was ham, plain and smoked. There was a bowl of potato salad and a host of other dishes.

"Take a plate and serve yourself," the Duke instructed me.

"Are there just the two of us?"

"Yes, yes. Don't worry. Nothing goes to waste. I can indulge my appetites." With that, he took up a massive silver serving spoon with a long handle and lunged at the terrine. "Wild boar, my favourite. Now watch. This is part of your education. You must recognize these dishes and know what each is. Try them. Don't take too much of any. That's the secret."

Even taking a little of each made my plate full to overflowing, but it was all so good—all those flavours. The dried and smoked hams were such treats, but it was not as though I was tired of cured ham. We ate and talked and returned to the buffet and helped ourselves again.

His Grace just enjoyed the company of a younger person—to say nothing of prodigious amounts of wild boar terrine—who was not caught up in the daily affairs of the castle. Unless you consider the demands of Susannah and Beatrice as daily affairs. Now I had to consider Anna's feelings. Whatever was going on behind that entrancing face was incompatible with a peaceful life of quiet contemplation. Not that I was considering such an existence, but to be allowed the choice would have been nice.

"You should have asked my permission before you accepted Anna's outrageous proposition."

"Sir, I appreciate that. But we both know it would have made no difference to the outcome."

The Duke laughed.

I turned serious. "Sir, at some stage I must tell Anna."

"Now is not the time. To make it easy for you, I forbid it."

"That certainly makes it easier, but the deceit remains."

"It's not really deceit. It's protection. How's your plate? Looking empty? Shall we try one last time?"

And so we did. I promise that the Duke's plate was no smaller than mine, but he chose his ingredients with greater skill. He made "pom-pom" singing noises as he stalked the dish he intended to attack with the giant spoon.

I forget now all the topics the Duke talked about. I had to be precise when we discussed what I should tell Fougas and also when I repeated the questions Dumarque had asked. The Duke stored it away and said he would send word how I should reply.

After the third foray to the buffet, the Duke drained his glass and smiled. "We really shouldn't call it a smorgasbord because that should be for cold food only. A buffet can contain hot food."

He stood and smiling with pure mischief, made his way to the fireside. I realized why it had been lit. Using his napkin, he raised the lid of a pot to release the aroma of sauerbraten. He sniffed. "This is a stew of venison in wine. It's delicious and I do recommend it." He replaced the lid. "But I am looking for other game." He lifted the lid of another pot. "Ha, I have not been abandoned by the kitchen! Hasenpfeffer: jugged hare. Now, am I to be treated?" With a look of pure greed and expectation, he lifted the top from a silver chafing dish "Yes, *bratkartoffeln*. This is potatoes, boiled and mashed and fried, very slowly." He smiled. "Hee-hee!" he giggled, "with sea salt in goose fat."

The Duke let the silver lid fall to the grate with a clatter. He blew on his fingers. "Hot! Now I'll get into trouble." He scooped a huge mound of the potato onto his plate. "It's totally impossible to digest and it will keep me awake for several days, but what an experience!" He covered the potato in hare stew. "I wonder if I dare have a little of the red cabbage." He looked around and succumbed. He placed his dish before his place and spooned up red cabbage from the buffet, or smorgasbord, onto another plate which he left by the fireside.

"Now, young man, here is food to build you up.

I knew stew from Albert's cooking, but these smelled so good. I followed my mentor's example and scooped up the bubbling potato. It was a crunchy brown on the outside and a thick paste on the inside. I swear there was more goose fat and salt than potato in it. I tried both the jugged hare and the deer stew. We ate and we drank.

To my credit I finished my plate. To my surprise the Duke finished his.

"Have you eaten enough?" he asked clearly hoping for the answer, "no."

"Sir, I have never eaten so much or so well. I hope to remember every mouthful for all my life."

"I will tell the cooks. It's what they long to hear."

He rose from the table and helped himself to more wine. He stared at the lights glimmering from the houses nearby.

"Should I move these dishes away from the fire, sir?" I asked. "They may spoil."

"Very good idea; best not to put them on the table, though. Might burn it and I would get into even more trouble."

With my napkin as a guard I pulled the dishes away from the fire and took the opportunity to open one we had not touched.

The aroma was quite different and fantastic, even though I could not contemplate one more mouthful. There were white beans, a lump of goose, as I supposed, a hunk of bacon, a juice that must have contained tomato, being the only red thing I could think of at that moment and goose fat.

The Duke's voice came over my shoulder. "That is cassoulet of goose. It's delicious, but if you think *bratkartoffeln* is indigestible, you have not examined the dimensions of possibility that you would after a few mouthfuls of that." I was grateful to stand even though the effort was almost more than I could manage. I exhaled noisily and joined the Duke by the window.

"Would you like more wine? I have not offered it or poured it because that might make you feel obliged to drink it. Be careful of wine. At your age be careful of people who offer it. Take it with water and mix the water yourself."

I returned to the table and poured.

"Half and half is what you've been drinking," he told me.

It was the formula I stayed with.

"I told you I would write to Gebhard Blücher, do you remember?" the Duke asked.

"Yes, sir."

"I have received a very prompt letter from Carl Clausewitz in reply. He's grateful to know where you are and he wishes you to visit him in Berlin." He looked at me over his glass. "And I regret, young Paul that he, together with the other army reformers, may want to keep you for some time."

The Duke smiled. "Don't worry unduly. You'll have your old role to play again. The Angel of Jena must fly once more."

He leaned forward becoming conspiratorial. "The men who wrote that note after the battle of Jena-Auerstedt have been reforming the Prussian army. We're nearly ready to stand against Napoleon again and they would like some help from Heaven above. I'm sure you take my meaning."

"I'll do what I can."

"That's all any man can do and all any man can ask. The question remaining is: Will it be enough? We'll drink to your success." We raised our glasses and drank. The Duke placed his glass on the table and withdrew a paper from his cuff to hand to me. "Go to this address. Start tomorrow if you can. With fair weather you should be there next week and that'll be soon enough."

The door shut quietly and we both looked up to see Jerome leaning on it. He stood forward sniffing the air and looked at the fireplace. "I smell cassoulet!" he declared.

"Help yourself, Jerome," the Duke offered.

Jerome smiled and walked towards us. "Later, sir. I'll eat all of it. But Fougas has received new instructions."

"Then help yourself to wine, Jerome and tell us what you've heard."

Jerome took a glass from the table and I watched him pour. I was intrigued to see that he, too, added some water to his wine, but not so much as half.

"Two French travellers arrived in town this afternoon and asked at the inn for directions to the residence of Paul Brandt." Jerome drank and savoured it. "The innkeeper is, naturally, primed to report any such enquiry to me. He was happy to provide directions but said you were away from home."

"That was intelligent of him." The Duke nodded.

"Indeed it was, because it produced the information that the travellers were really hoping to see the manservant, Fougas. What is interesting is that they are a couple: husband and wife. The innkeeper is convinced of it."

"I'm curious," said the Duke, musing, "to know why a couple has been sent to Fougas. It's not what one would expect. I think we should take the evening air."

Chapter Ten: Deaths and Duplicity

I waddled through overeating as we made our way home taking the shortcut through the woodland. I paid little attention to all those mysterious scuttling noises and sudden silences that betray the work of the forest night.

A lamp still burned in the room we used in the evenings and I concluded Fougas and the new arrivals were there.

Suddenly, I collided with the possibility that Fougas had received instructions to kill me as everyone said would one day be the case, just as Jerome's hand touched my shoulder. That made me jump. He smiled and slipped through the open door leaving me outside with the Duke.

Jerome returned instantly. "Be prepared for a shock. Fougas and your Uncle Albert are dead."

The fantastic evening of pleasure dropped into a pit of despair.

I entered my lodgings to see them lying on the floor. Albert's arm was clamped tightly around Fougas's throat. A sideways thrust from the assassin's blade had killed dear, kindly Uncle Albert.

I concluded my uncle had stood behind Fougas to throttle him probably while he sat at the table. Fougas had drawn his blade to stab backwards in defence. Albert had taken time to die and during his last moments had strangled the Frenchman.

But why? Fougas was an unpleasant man to be sure, but we'd lived with him for a considerable time and had become used to him. I thought about the scene.

Albert's sight was failing but he knew the house. Fougas was a slow reader and sometimes spoke aloud when he did it. We'd all heard him and secretly listened as he tried to unravel the messages from his master. But they were, for the most part, commonplace or dull.

Jerome separated the dead men and extracted the slender blade from Albert's body before he searched Fougas. Finding nothing of significance he covered the man with a blanket.

I knelt beside the body of my uncle and studied the stilled bearded face of a kind man who treated both animals and people with respect. He was a man who lived by the laws of the countryside and who had done his duty to the best of his ability. Now he lay dead on the floor of a house, not his own, and a long way from the land of his birth. I took his big rough hands and crossed them on his chest. "Good-bye, Uncle Albert. I promise I'll find out why you died and make sure your death is not wasted."

I stood and Jerome spread another blanket over him. It was as though Uncle Albert had suddenly disappeared.

In the grate lay fragments of burnt paper. On the table lay one last sheet and the reference book Fougas used to translate messages from their coded state. We'd seen it before but had never discovered where he hid it. It took me some time to get the idea of translating the few coded words in the text, but eventually I was able to read the following lines: "*People must think the boy killed him. So kill him where he will not be immediately found, but in the lodgings. You will inform the authorities that you saw the boy leave home wearing bloody clothes, but you do not know the direction he took. The letter will cause his departure.*"

I looked up. "What letter?"

"This one," the Duke answered taking a note from the mantelpiece. "Do you mind if I open it?" He didn't wait for my permission but tore the paper at the fold and read: *"Brandt, you are betrayed. There is no time to waste on partings. Come to me in Weimar. Leave by noon tomorrow."*

The Duke turned the paper over. "There's no signature, but then one is hardly required."

"Du Vallois?" I suggested.

"That conclusion is the intention of the writer. But what if it was Dumarque?"

"We can conclude that Fougas received instructions from Dumarque that Albert tried to thwart," Jerome suggested.

"I agree Jerome," His Grace answered. He rubbed his mouth as he thought silently for a few moments. "The question is what those instructions were." The Duke pursed his lips. "Is there more on the page? Perhaps there's more to learn."

I read: "The woman and her husband must leave on the Weimar road the forenoon following. When you have informed the authorities, follow them yourself. Report to me alone and speak of this to no one."

I looked up at my mentors. "I don't understand," I admitted.

"I fear you're cast in the role of culprit, young Paul," the Duke concluded.

"And of murder—but of whom?" Jerome thought out loud.

"That's correct, Jerome." The Duke looked at his factor nodding his head absently. "We need to think. Who is me and who is him?" asked the Duke. "Is the sender Du Vallois or Dumarque?"

"Or is it someone else?" I asked. "There's no signature."

"No one would put their name to such a document." The Duke dropped my letter on top of the letter to Fougas. "And we don't know who the victim is. Is there no more?" The Duke looked at burned paper in the grate.

We were denied further discussion by the sounds of a man and woman arguing outside. We heard the man hush the woman, whose objections continued in a ferocious whisper. The voices came closer and the door pushed open.

"Father Pym!" exclaimed the Duke and Jerome simultaneously.

The terrified priest stumbled into the room and fell to his knees before the Duke. I think he would have kissed his boots had we not been present.

"Who are you?" asked a young woman standing in the doorway. She was remarkable for her fair hair, her stature and her heightened colour. She was also remarkable because she wore some of my spare clothes. We all considered the similarities between us.

The Duke glowered at her. "You may address me as Your Grace. Your Highness is also appropriate. And you? Who are you?"

"I am Marie Delbarde, Your Grace. This is my husband, Daniel." She indicated the tall man dressed as a French infantry private standing beside her.

"And what are you doing here at this time of night with a priest? Do you wish to confess?"

"No sir, I've committed no sin and if I had, the priest would be in no state to hear it."

"Your Grace, she has come to kill me." The priest wailed from his knees.

"Unfortunately you're safe." The Duke turned his attention to the Frenchwoman having admonished the priest to stop his noise. "Shut the door and tell me why you've come all this way to kill this unfortunate priest. Appreciate please; it is by no means a criticism. The world will almost certainly be improved without him. I ask from curiosity, merely."

The priest emitted a faint mewing noise.

"I have not come to kill the priest. I have come to bring him to this house and to be seen doing so."

"By walking past the inn?" asked Jerome.

The woman nodded. "Why, yes, sir. Those were my instructions."

The Duke and Jerome looked at each other. They were thinking.

Jerome put his knuckle to his teeth. "I think I understand so far." He looked at the woman. "Go on."

The woman looked at the Duke. "My husband is a conscript in the Grand Army of Bonaparte, Your Grace. I came to beg for his release. I'm with child and it's growing harder to manage our small farm. Even before Daniel was conscripted it was difficult to manage. Every day my situation gets worse. I will not be able to plough or harvest in my condition. To make things worse, the mayor is casting longing eyes over the farm—and me—and he's been sending bailiffs to make trouble."

"Sit, Madame." The Duke pulled a chair back for her. The woman sat. Her husband continued their story.

"I'm the younger son of a stonemason. My brother works with our father, so there's no exception for me and I was conscripted."

"That does not explain what you're doing with the priest."

"She is going to kill me," Father Pym bleated.

Everyone in the room shouted, "Oh, be quiet!" or words with that meaning. The priest subsided into mumblings that might have been prayer, confessions, or the incantations of a necromancer.

"Be quiet!" snapped the Duke.

The woman continued, "I went to Daniel's officer. A man had been sitting and talking with him at the time. The officer said there was no possibility of release and that my husband must do his duty. But the man looked at me very hard. He made me feel uncomfortable. Eventually, he said there was possibly a way."

"Do you know the man's name?"

"No, sir."

"But if you saw him again?"

"Yes, sir. I would know him."

The Duke prodded the priest with the toe of his boot. "To whom do you report? Before you answer, I do not mean the Almighty. And I do not mean myself. I am expecting to hear a French name, one of only two, so be precise."

"Dumarque," admitted Father Pym.

We stood, despondent in chilly silence, as we digested the priest's confession and what it meant for each of us. The Duke shook his head. "What a disgusting web they weave." He addressed the woman, "Continue."

"The man said I could be of service to the Emperor and I would be rewarded with my husband's liberty." She opened her hands wide. "So we came here."

"I told you she is going to kill me," protested the priest, shuffling round on his knees to face each of us in turn.

"Oh, do be quiet!" came the chorus.

"To do what? Be precise," the Duke addressed the woman again.

"The man told me to bring the priest here. He said the priest was evil and it was time to end his villainy."

"Now do you believe me?" Father Pym insisted.

"Be quiet," came the chorus.

"In that respect the man who gave you instructions is quite correct. The world will certainly be better off without the priest and his villainy. But why are you dressed in the young man's clothes?" asked the Duke.

It was Jerome who answered, "She looks a little like Paul, Your Grace. At night the mistake would be acceptable. Anyone who saw her at a distance would say it was Paul. They're not expecting to see her and they don't know her. And as you say she's in Paul's clothing."

Jerome looked speculatively in the Duke's direction and saw he was studying the appearance of Marie Delbarde in Paul's clothes. Jerome cleared his throat.

The Duke seemed to abandon his train of thought and glanced at Jerome. He smiled slightly and turned to me. "Paul you were to be seen in the company of the priest, on your way here tonight, by people in the inn. Today possibly, the priest would be found dead here. Fougas would have given information to the authorities that he had seen you leave in bloody clothing." He ran his hand over his face while he thought more.

"So Paul, it was to be you who killed the disgusting priest, apparently." The Duke turned to the woman and asked, "That's the intention, is it not?"

"The man said I was to dress in spare clothes that Monsieur Fougas would procure and I was to lead the priest to this house. I was to return with him by way of the inn."

"How were you to do that?" asked Jerome.

"Fougas suggested I knock on the priest's door and stand back in the shadow. When he opened the door I was to beckon him."

"And he followed?"

"After he had put on his cloak."

"And when he discovered you were not the boy?"

"By that time my husband had joined us."

"Naturally." His Grace rubbed his mouth and then shook his head.

The priest, remaining on his knees was now silent. He assumed the expression of a hound that doesn't know what's coming next. It would either be food or a beating.

"I can't win my husband's release unless the priest is dead and I was to bring him back here for Monsieur Fougas to deal with him," Marie explained frowning.

"Why couldn't your husband do it? He's a soldier."

Daniel spoke again. "I do as I am ordered, sir, but I'm a good Catholic and I will not kill as an assassin kills."

"Why didn't you just run away together?" I asked.

"The officer sent two soldiers with us. They wait at the inn to see Marie play her part and bring us back tomorrow," Daniel answered.

"Then Daniel will get his discharge papers," added his wife.

"And without those he's a deserter?"

"Yes, Your Grace."

The Duke turned to his factor and asked, "Jerome what do you make of all this?"

"Your Grace, it's perverted in the extreme. It makes a mélange of expediency and opportunism with policy. Think on this: it must be French policy to kill the Angel of Jena. No disrespect to you Paul, but in truth they want you and your legend in your grave. To have you involved in a scandal that involves you and a priest with—" Jerome looked at Father Pym, thought and continued, "predilections would be an advantage especially as you would suffer the death penalty for having killed him."

Jerome was interrupted by an extraordinary whining noise escaping from the man kneeling on the floor. I began to have a little sympathy for the priest, but only a little.

192

"I suspect also Dumarque would like to discredit Du Vallois, his superior, in the eyes of his masters. For his own advantage and promotion, you understand. So in this ramshackle plot it would appear that Du Vallois's man—that's you, Paul and also the Angel of Jena—killed Dumarque's man, being the priest Pym, here."

"With predilections," added the Duke.

"Quite." Jerome nodded his head and smiled. "But there has to be more. It seems so casual. Also, I don't like the idea of people returning on the Weimar road tomorrow. That seems deliberate." He ran his hands over his mouth. "But there must be a good reason and I don't like the one that comes to mind."

The Duke watched him but concluded that Jerome was thinking. He turned his attention to the woman. "I regret to inform you that Fougas is himself dead. Currently he's lying under that blanket. You'll have to kill the priest yourself after all. Would you like Jerome to fetch another blanket?"

The Duke was not being helpful to the woman just as he was certainly basting the priest's head with misery. The conversation was tending towards the beating and not the food.

"Perhaps you could do it more readily with a pistol? If you stood close enough you probably would not miss," the Duke suggested with false innocence. He turned to face Jerome who looked back at him balefully.

"Your Grace, I do not have a pistol to lend her. However, there's a horse pistol in the night watchman's chair. I could fetch it."

"Upon reflection it would wake everyone, would it not?"

"For a considerable distance I should imagine, sir."

"True. But a swift end, don't you think?"

"Yes, Your Grace, but messy and someone would have to wash the floor."

"And the walls," added the Duke.

I glanced between His Grace and Jerome and I understood how close these two men understood each other and how their sense of humour sparked. This was made all the more exciting because the conversation was conducted with straight faces.

The priest's eyes were as large as the moon and his mouth worked but without making any intelligible sound.

"We cannot be free unless the priest is dead," Daniel stated rather obviously.

"Even when the priest is dead you'll not be free," Jerome spoke like a schoolmaster to a slow-witted child.

The cleric squealed shuffling across the floor on his knees. The Duke kept him away with his foot.

The Duke asked Marie, "Where did this meeting take place?"

"In Weimar, sir."

"And you came from?"

"Orleans, sir."

"South of Paris?"

"Yes, sir."

"A long journey. How did you accomplish that?"

"I was fortunate to secure a place in a coach that brought me practically all the way. I travelled with the wife of an officer as her maid and companion."

Jerome shuffled on his feet as though changing his weight while he refined the various conclusions in his mind. He nuzzled the knuckle of his index finger for a moment and then explained, "We know that Fougas had instructions to send you back on the Weimar road tomorrow forenoon. I suggest Dumarque has made arrangements whereby you will meet your end on that journey. Just travellers killed on the road. The blame for the priest's death falls on the young man here whose clothes you're wearing. He becomes a fugitive."

"But he is also bidden to Weimar." The Duke waved the letter he had taken from the mantelpiece.

"And so the Angel's death, or arrest for the murder of a priest, is accomplished on the road also," continued Jerome.

The Duke nodded in agreement and turned to me. "I think you should ask for your clothes back."

"Sir, I beg of you!" the woman protested. The Duke smiled.

"Later, later." The Duke paced the room and stood before Jerome. "As you said before, this murder is to appear that Paul, Du Vallois's man, killed Dumarque's man, the priest. Without knowing more it would appear that three or four lives will be sacrificed because Dumarque wishes to disgrace Du Vallois." The Duke turned to study the assembled company for a moment and then returned his focus to Jerome. "This plot cannot have existed before Dumarque saw the similarity between Madame Delbarde here and Paul."

"I think you're correct, Your Grace," confirmed Jerome.

195

"And you think the Delbardes will die on the Weimar road?"

"Yes. I think that would be part of Dumarque's plan."

"But they have two soldiers with them."

The Duke turned to the Frenchwoman and asked, "You realize you cannot go home and your husband must not report back to his regiment?"

"I had not thought, sir."

"That much is evident. However, you were put into a position where you were ordered to assist in killing someone or else your request would not be granted."

"That's true, sir. I had no choice."

The Duke turned to me, "Paul, we have discussed what's wrong with the Code Napoleon and here's a manifestation of it."

He frowned and sat. "If any of you set foot on the Weimar road tomorrow you will be killed there—of that I am now convinced."

He turned to the priest. "I have no objection in your case."

He thought for a moment and looked at the French couple again. "I suggest that when you leave tomorrow—and you will—you must head in any direction other than to Berlin." He ran his hands over his face as though to clear his thoughts. "You are to be pitied. To be given such a terrible task is unforgivable. Somehow and somewhere you must start a new life." His Grace was interrupted by the castle clock striking the hour. "But it's too late to plan tonight. We'll consider everything in the morning."

The Duke addressed the priest. "You are dismissed my service. You are never to return or to speak of your time here."

196

I was staring at the blanket that covered Uncle Albert. "I must tell my uncle Franz." I said as tears overflowed and poured down my face. I felt like falling to my knees and begging Uncle Albert to come back.

"No, Paul." The duke hugged me. "I'll do it. You go to bed."

With those words Jerome and the Duke left with the hapless priest in tow. The only accommodation available for the French couple was the empty bedchamber of either Fougas or Albert. They chose Albert's room and made do with such linen as we could find. A totally unexpected world, a world full of promise and hope, was opening before Daniel and Marie.

Chapter Eleven: A Trap Is Set, but I Am the Bait

I didn't sleep well. It was not surprising given the volcano inside my stomach and the sadness inside my head. I had overeaten in spectacular style and my stomach took its revenge. It interfered with my sleep by inflicting me with dreams of geese flying out of cooking pots and bowls of food that wanted to eat me. In my waking hours I thought of all those things I had meant to ask Uncle Albert about.

I entered the kitchen the next morning to make *biersuppe* and eat bread and butter. Nothing was organized and I remembered Fougas was dead. Another wave of depression overwhelmed me as I thought of dear uncle Albert. The stove was so low that it took a long time to bring the kettle to boil. I assembled breakfast, but I remained distracted by the past and fearful of the future. I peered around the door, but the bodies were not there. A French infantry uniform lay on the table.

Outside I saw the Delbardes talking with the Duke. She wore her own clothes and he some of Fougas's. A lot had been happening while I had slept, even though I was convinced I had hardly done so. The Delbardes turned to walk hand in hand up the path and away into an unexpected future.

The Duke entered. "I've told them to make their way to the next village before taking the coach south. That's all I can do." He frowned wondering if he should have done more. It would be like him. He looked up. "I've spoken with your uncle Franz and he and the sexton have called already." He looked at me to make sure I was listening as he changed the subject. "I have also spoken with Jerome and we're in agreement." The Duke stood in the doorway. I stood with my mouth full of bread and butter. I indicated if he would like some as I chewed. He shook his head. I continued to chew.

"He considers that the French couple, you, and Fougas would all be assassinated on the Weimar road today. At least we think that's Dumarque's plan. But Fougas has met his end already."

I swallowed. "And the soldiers at the inn?"

"They're either assassins or victims. There's no alternative and from what Jerome told me, I suspect the former. They left early this morning. And they left on the Weimar road. The innkeeper's people watched them go.

"Last night they were drinking at the inn waiting to see you—or your likeness. And now they're gone. I regret the risk, Paul, but I want to know if we're right. Jerome suggests that if they are assassins, they'll set their trap in one of the woods with open road to and from it. A place where riders may be observed from some distance and where those lying in wait can be certain their prey is alone."

I broke the loaf again and buttered another piece of bread.

His Grace continued, "There are only few such places on the way to Weimar. Our plan is that I will lead a large group up the road first. We are not part of Dumarque's scheme, so we should be ignored. As we ride through each wood we'll search for any ambush. Two riders will stop on the far side and ride back to meet you and Jerome."

The Duke ran his hand over his mouth and walked over to me. "This is the part I do not like." He pointed his fingers at me, wagging them to emphasize his point. "You and Jerome will ride up the road after us. Jerome will be wearing the Frenchman's uniform and you your spare clothes."

I nodded not liking the plan either. But there it was.

An hour later the Duke and a party of six armed foresters rode slowly onto the Weimar road. It was midmorning on a beautiful autumn day. The sun's rays flickered through the gaps in the delicate leaves and the sounds of the forest were of plentiful contentment. And I felt cold.

Jerome and I followed sometime later trying to enjoy the open road as it meandered through meadowland. We watched the advance party pass through the first spinney and emerge at the far side, less two. We lingered and rode off the road.

We waited, opening the gap, in the shade of a lone oak. The breeze held all the scents of the countryside. Our horses tossed their heads to rid themselves of flies. Their bridles rattled. The birdsong was muted in the warmth of the day and we watched the shadow of the occasional cloud darken the fields as it swept by. Our senses were heightened.

I admit to becoming exceedingly nervous as we came into accurate musket range from the copse, but when we saw the Duke's men, our fear evaporated. We passed though the spinney and onto the next stretch of open road. The Duke's horsemen would wait where they were and join the party on our return.

We approached the second spinney, but even as we closed on it, we saw no sign of the foresters. We rode more slowly and became tense.

At a hundred paces a musket ball will probably miss, but if it hits, it will kill or maim. As the range reduces the probability of being hit and killed increases with each step. One must have such compassion for those blocks of infantry who were marched about battlefields like toys and not men of blood and bone.

We reduced to a walk and separated across the road splitting the target. At seventy yards there was still no sign of the advance party. They should have doubled back through the spinney to show it was free of ambush.

At fifty yards there was a crash from the spinney and two plumes of smoke rose from the spot where the weapons had been fired.

My horse shuddered and staggered. I leaned on the pommel and leaped from the saddle before she fell and trapped me.

"Come on!" I shouted and ran towards the spinney. It takes between one-quarter and one-half of a minute to reload a musket. I assure you it is possible to run the distance between my horse and the plumes of smoke in that time. Consider the penalty for tardiness.

I never took my eyes from the patch of brambles where the musket smoke had erupted. It started to disperse in the lower branches as I ran straight for it.

I saw two partly uniformed French infantrymen. I drew my pistol as I approached and even though they heard me, neither had finished reloading.

I pointed my pistol at the nearest and panted. "Throw your weapons to the ground!" They did as I commanded and without reluctance. "How many of you are there?" I demanded.

"Just us two."

"Very well. I will shoot you in the leg and you'll bleed to death unless I staunch the flow, which I will not do unless you tell me the truth." I aimed my pistol to threaten the elder soldier's very manhood.

"We were told to expect two riders first. A French soldier who is a traitor and a woman dressed as a man. We have orders to kill them both."

"We thought we would kill the man first and the woman after," added the other with a shrug.

"But as you see—"

"You are no woman."

"And the man is no traitor. He's not even French," I looked around and to my horror saw Jerome's horse in the paddock with Jerome slumped on its neck. I returned my attention to the two ambushers. "We'll walk to that horse as we continue this conversation. You haven't answered my question. What were your orders?"

They stacked their muskets and led the way to Jerome talking as though discussing prices at a market. "After the traitor and the woman, there was to be a man alone like you and a man called Fougas, whom I know. We were to shoot them also."

"And?"

The older man indicated his fellow soldier and added reluctantly, "I was ordered to shoot him afterwards, but I wouldn't have done it."

"Naturally." I agreed, although my expression showed I did not believe him. "But why?" I asked.

"I don't know the reason. I have orders and I must obey them."

"To whom will you report?"

"Monsieur Dumarque."

"And where is he?"

"He awaits further up the road by the fork to the left."

We waded through the swishing meadow grass to reach the standing horse. The side of Jerome's head was covered in fresh blood. It had poured across the horse's neck, but now it trickled.

"Get him out of the saddle," I ordered.

With remarkable gentleness one supported his weight as the other guided Jerome's leg over the horse's back. They lowered him to the grass and removed his hat. The ball had cut a swathe between its brim and the side of his head, clipping the top from Jerome's ear and furrowing the skin deeply. Where the ball had gone I had no idea, but it was not in Jerome's brain. He lived, but blows to the head so close to the repository of the soul can cause terrible changes in a man.

The French mumbled to each other. One knelt on the ground behind Jerome to lift his head and rest it on his thighs. The other examined the wound. It was accomplished with as much tenderness and care as could be wished.

"It is now it should be done. Pour the unction on while he sleeps." The other looked up.

"I agree." With that he rummaged in his pack to produce a small flask. He poured its contents into the wound. Even in his unconsciousness Jerome cried out terribly.

"It is done as it must be." The kneeling man held Jerome's head so the other could bandage it. Jerome lay dead to the world but living. They rested his head on the side of his dismounted saddle. One of the French rubbed the horse's neck with grass to remove the blood. I thought of the soldier who had looked after the horses in the forest all those years ago and tried to remember his name, but could not.

It was then that I considered my own horse. I looked around but couldn't see her. I ran through the grass that grabbed at my boots.

My horse had taken only a few steps off the track and had lain down bleeding and weakening. Her breath was shallow and there was blood. She raised her eyes to me as I untied her bridle and slipped it from her head sliding the bit from her mouth. I unfastened the girth. She stretched her legs, quivered for a few moments and then quietly died.

I returned to Jerome.

The older soldier complained, "Monsieur Dumarque said I would be rewarded."

"And that is why you agreed to do it?"

"No, sir; I did not have to agree to do it. I was ordered to do it. Monsieur Dumarque is in the employ of the Emperor and we must do what the Emperor commands."

The sun's brightness was suddenly eclipsed by neither cloud nor heavenly body, but Dumarque. I had long since put away my pistol. I made to reach for it.

"There's no need, Brandt. Dumarque is my prisoner." It was the Duke.

I stood, but one glance showed how angry the Duke was. He was as angry as I had ever seen him. "How is Jerome?" he enquired.

"I fear sir, he's badly hurt. I don't know what is required."

It was one of the French soldiers who spoke, standing respectfully before the Duke. "He must be moved as little as possible and kept warm until the wound has healed and until he has recovered his senses. Sometimes there is blindness caused by bleeding within the cranium, which is beyond all help."

"He must be moved to the castle."

"No, sir. It's too far. There's a barn across the field. We can move him there, but no further."

"But who's to look after him?"

"We will." The two French agreed the notion between them. "If Monsieur Dumarque is your prisoner we have no orders to prevent us. We are your prisoners also and we are happy to preserve life as we have been taught to do."

The Duke gave his blessing to the proposal. He turned to me and said, "Paul, this must delay your departure. I need you here to supervise Jerome's recovery."

I nodded. "Yes sir, of course."

The Duke instructed me to examine the hut, to determine what was needed and to have a wagon loaded at the castle with the necessary supplies. With that said he turned his horse and headed home with his men and their prisoner.

The soldiers stripped off their jackets to make a crude sunshade to protect the invalid from its direct rays. The three of us walked to the barn.

I listened as they talked. They spoke of home and family life. Their worries centred on their businesses. One of them had a son. They both had smallholdings that needed attention. They pulled blades of grass and chewed them.

I was lost in confused thought and had to be brought to concentrate on the Frenchmen's list of requirements. It was a long one, and as I had no means of writing, I had to commit it to memory and therefore to concentrate. Concentration was made more difficult by distracting insects buzzing in the evening sunbeams penetrating the gloom through the open door. We walked back across the meadow with the French carrying two long poles.

I watched as they dismantled the sunshade and inserted the poles into their buttoned-up tunics. The result was a crude litter onto which Jerome was moved and gently carried across the meadow to the cool of the shade. There he would remain.

I saddled Jerome's horse, and rode back to the castle catching up with the Duke's party. I fell in with a group of surly foresters.

There was no conversation, just angry resolve.

I could not contain my curiosity and asked, "What's happened?"

One forester wheeled his horse away from the column and we spoke under the shade of an aged beech tree. "My father and one other are dead," he told me. "They turned back into the spinney to check for the ambush and fell into a trap set by Dumarque. He used rope rocks."

I digested this. I expressed my regret and thought in silence. My first conclusion was that Dumarque would certainly have set a trap because his plan relied on his assassins killing one another until the last reported to him. He, expecting his reward, would also meet his own death. Dumarque intended to destroy Du Vallois regardless of the number of lives taken to do it.

I also thought of rope rocks. Cavalry will avoid walking their horses through woodland for many reasons and fear of rope rocks is one of them. The idea is simple enough. A rope with a rock at one end is attached to a bough so the rock hangs about head height in the path a horseman might take. Another rope is tied to the rock at one end and to a nearby bough at the other so that it hangs slack. The rock is hidden on a bough so that it can be dislodged. The rope rock swings at, or past, the rider and the slack rope snags his neck dragging the rock back as a garrotte. If a horse bolts, its rider might be dragged from his saddle and throttled. In former times rope rocks were never used in isolation. Pikemen would rush from cover and thrust upwards into the struggling bodies. It's crude, easy, reliable and effective.

I wondered who Dumarque had recruited to set the rope rocks because he would have to deal with them also. Or had he set them himself? It was easy enough to do. I made a mental note to ask the soldiers looking after Jerome.

I added the totality of Dumarque's plan. First to die was to be the priest with me as culprit to follow and then the French couple and Fougas. Following that slaughter would be the deaths of the two ambushers. Seven lives lost so that Dumarque could destroy Du Vallois.

"It's lucky you turned back," I said aloud.

"When we heard the musket fire, we knew something had gone wrong," the forester replied.

I nodded.

When Dumarque had looked at me, I'd seen pure contempt.

As it was, Fougas and Albert were dead, Jerome was terribly injured and two foresters were also dead: four deaths. But there would be a fifth if there was any justice.

"We must rejoin the others," I suggested.

207

We entered the yard where I was immediately admonished by the Duke. "Where have you been? This is no time to delay. You alone know Jerome's requirements. After you've delivered them, bring back the bodies of the foresters. See me when you have completed these tasks."

With that he strode into the sanctuary his home represented. Where Dumarque was by that time I had no idea, but I hoped it was very dark.

Chapter Twelve: His Grace Bids Me Farewell

It's all very well, but horses and wagons are not left standing idle on a busy estate. I dashed about from housekeeper to kitchens and from forge to storage sheds collecting palliasses, a cooking pot, iron stand, water barrel, wine butt, stores of food and spices, ingredients to cook with and bandages for Jerome's head. Wherever I went in search of something, I remembered something else that was only to be found, as it seemed to me, at the other end of the estate.

All these things I collected in separate caches so that as I dashed about I did not have to do so laden.

I tried to remember the soldiers' list. I thought of the tools we had needed on the road and returned to the kitchens for a flensing knife and to the storerooms for game traps.

At the stables I arranged for a horse, but the wagons, all three of them, were out on the estate delivering winter firewood. They could be anywhere and they wouldn't be back until dusk or later. That much was certain. I thought what Jerome would do, but he had authority that I had not.

I ran to the wheelwright's forge on the other side of the village because I remembered seeing a wagon there.

I panted at the glowing entrance to his barn. "I need a wagon urgently. Mister Jerome has been injured and I have to take all sorts of things to where he lies. He cannot be moved."

"I have nothing, young sir," replied the giant wheelwright, placing a wooden mallet of the size of my head by the door.

"What about that one?" I gasped with my hands on my knees.

"That's not rolled in years."

"Will it?"

"Fall into pieces more likely and it's all covered in weeds."

It stood with its grey wooden prow standing above the brambles like a stranded ship. Its wheels were entirely hidden in undergrowth. Time was slipping by.

"If I don't deliver him supplies he may die. I don't want that on my conscience."

"Let's see." The wheelwright waddled into his barn to return with a scythe. In two or three stokes of a stone he'd set up the blade and started to work. The grass, nettles and brambles fell before his sweeps. I found a wooden rake and pulled the cut material aside. Underneath the wagon nothing much grew except baby pheasants.

"That'll give the dog something to chase." He laughed as the birds clattered off. It was almost as though they were shouting, "Come and get us!"

"Stupid birds," exclaimed the wheelwright.

His dog, about the same size as a cavalry horse, pounded out of the barn barking like a pack.

The giant laughed. "They're safe enough. Old dog's as blind as night. Hearing's all right, though."

He rocked the cart and fetched a tub of grease. He smeared the axle hubs freely and rocked it again. I noticed one of the shafts was split.

"Ah, yes, now I remember." He peered at the kingpin on the front axle." It's broken. I'm going to need your help."

"Of course."

He handed me two giant wooden chocks as though they were a pair of slippers, but I nearly dropped them—they were so heavy.

"Get those in tight behind the back wheels. And I mean tight."

I was pushing the second into place when he peered over me. "That'll do. Now when I lift the wagon, I want you to pull the front wheels away and when you've done that, I want you to chock the wagon body up on these."

He tossed two substantial baulks of timber under the wagon.

"I want you to get them leaning backwards a little to keep pressure on the back wheels and I want you to place them under the body behind the fifth wheel."

"Fifth wheel?" I asked.

"It looks like a small table. Then we'll be able to get the front wheels back into place."

With that he pushed a pole, made out of a whole tree it seemed to me, between the body of the wagon and the front axle. He lifted the front of the wagon separating it from its own front wheels. I pulled at the shaft and, at the second attempt, made the front wheels roll forward a little. I was about to congratulate myself when I remembered I had to burrow under the body of the wagon to erect the two supports.

The wheelwright lowered the pole and the body rested on the two jacks, I hoped securely.

He turned his attention to the front axle. "This is the problem." The kingpin sticking out of the fifth wheel was broken. It is the kingpin that enables the wagon to turn corners and it is also the one part that holds the front axle to the body of the wagon.

I was about to ask how long it would take to repair when the wheelwright took up his mallet and with one blow drove the broken kingpin out of its hole. New ones were regularly required and he returned from his barn moments later with a selection. He nodded when he found a satisfactory replacement and, holding his huge mallet close to its head, tapped it into place. He greased the fifth wheel, shaped like a wooden plate, with the kingpin sticking up in the middle.

We pushed the front axle back so the wheels stood in the ruts they had made for so long. Lifting the body of the wagon again caused the jacks to fall and he lowered the wagon so the kingpin on the axle passed through the hole in the middle of the fifth wheel on the body. The two parts of the fifth wheel came together with the kingpin sticking through. But for the split shaft, the repair was complete. He glued, pinned and bound that together.

"Where's your horse?" he asked.

"At the castle."

"We'll use mine, but only to the castle."

I nodded.

The wagon didn't want to go anywhere and it weighed. By heavens it weighed, but we pushed it from its ruts and started it on its journey giving the horse a chance.

"It'll be easier once the grease has worked in a bit," the wheelwright said confidently.

And so it proved to be.

At the castle we scooped out sprouting seed and dead leaves from the wagon and loaded it with supplies. The giant picked up the water barrel without demur. I wondered how we would get it down without relying on gravity exclusively.

"Put a straw bale under it," the wheelwright advised reading my mind. The ostler backed a horse into the shafts and I and a stable boy set off to Jerome without further delay.

"Thank you," I called to the wheelwright. "Can I settle with you when I return the wagon?"

"Quarter day will suffice."

I nodded. "Thank you."

I rode on the wagon to show the stable boy where Jerome lay and where he would have to make his subsequent deliveries.

We rattled and shook over the meadow grass to the hut as the sun began to set behind a small copse. When I thought about it, I considered that, given the problem, I hadn't done so badly. But I wasn't the judge.

The two French soldiers stood at the doorway as they heard our approach. I would have to do something about those uniforms.

I made a mental note to inform Frederica Storch while I listened to their requirements for the morrow.

Having unloaded we bade them good night and drove off to recover the bodies of the two woodsmen. To leave them out at night would be to insult their memory. Between me and the stable boy, we hefted the foresters onto the bottom boards and covered them under their capes. I collected the muskets and my tack on the return journey.

"Drive to the chapel," I told the stable boy. "I cannot think where else we should go with them."

The day was just a glow in the western sky by the time the horse was stripped of its harness and rubbed down in the castle stables. I was exhausted and scuffed my way up the stone steps to His Grace's private apartments and knocked.

He opened the door.

"You bade me attend you, sir."

"You've completed your tasks?" The Duke turned and made his way slowly back to his desk and sat. He had obviously been working because the space before him was strewn with letters.

"Yes, sir. The Frenchmen looking after Jerome have all they requested and a groom will ride there each day to hear of progress and deliver fresh supplies."

"How was Jerome when you left?"

"Sleeping deeply."

"I suppose that's a good sign."

"That is certainly the opinion of the French, sir."

The Duke grunted. "The French! I do not understand them." He rose and walked to the fire and stirred it with an ornate brass poker. He stared into the flames for a moment. I studied the walls, particularly the portrait of an elegant young lady whom I supposed to be the Duchess. The Duchess was a forbidden topic. I changed my gaze to study a pair of wooden panels mounted on the far wall. They were ornately carved, but the wood was so dark that it was impossible to tell what they depicted. Other than those features, the study could have been built from books: rows and rows of them.

The Duke breathed in noisily and stood back from the fire. "They are ordered to kill one of their own, and they accept it. When circumstances change, they continue as though those previous circumstances never existed. What can drive such people?"

"I don't think it's what, Your Grace; I think it's who. They are subjects, not citizens and they have to obey. I listened to them talking, sir. It was all about their families and their life's burdens and home. They aren't killers. I don't think they're really soldiers. Those two are a smallholder and a craftsman. They're caught up in something and they must obey."

"And people like Dumarque give the orders."

"But what's his authority?"

"He speaks for Napoleon."

"And Napoleon means terror."

"Nothing has changed for the French. They disposed of a barbaric king and created a barbaric Emperor."

"Did such people as Dumarque exist under the king, sir?"

"That's a good question." The Duke considered it as his stare returned to the mesmerizing flames. "They must have done. Remember also the Inquisition. That was torture and death at the hands of the Church—so terror is nothing new." He looked at me. "The question is this: Are we looking at something new now, or even worthwhile, in Bonaparte? I have a premonition there is

215

something hidden very deep in Bonaparte's France that goes far beyond simple conquest and it is yet to show itself."

"Competence either exists, or it doesn't. Competence in administration is imperative and competence in suppression is also imperative particularly when administration fails. Bonaparte is competent as an administrator and also as a suppressor of dissent."

"But yet there is more." He looked at me and smiled. "Hegel and the others have taught you well. Heed your lessons." He left the fire and walked over to me. "Before I go to prepare for a short journey, let me tell you what I believe and what I hear. First, from Spain it is said that things no longer go reliably for Napoleon. The English are there and they are learning. So are the Spanish and the Portuguese. Jean-de-Dieu Soult has some three hundred thousand French troops, but only a quarter of them can confront the new English commander Wellesley. The English force grows and the Spanish guerrillas contain the balance of the French forces using tactics the patriots used against the English in North America."

The Duke took up a goblet and poured a generous amount of wine into it. "Would you like some?"

"No thank you, sir. I am quite tired and I think it would go straight to my head."

"Well done, young man. I, on the other hand, seek exactly that result." He drank. "Let me continue. The English raided the Netherlands at Walcheren. It was a disaster because of an outbreak of a fatal disease called malaria. But it shows the English are becoming more engaged in causing Napoleon's downfall and I believe that downfall will come. It's not assured because young men like you will have to push the monster over. But it will come. I had hoped it would have started at the Battle of Wagram last year, but the Archduke missed opportunities as well as his brother's timely support."

The Duke mused at the failure at Wagram and shook his head as he rocked on his feet. He replaced his goblet and coughed. He dabbed his mouth and smiled.

"Sorry about that. I don't seem to be able to rid myself of this affliction." He patted his chest. "To continue, I believe I told you before that the English would tie the monster's feet together in Spain while they pushed him onto a sword, which I believe is Russia." He looked at me and added, "And that will be very dangerous for a large number of our young men." He picked up his drink. "I have come to be fond of you, young man. That doesn't mean I approve of all of your actions, especially some that have taken place in this palace, but you are young. You will do your duty as you see it, of that I am certain. I pray that you will be spared because it will be more important to all of us that you live to build the new Germany—as it will become—than die trying to liberate this one. Germany will be liberated from Napoleon. That is certain and many fine young men will give up their lives to achieve it. My point, Paul Brandt, is that only a few have the intelligence and strength of purpose to build on the freedom the others have won."

He rubbed his hand over his face. It was as though he was turning a page in his head because he asked after Jerome.

"In two weeks he can be moved back to the castle, Your Grace, but not before. The French say that even though he may feel recovered, he must remain where he is for that time. Even when he is back in his own rooms, he must rest in bed with no excitement for a further month."

"That being the case, young Paul, I require you to stay here until Jerome is safely in his own bed and when that is accomplished—

and not before—you can start for Berlin. I will write to von Clausewitz and tell him you are unavoidably detained."

I bowed as I had been taught, but the old man beckoned me into his arms and hugged me.

"I must make a short journey myself. I leave tomorrow. I don't know if we shall ever see each other again, but I'm glad to have known you and I am glad to be parting from you tonight on terms of ease and amicability. I also have come to trust you. I have a steward naturally, but I want you to sit in Jerome's chair while I am away and deal with matters arising. Can you do that?"

"I can try my best."

"That is all any man can do."

Chapter Thirteen: Into Berlin—Winter 1811

The weather became poor early that year and I fretted because it proved difficult to keep Jerome warm in the barn. But the French were adamant that he must not be moved. I considered having a small hut built around him, but the soldiers ruled it unnecessary and relied on the brazier. Jerome was talking by this time and he looked forward to my daily visits, I think.

Time slipped by and I was at a loss what to do for the best. His Grace was away and word had been received that his business, which he never specified, would take longer than he originally expected. For my part I had the demand of von Clausewitz to consider and I had neglected it for a considerable time.

When Jerome's recovery was advanced enough for him to be moved to the security of the castle, I exceeded my authority and commandeered the Duke's Hungarian carriage. It was the only vehicle left with any sort of springing and I thought it better to carry Jerome sitting in that rather than risk jolting him lying in the back of a farm cart. Naturally, the coachmen wanted me to take all the responsibility and I wondered just how far that would go as he drove the dainty vehicle across a muddy field.

The two French troopers had begged for clothes so that they could pass unremarked and I had approached Frederica Storch with their request. She continued to conduct herself as though we had never met but she agreed to see them. It was not me, but one of the farmers' wives, who remarked sometime later that the younger of the two Frenchmen seemed to need a lot of fitting for his outfit. I considered this and concluded Jerome would have at least one willing servant for as long as he wanted.

I stayed on not wanting to desert Jerome who, by then, was beginning to fret and behave badly. I felt I was the only person who could persuade him to remain resting. Finally, I told him I was bidden away and could tarry no longer. I left him in charge of his faculties and the castle. To be honest, quarter day was approaching and the reconciliation of accounts required a series of negotiations that one needed to be properly trained and prepared for.

I had to leave the sanctuary I had grown up in. It was, by then, late autumn of 1811 and we had lived near the castle since the spring of '07. I was a man of twenty and it was time to spread my wings. That thought made me smile even as I rode. Could I, as a young man, still fly as I had as a boy at the Ilm River? The Angel legend had begun there. Now the Angel must fly again.

The mood in the village remained sombre. It was not just because of Albert's death but also those of the two foresters'. To say nothing of knowledge of the priest's treachery.

On the road to Berlin, that took me beside the abandoned and forgotten battlefield of Jena-Auerstedt, I also thought of my parting from Rosina, Franz and dear Anna.

Our family conversations seemed not to fit together properly anymore because we missed Uncle Albert's contribution. I often looked around to see if he had something to say. We were sad without him and more than that we were incomplete. Rosina and Uncle Franz felt it also and they postponed their marriage in deference. Anna wanted to accelerate ours to the same day because I was going away and into danger. Anna did not want to die a spinster and she didn't want to marry anyone else. My promise made at the lakeside to marry her had grown into a desire to do so.

And it was a strong desire.

220

It was no longer an obligation made under duress and it was certainly no passing remark. I enjoyed holding her and smelling her hair. We enjoyed the feel of each other's bodies and we laughed and learned to love each other. A whole dimension of my life opened and I think it did for Anna, too.

It was eventually agreed both marriages should be postponed. Anna's mood changed and she became fearful, not just for the future but also for me. She was no more a demanding, frightened child. She had become a demanding, frightened adult. All risks had to be avoided. It was as though she had lost the skill of identifying risk and managing it. Possibly she feared that I had lost it, too.

I begged her not to imply choice where there was none. I had to do my duty. I had to report to Berlin where the army had need of an angel. Under these rules, Anna accepted very reluctantly that I had to go and promised not to place obstacles in my way.

I gave up my lodgings. Those possessions I could not take I vouchsafed to Anna. For a young man in 1811 my possessions were few. But many had nothing and any possession is better than nothing. I left most of my money with her and the admonition to use it sparingly or keep it safe. She seemed not to have any interest in it preferring instead to hold an old neckcloth of mine to her face.

"I will keep this always to remind me of you." She almost sobbed.

My last sight of them was Anna waving my neckcloth and Rosina holding hands with Franz outside the farmhouse we had made our home. The sun shone and the geese called. The golden leaves fell once more. It was peaceful. I regretted leaving them and all the comfort, love and security they represented until I faced forward and the opportunities ahead.

Muddy and smelly it may be, but Berlin had a tension running in it. The citizens hurried about their affairs paying no attention to a country boy on horseback. The city was grand in some places to be sure. In other places it was desperately poor and in some quarters even decaying. It was the French, with their dash and élan, who made the most show as their horses clattered down the centre of the street. The French cavalrymen with their sabres drawn and resting over their shoulders scattered everyone.

I had debated whether to spread my last day's journey over two days or to spur on and complete it in one and save a night's lodging. I had chosen the latter and, by evening, regretted it. My horse was as exhausted as was I, and he'd done all the work. It was a question of finding lodgings again unless I could present myself to von Clausewitz promptly. I headed into one of the better parts of the city. There the problem resolved itself.

"Brandt! What are you doing in Berlin? Follow this coach."

I could see the coach but couldn't be sure I had recognized the shout with so much noise in such public a place. The coach rumbled on. I did as I was bidden and followed it through a pair of substantial iron gates into a courtyard behind a high stone wall. On the far side stood steps up to the front door of an imposing stone manor.

As the gates closed behind me, I rode to the coach, which rocked as the passenger alighted onto the gravel. He walked around the back where I saw Du Vallois emerge.

"I do not recall that I gave you permission to come to Berlin!" He shot the words at me angrily.

"On the contrary, sir, I have a letter from you urging my instant departure. It's somewhere in my possessions. I'll find it for you. I have been delayed, but I have come as soon as I could."

"I gave no such instructions."

I must have shrugged because he took offence at my arrogance and shouted. "How dare you question me? I tell you I sent no instructions and that is the end of the matter. It is not for you to question me now or ever again."

"Would you like me to find the letter? While you make your claim, you also call me a liar and I will not accept that from any man." The fact that I was wrong did not occur to me until later. I was too tired.

Du Vallois was no longer the urbane doyen: an aristocrat of manners and breeding. My mild opposition to his stance had changed him into an enraged purple-faced tyrant.

Both I and my horse were saddle-sore as well as being tired and hungry. My frame of mind was as frayed as my horse's halter.

"Get off that horse and I'll give you a thrashing for your impudence." He strode to the coachman and ordered that he hand down his whip. I could not believe it. He intended to horsewhip me. I had seen the results once before, and once seen they are never forgotten. I remembered them vividly from my childhood. As a boy I had stared at a serf, who had fled early on, and who had stopped by our shelter to ask for water. His face had been crisscrossed with deep scars that turned it into a hideous writhing mask when he spoke. He had told me it was from a horsewhipping by his master.

I was too tired to think of any response save the easiest.

Du Vallois turned to face me with the whip held high in the air. The colour drained from his face. I remained on horseback and held my pistol levelled at his body.

"You would not dare," he sneered.

"You know you're wrong. Throw down the whip and undertake never to raise your hand against me again."

He raised the whip higher and scowled. "You impudent beast! Take your punishment!"

"Drop the whip."

His nostrils flared and his hand turned to start the thong flicking towards me. His wrist began to lower.

I shot him in the head. The whip fluttered past my face as Du Vallois collapsed against the wheel and then to the ground with his cloak caught up on the rim.

I blew into the barrel and rode to the coachman. "Give me your pistol," I demanded as I reloaded. He was still dithering even as I finished and he realized he had no choice. "Tell me, who's in the house? His wife?"

"As far as I am aware, Monsieur Du Vallois lives as a single gentleman."

"No longer. Are there servants?"

"Oh, yes. There is house staff, but he has no wife."

"That doesn't surprise me in any degree. Is there any other gentleman there?"

"Why, yes. Monsieur Henri Castel. He arranges most matters as I understand it."

"Is he also French?"

"Yes, sir, but the house staff is Prussian."

"Tell me about Castel."

"He is a little older than Monsieur Du Vallois. Very thin, and watches everything."

"Care for my horse. Oh, and get rid of Du Vallois."

With a pistol in my hand I scuffed up the steps and opened the front door stepping into musty gloom.

"Sir requires?" asked a lugubrious footman.

"Monsieur Castel."

"He is in his office: at the top of the stairs to the left."

I looked up a flight of magnificent marble stairs. Everything was of the highest elegance but was—I struggled for the word—neglected would have to do.

"Your master is dead outside. Take him away." I trod wearily upwards and opened the door to the office of Monsieur Castel.

"Du Vallois is dead. I presume he worked for you?" I announced.

The man—Castel as I presumed—sat at a catastrophically disorganized desk. He placed his pen in its tray and looked up at me. He immediately adjusted to an entirely different situation to any he could possibly have expected. He was utterly in charge of himself and his reactions and therefore, I supposed, in charge of every situation.

"And I presume you killed him. I heard the shot. I suppose you have no qualms about killing me also."

He moved the branch of candles, which illuminated the letter he had been writing, aside and leaned back in his chair.

"I never kill for sport and seldom on a whim, so you're safe."

A mere twitch of a smile touched his lips. "That is encouraging in a mild way. What do you want? No, before you tell me that, do two things please. Do not tell me who you are. I will deduce it in time. But do put your pistol away. Unless you want to fire it, in which case there is little point in conversation."

I placed the pistol at half cock on the desk.

Henri Castel spoke, "To answer your question, Du Vallois worked for himself or, more accurately, a demon within him. He knew that, should he fail, his Emperor or his proxy—myself in this instance—would have no hesitation in ordering his execution. Therefore, he was ruthless in fulfilling his duties. First to avoid punishment, second to win accolades and third, I suspect, because he had come to like it. You must know there are several of his type who we keep in fine style to show the rewards for diligence."

He studied me for a while and then added, "But we do not add to their number."

"Is all France like this?"

"Those with authority, such as myself, do not normally talk with those who have none. We move silently above the herd and if we ever mingle in the herd, it never detects us. Amongst our own kind, our lives are unremarkable. We are exclusive, refined, exalted and considered in our every movement. We feel no pressure. The strains are all at the seam: between us, who plan and rule and the masses. Du Vallois is part of the seam. Do I make any sense to you? Do I know you?"

Castel studied me through narrowed eyes.

"Yes, now I have you. There are very few names crossing my desk that are always accompanied by a physical description. In your case it is always: fair haired, with a fresh complexion and a countenance that attracts. Essentially, those are your attributes. You are Brandt—let me think...yes, yes—Paul Brandt, but in truth a Russian serf and also," he paused and smiled, "the Angel of Jena. What an important moth has been attracted to my lantern. Du Vallois's death was hardly in vain especially when you consider it is you who is to be charged with his murder."

"Hardly murder. I defended myself merely. He was preparing to attack me and there was a witness to his intentions."

"If a member of Bonaparte's Imperial Police attacked a Russian serf, it would not come to the attention of the authorities and if a Russian serf killed a member of Bonaparte's Imperial Police for any reason, it would be murder."

He clapped his hands as he came to his conclusions. "Now I know who you are and before I have you arrested, I shall ask some pertinent questions of my own. Do you know Viscount Castlereagh?"

"Not that I know of."

"Oh, but you do. Tell me of the Tsar's army of one million men."

"One million, a thousand times a thousand. It's an army imaginable by Russia alone."

"But is it true?"

"Do you care?"

"Passionately." Castel rose from his desk and moved in an exaggeratedly delicate way around it. His fingers worked like the feelers of some extraordinary spider along its littered top as he made his way towards me.

"Why? What difference would it make? France and Russia are allied, are they not?"

"No—no longer," Castel corrected me. Now he used his hands to conduct the words that left his mouth as though sending them on a further journey. "The Tsar trades with England in defiance of Bonaparte's Continental System that forbids it and the Emperor will end the treaty. It is certain."

"But even so it cannot mean they are going to war against each other."

Henri Castel studied my face. "If the Tsar has an army of one million men it would be a threat to the French Emperor and Empire." Now he changed his demeanour and his effete posing faded. He stepped away and began to tour the room almost as though dancing, very slowly. He thought out loud. "Do you appreciate that the battles of Austerlitz and Jena were fought between armies of approximately one hundred thousand men on each side?" He grimaced as he considered the proposition.

He turned halfway across the room and his fingers resumed their hypnotic movements. "Can you imagine all those souls marching about in ranks and files preparing to slaughter each other?" He shuddered dramatically. "Now we hear the Tsar has an army of ten times that size."

He turned his back to me.

I spoke, "You could never convince Emperor Bonaparte whatever you said. If you said, 'No such an army exists,' he would say that you must prove it and you know you cannot prove a negative. And if you said, 'Yes, he has such an army,' he would make preparations for combat, would he not?"

Castel turned and asked, "But is it true?"

"What I'm saying is that it doesn't matter whether it's true or untrue."

"So whatever intelligence I offer the Emperor, he will invade Russia?" Castel mused. A tiny handkerchief came into play.

"Is that his intention? Does he see a Russian monster he must destroy before it destroys him?" I asked.

The handkerchief disappeared into the cuff it had appeared from and Castel's fingers crossed over his mouth, delicately tracing and eclipsing it, as he thought.

I stared at this earnest inquisitive man for several seconds just as he watched me. I added, "Can you imagine an army of one thousand times one thousand? Can you imagine its cavalry, its cannon?"

His hand dropped and Castel demanded, "What if America was to declare war on England at the same time?" The hand returned.

"The English are not in Russia, so it'll make no difference. The English will grow in Spain and they will arm the Spanish."

"As they arm the Russians?"

"As one hears," I said. "Everyone knows of the Golden Cavalry. I'm sure you've heard of it. I see no reason why the English shouldn't extend their largesse to the Russians. But the Industrial Revolution is not something I fully understand. Possibly a million muskets and a thousand heavy cannon are no difficulty for the English to manufacture. As I say, I'm no expert on such things. If they can make them, I am sure the English navy can deliver them and the Russians can be taught to fire them."

"A thousand cannon, you said?"

"Did I? I thought I said a thousand heavy cannon. It sounded a lot when I first heard it and even after several months it still sounds a lot. How many horses would be required do you think? And where would those horses come from?" I thought for a moment, challenging the thin man who weighed every word like gold. "Ireland, I suppose."

"What would make the English leave Spain?" asked Castel.

"They left Walcheren and I understand that Sir Thomas Moore's troops left Corunna. They'll leave if conditions dictate, but they'll come back."

"And America? The president has threatened war because the English harass American shipping," Castel challenged.

"President Madison knows the English do this for two purposes. The first is to make sure it is only the English who profit from running the English blockade of Europe and not the Americans and also—and I am not sure I understand this correctly - because it will bankrupt the British involvement in the slave trade, a vital first step towards the abolition of slavery. There is also the American desire to invade Canada to consider, but Britain will not recolonize America, so if there's war between the two, it will be a squabble between relatives: a piece of family business."

The hand dropped. "And therefore not of consequence?" The hand returned.

"Every war is of consequence to those who fight in it. But to history? I would not have thought so. There will be battles and the zealots will fight them, but I doubt the people will engage. That's certainly the opinion of my tutor."

"Will Napoleon lose?"

"In Russia?"

"Yes."

I thought before answering, "If not there, then somewhere else. He'll not stop because he's an addict as surely as if he smoked opium. He believes in total control. There will always be someone somewhere who disobeys him. The English and the Spanish will not succumb to Napoleon's demands and neither will the Portuguese. In time German speakers will not. There will always be someone."

"Then what's to be done?"

"You ask me?"

"I see no one else."

"You prepare for his successor. If this government of France disappears, will France disappear also? No, of course it will not. It will change. It will accommodate the demands of the victor for as long as those demands exist. It is a skill of government to assuage them quickly and faster than most would expect."

Castel's hand finally dropped and he resumed the appearance of a normal man and not some reincarnated hypnotist from mythology. He took a small pistol from his waistcoat and allowed it to clatter onto the papers scattered before him. He shrugged. I winced. I hoped it was not cocked. "It is France's destiny to rule over Europe," he announced.

"I've heard that view expressed before, but what is France that it has such a right?"

"The country of Napoleon."

"Never. Bloodshed and tribulation will follow every attempt. You are not fit to rule because Napoleon wants power over people. He has devised his code to rule over subjects. There are to be no citizens."

Castel looked at me curiously for a long time. "What an extraordinary philosophy roils inside your head. I am almost jealous. But that doesn't mean I agree you're right. Do you not believe in supremacy?"

"Naturally. There's always a victor."

"Then?"

"When France loses?"

"In the scheme of things, France must lose sometimes, but defeat does not represent an end, just an obstacle. And to whom would we lose?"

I looked around his scruffy, dim study and thought that if this represented the summit of achievement I wanted no part of the climb to it. I noted the dirty windows and the smoke-stained mantelpiece. Even the chimney breast was smoke-stained with dark patches across the ceiling. It was just negligence. No one had bothered to clean the chimney. I glanced at the fire burning fitfully in the grate and saw a waft of smoke curl into the room. Castel was elegantly attired in grey silk, but in those surroundings his jacket and pantaloons just looked worn out. "You should consider France does not actually have any friends."

"Do you believe that is true? What of Russia?"

232

"It was you who told me the Tsar was raising an army of one million men. Against whom would he use such an army? The Tsar would not need it if he was an ally of Napoleon. Surely he would not. He would only need it if he proposed to defeat Napoleon with it. I'm a Prussian now and we have more friends than the French who have none in Europe—none, emphatically."

"What would you do in my place?"

I thought, stared at Castel and then looked around the room. I wished I was not so tired. I thought and replied, "You should travel—to America or to Paris. Probably Paris is better. In Paris, soon you will meet the Germans, the Russians and possibly the Americans—oh yes and the English. What was his name?"

"Viscount Castlereagh as I am convinced you well know."

"Yes. You will also meet the English. When you are amongst them all, you'll find the spider's thread that will extend your career amongst new masters. But what they'll demand and who they'll be, I have no idea. Skill at playing one consideration against another will be needed if France loses in Russia."

Castel squinted at me. "And if France wins in Russia?"

I thought for a moment. "In Russia you ride from one horizon to the other and you achieve nothing. Its size will fully occupy a reformer like Napoleon probably for his lifetime. But he has to win her first."

"I will now tell you something." Castel started at me intently. "Even though you claim to be a Prussian, I know you are really a Russian peasant. Napoleon will win in Russia because neither the Russians nor the Prussians, especially Prussian aristocrats, can believe a Corsican corporal can possibly beat them. They

233

think it's luck. They cannot concede it's his ability. That's why Napoleon will win."

"I do not debate his ability. I question his judgement. I'm not at all good at playing at cards because when I lose, I think my luck will change and so I continue to play and lose more. When I win, I believe my luck will never end and when it does, I lose what I've won. Napoleon also does not know when to stop."

Castel leaned back on his desk studying me. "As I said before, the battle of Jena was fought between two armies each of approximately one hundred thousand men." He smiled and chuckled. "And one Angel. I will now tell you that Napoleon will enter Russia next year with as many as three quarters of a million men and very possibly more. And you think he will lose?"

"Now I know he will."

Castel's eyes opened wide in genuine amazement. "Why do you think that? How can you be so sure?"

"What did you call me? Paul Brandt, but in truth a—?"

"Russian serf, or was it peasant?" Castel shrugged.

"It's no matter. I am of hardy stock and most of us died coming out of Russia. Napoleon is going in."

We looked at each other for a considerable time. Eventually, I detected jealousy. Well, perhaps not that, envy certainly. "Napoleon has many able generals to aid him."

"Certainly and they've been successful. Therefore, they'll do what they know and they'll expect to be successful again. But they don't know Russia."

"They don't know Russia," he repeated and pushed himself from the table. He stood very close to me. "Is Russia so terrible?"

"How terrible can you bear? What would you do to stay alive? My uncles Franz and Albert used to tell me stories of what we left behind to make sure I never went back."

I broke away from his proximity and turned about the room to give myself space and time to think. "When were you last hungry? Can you remember?" Castel shook his head. "Imagine not being able to remember when you were last not hungry. Now think of the newly buried."

I saw Castel wince with distaste.

"That is what Uncle Albert and Uncle Franz told me and I believe them. Children who died of hunger were buried secretly deep in the soil and far into the woods. They were buried very deep in the ground so the animals of the forest would not find them and dig them up. And man is the worst of all the animals."

I walked close to Castel and said quietly straight in his face, "In approximately five hours, possibly less, you can walk from one settlement to the next anywhere in the northern states. In Russia, to walk between one settlement and the next, you'll have to walk for thirty hours. If it has rained, you'll not walk at all because the road will become a stinking soup and in places it will prove to be a bottomless quagmire. Your legs are not long enough to stand above the mud and you will drown. It is entirely unable to bear the weight of a man and certainly not one who carries his house on his back like a soldier. A horse can only be saved by its cart. Napoleon will lose in Russia. It won't be the Tsar who kills Napoleon. It will be Russia herself who kills him."

Castel put his handkerchief to his mouth as he considered me and suddenly spun around like a child's top. "You will dine with me here and give me company. And look at the time! I think some wine is in order." He tugged a cloth bell pull. I heard the clattering sound in the distance. "Tell me, what of Dumarque?"

"The last I saw him he was in the custody of His Grace the Duke and charged with—" I thought and rubbed my face in perplexity. "Planning the deaths of others. Is that a crime in France?"

"Indeed. But whose deaths was he planning?'

"Mine." I counted off on my fingers. "The priest's, a French couple, two French soldiers, Fougas and I'm sure some others. He had a plan to involve Du Vallois as someone guilty in your eyes. I presume he worked for you?"

I received no answer while the servant was instructed and dismissed. I waited for an answer as Castel stared out of the window. The clock ticked and Castel thought. At length a tray was placed with a tinkle of glass and Castel instructed the servant that I was to dine and rest the night, so all should be prepared. It was to be a great feast—for two.

"A celebration," he said to the hapless servant who answered in monotones and who avoided eye contact with me.

Such clothing as I had was to be brought in from my horse and anything of Du Vallois's, which I required, I should consider as mine. He would not require it.

Castel addressed me, "I am a more cautious chess player than Dumarque. I do not even trade pawns without good reason. So, I do not always win. But I never lose and there will always be another game. You should bear in mind that I speak for France as well as myself. We shall continue with our games of chess until we control all that happens in Europe." He looked at me squarely and added, "And all who live in it."

Castel smiled and I understood my life was safe from him—if he was to be trusted.

I was treated with both suspicion and deference by the household staff and my room was prepared quickly and efficiently. I was shown into Du Vallois's suite to see if I wanted anything. The rooms were opulent, but that was all. They demonstrated excess without purpose, so they were vulgar. The fact I had killed Du Vallois was to my credit with the staff but that I had spent time with Castel seemed to work against me.

I sat on the side of an enormous bed as my boots were pulled off. I lay back and slipped into sleep.

A face I did not know came into view as I opened my eyes. It said in German, "Sir, you are to dine with Monsieur Castel and you are not yet changed or washed."

I gathered my wits and with the help of the servant, Luc, managed to present myself in the empty dining room both clean and well dressed. With a glass of wine and water to hand, I looked through the window at the small garden and noted its neglected state. Once it must have been a charming sanctuary for a mother and her children. Probably a daughter, I thought, because the garden seemed to have been set out with a woman's touch. Now it was just a neglected wilderness. The stables stood at the far end. I hoped they were not as neglected, and that my horse was being properly cared for.

I tired of waiting for Castel and went in search of him. I found him in the study assembling papers and ledgers in different stacks. He broke off his work to pour wine. He sipped it delicately and replaced his glass.

"I have decided to take your advice and travel. I shall go to Paris," he said by way of a greeting.

"Most enjoyable. When do you intend to make this journey?"

"I think it will be and I intend to make a start tomorrow, if at all possible."

"Is that why all these papers are stacked up?"

"I think this should not concern you."

Castel took my arm and led me from the study back to the once-impressive dining room. The table had been set for two at either side of one end.

"May I ask how you came to own this house?" I asked.

"I do not own it in the sense you mean. It was the property of an English cotton merchant and it fell under the terms of the Berlin Decree therefore."

"Berlin Decree?"

"The Berlin Decree introduced the Continental System—"

"Yes," I interrupted him. "So it was sequestered."

"Just so."

"And therefore the French state owns it?"

"Why, yes. And if the ownership was ever to be challenged, then the matter would go before a court and as the courts are French I see no difficulty."

"But if the courts were not French?"

"Then there would be no Frenchmen in Berlin. I would lose interest therefore."

"What will happen to this house when you leave?"

"I have no interest."

"But you won't be able to remove all your papers or effects by tomorrow, will you? They'll remain here while you're on the road to Paris."

He looked at me rocking his thin head gently from side to side. He thought while his food was served.

"Brandt, let me confide in you. I appreciate you are an enemy even though I find it difficult to treat you as one. I would not treat you like this if we met on a battlefield. There I would regard you as the greatest threat. Here, I think you are constrained." He continued speaking after taking some time to consider, "I shall go to Paris because I'm convinced that if Napoleon wins in Russia, it will occupy him for a long time, as you say. And Paris is the centre of the Empire and therefore the civilized world—not Berlin, let alone Moscow. There are also England and Spain to think about. Neither is quelled and I suspect never will be, again as you have concluded. A different approach will be needed."

I was served, but I hesitated to ask with what. I leaned forward and sniffed. "Coq au vin, Monsieur," the footman mumbled.

"If Napoleon loses in Russia, I will meet the Russians, the Prussians and probably the English in Paris. As a Frenchman I will meet no one in Berlin."

"Another piece, please. I am very hungry," I whispered to the footman.

Castel continued, "A new French government will be required and to be part of it I must be established in Paris. It's not possible to be credible unless I'm first established. The allies would

239

negotiate with those who represented the nascent power and those people would already hold authority in the Capital."

I ate. It was as good as anything the Duke had served. "Therefore Paris is important to your future?" I asked as soon as my mouth was empty.

"Imperative," agreed Henri Castel.

"And your papers will remain here?"

"Brandt, what is on your mind?"

"Two things. The first is that this dish is delicious and I am very hungry indeed. The second is that it occurs to me that you are preparing to move into unknown territory." I was absolutely torn, but I placed my knife and fork on my plate. "The first rule, surely—and I cannot remember which Roman general said it—is you must always have a secure base. Berlin is that base and you cannot desert it, because if you do and were seen to be manoeuvring in Paris, Bonaparte will behead you for treachery. Is that not so?"

Castel put down his fork and looked at me bleakly.

I went on, "Therefore, you could only pay a short visit to Paris in the first instance. And then, apparently, you become delayed at the request of others. Everyone would know you intended to return to Berlin and it would only be after considerable persuasion that you would agree to extend your visit." I was looking at my food by this time. "You would necessarily have to send for more papers, clothes and so forth. Also you would have to ensure you received reliable and regular reports from Berlin."

I picked up my fork and ate.

"And you would arrange all that for me?"

240

Castel also ate. There was a truce for food and it lasted quite a long time. It was so good and underneath the meat, I found a square of bread that had been fried in what? Ah yes, goose fat. The juice had begun to soak into it. It was heaven. With my plate empty, I resumed, "Certainly, but there's a problem."

"Which is?"

"I would need money for the running of this house."

"Ah." Castel looked at me.

"Surely, the Englishman who so casually forfeited his home also failed to protect his fortune?"

"It's true that he left some of his wealth in his haste to flee."

"And that wealth you have at your disposal?"

"As you ask, yes."

"To avoid the accusation of pillaging, you would leave that wealth here, would you not?"

"I wouldn't want to discuss that tonight in case I failed to wake."

I smiled at Castel. "I did not trust Dumarque or Du Vallois because neither was their own man. One can never trust a subordinate, surely. But you're different. You can be trusted because you make decisions for yourself. As I hope I do."

"Is trust enough?" asked Castel.

"Certainly not, but it gives me a beginning. May I make a suggestion?"

Castel nodded assent as he ate.

"It's this. You'll need a reason that is imperative and important for journeying to Paris. The matter of the Tsar's army satisfies both criteria. I propose you go to Paris because you've heard the English are to supply the Tsar with a thousand heavy cannon as well as muskets. That is a critical addition to the Tsar's strength and you need to know if it's true. The path into English secrets surely starts in Paris. It is also certain such a message and such a request is too sensitive to be entrusted to any messenger, especially from Berlin."

Castel pushed back his chair and tried to assume the role of cat regarding a mouse rather than the opposite. He didn't interrupt me as I spoke.

"I would add that I have spent time with a craftsman at Sömmerda who knows all about guns and especially English ones. What I now suggest is valuable to you. It would be difficult for any agent to discover if the English had made so many cannon. They have the Worshipful Company of Gunmakers, but it has many members and you will never find out which have been making the cannon before they detect you asking about them. However, there is the Proofing House. This is not a perfect plan, but all barrels in England must be proofed. At the Proofing House you will hear if a thousand heavy cannon have been proofed recently."

"What is proofing?"

"They put a particularly large charge in a new barrel and if the barrel survives, it is safe to use normally. If it does not, the barrel is no good."

Castel ate, thought and then asked, "Your reasoning is that one enquiry would be unlikely to be detected whereas enquiries at all the foundries would be detected?"

"It must also be quicker and celerity is its own virtue, surely?"

Castel nodded. "Now tell me why you make this useful suggestion."

"Why do you treat me as an enemy?"

"That's simple. You are one."

"Not in the sense you mean. I have every need for an ally in Paris. Think of my position. If Bonaparte wins, I will need a friendly voice in Paris if I am to prosper wherever I am in the French Empire. If Napoleon loses in Russia, I shall have need for influence with the new French government, if I am to find advantage in France. For you to be an enemy of mine, you would have to pose a threat to me. But you do not. To be an ally of mine, you would have to offer something I want and you do."

Castel resumed eating, but so slowly that he was practically playing with his food.

"I would add one other consideration," I continued. "If you allowed me to stay in this house during your absence, it would obviously still be your home in Berlin. Should an enemy of yours seek to discover if your motives were false in returning to Paris, they would try to find out if you had left Berlin permanently." I gave him a sidelong glance. "Would they not? The answer they would receive would be, 'Monsieur Castel's staff awaits his return daily but has not received notice what day that will be.'"

Castel placed his fork carefully on his plate and sipped his wine. All the time he studied my face. "Brandt, you are possibly the most dangerous young man I have ever had the pleasure to meet. I don't know who taught you, but he was brilliant and you are fertile ground. You are young and, I hope, cautious enough to stay alive. Therefore, you will be relevant to the future as I

243

intend to be. On that thought I shall now retire. I will see you in the morning when, hopefully, we shall have fresh minds." He looked at me speculatively. "One last thought for your consideration is that you will be under house arrest here. I want to know where you are and here is better than a common jail."

He rose and taking up a fresh wine jug, poured himself a large measure. He crossed behind me and filled my glass to the brim. "I propose a toast to our future of benign cooperation."

We drank. I set my glass down and without knowing why, glanced at Castel's, as he placed it on the table. Mine was nearly drained, while his was nearly untouched. I was so tired I had made a mistake and it could be a fatal one.

Chapter Fourteen: I Become a Gentleman

I was shaken awake by the same servant who had attended me the previous evening and I will admit to a moment's panic. I had no idea where I was and my head told me I was falling. I felt terribly sick.

"Monsieur Castel has left. He bade me wake you at noon and give you this draught to drink together with this letter."

I sat up and immediately felt dizzy with my stomach churning. "I've been poisoned."

Luc handed me the draught and I drank it unprotesting. Suffice it to say the next hour was spent with my body taking its revenge for my not having protected it. I wallowed on the bed with my eyesight wavering, my head pounding, and my stomach either erupting or threatening to do so.

A further hour found me exhausted but washed and dressed in the stale-smelling dining room. It smelled of damp. I touched the wall by the window to confirm it was so. At table I was served weak coffee with a sweet pastry and jam.

"Am I to be poisoned again?"

The butler looked aghast. "It was not I, sir."

"Then who?"

"I could not say. But it would not have been any of the staff. You see, sir, we know you are the Angel of Jena."

"Ah," I thought aloud. There was only one person who could have told them. I ate and read the note:

Brandt,

I have taken your advice and also various precautions one of which you will now be recovering from. Do not be alarmed. The effects, while unpleasant, pass one way or the other and do not linger. I considered it a prudent precaution to ensure my own safe departure. I also needed to ensure my final preparations were not compromised by your knowledge of them.

You will find fuller particulars and a list of tasks I want you to undertake on my behalf in the study.

I am convinced that we shall meet again and if that occurs, I shall have to concentrate on preventing you taking your revenge on me. In the meantime, regard yourself as my guest in my home or, if you prefer, you may regard yourself as being under house arrest.

Henri Castel.

I felt better with food inside me and I surveyed the papers in the study. There were three large bundles all sealed in canvas with a vile red-coloured wax under an elaborate design. Each was numbered and very heavy. There was something in them other than paper. There was a letter with instructions where to find a supply of money that would last for some time and a request that I did not tamper with the parcels.

My head became clearer as the day wore on. I concluded Castel did not think very well for a man in his profession. He should have used paper, not canvas, to wrap his parcels. Paper would tear and disclose every effort at opening them, which I thought I might do. He must have considered that canvas would hold the weight better. I broke off a large fragment of sealing wax and slipped it into my pocket. I might need to match the colour.

I summoned the butler and dealt with housekeeping matters. Or, to be honest, those I could face that day. I surprised him by demonstrating I had dealt with staff before and asked to meet them. I thanked Jerome and to lesser extent, the late Fougas.

I settled down to write a letter to the address in Hannover that Mr. Brown or Mr. Stewart or, in truth, the Viscount Castlereagh had given me. It was a long letter that suggested the Proofing House would be subjected to questioning by agents of Bonaparte who would attempt to discover if the English had recently supplied the Tsar with a thousand heavy cannon. I was sure the master of the Proofing House would be at pains to complain of his exhaustion at the size of the task.

There came a tapping at the door and a small procession of men and women entered to stand respectfully before me. Each introduced themselves with their names and functions, some of which, I regret to admit, I forgot.

The butler's name was Walter and the groom's was Rolf. The household remained intact but the stables were empty. The coach was gone with Castel as was the undergroom, the coachman and the coach horses. Only the groom, one other stable hand and my horse remained, and Du Vallois.

"Who manages the household accounts?"

"I do, sir," replied a tired-looking woman.

"We will talk of them later today. Please be ready."

"Who manages the garden?"

They looked at each other. It was Rolf who answered eventually. He seemed disinclined to speak.

"There was a gardener, sir, but he died the winter before last and Monsieur Castel never replaced him."

"I want a gardener with the skills of a sexton and the silence of the grave. We must say our farewells to Monsieur Du Vallois speedily and with as few mourners as possible."

"There is a lavender garden beside the fountain, sir. The gardener died just after he had cleared the old plants. The new ones are still in the potting shed, but they need planting out," the groom answered.

"Rolf, will you arrange the burial of Monsieur Du Vallois there?"

"If you wish."

"Deep, facing east and with the respect due to any human."

"As you command."

"When he is interred and after you have planted the new lavender, I would wish to say a prayer."

The groom nodded. I dismissed everyone save the butler. I instructed him to take me on a tour of the building.

"The housekeeper, sir?" he asked me.

"Is busy with her accounts."

There were a number of tasks I needed to accomplish but they all relied on the loyalty of the staff and any such assumption would be unjustified. My letter to Mr. Brown would have to be delivered through the good offices of von Clausewitz.

The butler led me from room to room. All had been fine once, but they were showing advanced signs of neglect. I looked through the window at the garden and saw the groom carry a spade across the barren space to an idle fountain standing behind a tangle of dead winter vegetation. My hand came away from the windowsill wet. I looked at the butler.

"We have told Monsieur Castel, sir. But he does nothing and that is not the worst leak. Some of the servants' quarters are very damp."

"What time did Monsieur Castel leave?"

"I cannot be sure, sir," replied Walter. "But after you retired, he worked all night on his preparations. Luc, the valet, is exhausted this morning."

"And he's heading for where?"

"I cannot say, sir. He did not confide in me and as I understand it, the coachman left with no clear instructions about his destination except that it was distant."

Our conversation took place along a corridor where the butler pointedly failed to open the doors on one side. I tried them as we passed to discover all four were locked. It also became apparent the house was not symmetrical. There were two diagonally opposed areas on the ground floor, which obviously represented space but which, equally obviously, did not offer it. The upper floor was symmetrical. Thus there were spaces being held away from my eyes.

To the butler's surprise, I insisted on entering the roof space to examine the servants' rooms and then the cellars. Eventually we re-entered the study.

"Walter, I don't know how long Monsieur Castel will be away and as we have no secretary, his tasks will fall to you. Please sound out the proper people we need to protect Monsieur Castel's property until he returns. We saw slipped slate on the roof and we need to stop all these leaks, especially the ones in the servants' rooms. Enquire for the proper craftsmen. I also saw rot in some of the window frames. That must be corrected before there is extensive damage. I shall require a gardener, but not until Rolf has completed his work. And surely there should also be more parlour maids?"

"That is a question for Maria, the housekeeper."

"But you're in agreement with my propositions?"

"Yes, sir; they are urgently needed."

I devoted the remainder of the afternoon to the housekeeper. It became abundantly clear why her life was one of drudgery. She had been constantly starved of funds. That her accounts contained fraud was undeniable. But it was only to be expected given the gap between need and allowance. I increased all her allowances and paid overdues. I requested a suggestion for new staff hirings and set standards.

For that evening I dressed carefully. I did not dress as a Frenchman but a foreigner, not a nobleman but as a person of a little consequence. I stepped onto the streets of Berlin and sought the direction of von Clausewitz.

Chapter Fifteen: Golden Secrets, Paper Lies

A footman ushered me to a small library. The Duke's paper showed the address I was to attend and contained a note for von Clausewitz that read simply, "An Angel attends you."

I passed the time reading until darkness when I left having seen no one. I let myself out stepping into the chilly evening. Young men are not thought to have instincts except the base ones and that's probably because they've never been threatened by death. It's my experience that abilities develop with use. That is certainly true of self-preservation.

I stood away from the front door and wasted time in the shadows apparently looking for something in my pocket. I didn't detect a threat, but my eyes needed time to adjust to the dark streets of an unknown city. Possibly I had misjudged how safe Berlin might be.

I considered my position as I stood in the gloom. I carried neither pistol nor sword. I did carry a small dagger, but it would be of more use cutting paper than as a weapon.

I studied the street. There were groups of men talking. Others walked in one direction or the other going about their business. The centre of the muddy road was empty. It was too late for goods wagons and too early for the carriages of the wealthy.

As I watched one of the groups broke up. Consider my astonishment when I thought I recognized Castel's coachman amongst them. Of course I couldn't be sure. I had only seen the man once and now the light was poor, but I followed him until he entered a tavern. I saw no point waiting, so I made my way home to be met with consternation.

"I was becoming alarmed at your absence, sir and did not know what to do," said Walter.

"I'm afraid Berlin is far larger than I'm used to and I lost my way. But I'm home and hungry for my supper."

Having eaten I took the remarkable step—for the staff anyway—of descending to the kitchens to thank the cook for her efforts and to apologize for my lateness. It did no harm and I spent some time asking her about her needs. Her domain had been built without regard for economy, but like the rest of the house, there had been no maintenance and the evidence of uncorrected wear stood everywhere.

If the coachman was still in Berlin, then it was reasonable to assume Castel also remained in the city. This conclusion heightened my senses. I left the kitchens and rang for Walter to ask if he had been able to make any progress finding workmen because, as I said, "We must look after Monsieur Castel's home."

I received a reply that matters were in hand or that at least some progress had been made. I dismissed him for the night and said I would tour the house to see it better for myself.

The locked rooms that Walter had decided I was not to be shown stood on the first floor. I would enter those. The doors remained locked, but a light showed underneath the first. Basic locks are no barrier to anyone who has studied locksmithing, especially the locks of Mr. Winchester and von Dreyse. The door yielded and I slipped into the room.

I had heard of such places but never seen one. A *bureau-fantome* is where a subordinate prepares answers to the questions his master might ask. In this instance his master might be Le Prince de Talleyrand himself or a Director of the French Imperial Police.

I looked around standing in the corner of a grand salon. It would have been a quite formidable reception room once. Perhaps it might even have been a small ballroom. But now it looked shabby as though resenting its lowered status.

On the tables near me, lay piles of papers under the category "Matters." These small stacks of papers were further divided into "Old" matters and "'New." On the second group of tables, nearer to the plinth, lay "Matters of Current Interest." On the plinth itself stood a table alone that bore papers marked "Matters for the Secretary's Attention."

I familiarized myself with the contents.

It must have been a frustrating life because the flow of information was always one way. It would have been very satisfying to know what the American president had said about French government offers of help if the Americans declared war on England the next year as was rumoured to be the case. And what of the dialogue between Bonaparte and the Tsar? To say nothing about the entirely separate dialogue between Talleyrand and the Tsar? In that conversation it was rumoured Talleyrand had coached the Tsar how to deal with and thwart Napoleon.

The files contained tittle-tattle for the most part comprising compilations of shallow invective: information gratuitously given by those who sought favours, those who traduced their foes and those who sought to damage their competitors. This was the stuff of importunism, of sedition, deceit and vengeance.

Along the walls and entirely blocking the other three doorways stood more tables all covered with the same piles of nauseous accusation. A name on a file caught my eye: von Gneisenau. I swept it up and searched for the others who had signed my letter at the Ilm. I decided to put purpose to my pillaging and studied the requests for information lying on the top table. One instruction made my body chill. Because of its importance I stole it. I can therefore quote it accurately:

The Emperor is assured of 75,000 Prussian troops to serve in the Grande Armée of France following the terms of the peace treaty. It is now required to increase that number, first to 150,000 and, before the invasion of Russia, to 200,000, if not more. These troops will lead the Grande Armée. The privilege and honour of penetrating and defeating the Russian force will be theirs. The Emperor predicts one of the greatest battles of history. It will be a battle in which the victors will be revered throughout time. Thus the Emperor has determined a bounty will be paid at the end of a successful campaign to every Prussian and Austrian soldier surviving. Furthermore, grants of land and a pension will be awarded to each.

Arguments that, to remove so many young men from the Prussian state may destabilize the country, or that such conscription might render the Prussian army permanently impotent following losses in battle, must not gain currency. It is High Policy that Austria, Prussia and the other North German states each commit to raise these revised numbers immediately after the year-end festivities.

I added that paper to the pile I had purloined only to see a note beneath it:

Brandt,

If you are as astute as I suspect, you will have found this note. You will have been drawn like a moth to the candlelight. Had you not found it, there could have been a conflagration. I am pleased you have found it, so now I urge you to extinguish the candle to prevent one.

Henri Castel.

I was moved to swear, but His Grace disapproved of it unless it was he who did it. When he did his words would launch like an incoming tide of destruction to break in a spray of derision over the hapless victim for all to see and laugh at.

I recovered and said, "Thank you," out loud as I checked the tables for any other files of interest. I was rewarded by finding more than just my own.

I extinguished the candle and locked the door behind me. It occurred to me that a fire might have suited Henri Castel's purposes very well. He would be able to claim that because his house in Berlin had burned to the ground, he would unfortunately have to delay his departure from Paris. The fact that a few people, including myself, might have perished in the blaze would be unfortunate, nothing more.

I decided to examine the two diametrically opposed blank spaces on the ground floor. One showed an obviously false panel with a perfectly obvious release. It was obvious because dirty fingers had pressed it and whoever was responsible for keeping secrets had been negligent in cleaning them off. I pressed it and the panel opened a little. Pulling it back I saw stone steps leading down into darkness. I jammed the door open with my stack of files and trod gingerly into the gloom protecting the candle flame from a quite strong draught.

Cellars, passageways, cold, damp and the smells of mould met my senses. Had I known of this place before, Du Vallois would by now be in permanent residence. There was nothing of immediate interest but a lot to explore later. I wondered if there was a way out of the house and I spent some time looking for one. If there was it was not obvious. Then I remembered it had been an Englishman's house and concluded it would not be so.

Standing upstairs on the carpeted floor of the back hall again, I retrieved my files and gently closed the panel. I crossed the building to the opposing space. There was no panel betrayed by greasy fingerprints, but there was a panel and therefore there must be a substantial void behind it. I looked at a length of wall against which no furniture had been set. The disguise was better. I lifted a picture from its hook. Behind it was a keyhole.

I replaced the picture. There was too much to do and I was too tired to do it. I gathered up the files. They were evidence of my success so far and I made my way to bed.

I awoke elated and impatient to open the lock behind the picture, but I was cautious. It had occurred to me that Castel had yielded his home very easily—too easily perhaps. I had to assume his staff remained loyal to him and as such I was far more of a captive in it than I cared to admit. I was tethered, but it was a tether I could not see. I needed space and privacy, but with his staff present, all my actions would be reported to him.

The cat was away and this mouse needed to play. I had to cast off my leash.

At breakfast I suggested to Walter, "Christmas is a time for people to be with their families, isn't it? How many of the staff would make a visit if they could?"

"I could not say, sir. But if the opportunity presented itself, then I think everyone with a family would visit."

"Are they all from Berlin?"

"Some are not. Not far, possibly a day or two's journey."

"Please ask the housekeeper to attend me and tell the staff a holiday is awarded. They may go home. They must not be absent for more than fourteen nights without forfeiting their employment. The housekeeper will pay extra wages for travel and to contribute to their families."

"Who will look after you and the house, sir?"

"The house will survive two weeks and we are making plans to repair damage and wear, are we not? For myself well, I'm hardier than you may suppose. There will be some cleaning to do after everyone returns. That I promise you."

I spent the morning reading in my room. There was a great deal to learn even about myself. The thing that amazed me was how much of the information in my file was wrong. The afternoon was devoted to paying money to the housekeeper and discovering who was leaving for where and for how long they would be away.

Discipline disintegrated in the household and I was jostled by an inattentive footman bent on some purpose of his own. The following morning, I had a staff of three: the cook, an undergroom and an aging chambermaid. With only my horse in the stables it was easy enough to persuade the groom to take the role of night watchman and guard the front door.

My first task was to ensure there was no back door. I returned to the false panel and descended into the cellars carrying a large branch of candles. I tried not to waste time examining the various trunks and boxes lining the passageways. Some contained a collection of fossils and stones, put away for "the duration," one supposed. The cards describing each exhibit had faded with the ink spreading in the damp.

A tunnel stretched into the darkness behind a locked iron gate. Surely no one would do that? A lock here would be bound to rust. I looked at it more carefully. The tongue of the lock was thick, heavy and forbidding. But it was also fixed. It rested in a stout iron valley anchored in the wall. One could rattle it back and forth all day and it would never yield. Furthermore, no key would ever engage through the keyhole because there was no lock. But would it yield if you lifted the whole gate? One glance at the spike hinges gave the answer. With a piece of wood taken from an ancient sedan chair, I levered the iron gate up so the tongue lifted out of the valley and pushed the gate open. It made no noise. It had been greased, so it was in use.

I moved along the passageway to find stairs upwards that ended on a small landing facing a wooden door. I guessed I was at ground level. I listened and heard conversation, but not clearly and not nearby. I pulled the door to find myself attacked by a thick mass of coats and cloaks hanging on pegs. Making sure I knew how the latch worked on both sides, I slipped through.

I stood in the dingy corridor to the back room of an inn. It smelled of beer and wet woollen coats. I moved closer to the noise hoping to observe without being observed. It's difficult to see faces in taverns. People lean towards each other, or they hold mugs to their mouths, or they face away in the normal way of things. I looked through the window to the street to see a church I recognized from the previous evening.

This, then, was the inn the coachman had entered. I slunk back into my coat-covered refuge and returned along the dank tunnels to the house trying to make sense of it.

I returned to the corridor and closed the panel with its secret behind me. As an adjunct to art and as a tribute to sycophancy, there stood a pillar with Bonaparte's head in bronze on top. I pushed this monstrous edifice across the carpet so that if someone opened the door from inside the passage it would topple. But because of the carpet, I needed to amplify the sound, so I arranged a table with a German-silver tray and glasses in its path should it fall.

I reasoned that it would be preferable not just to have warning of someone entering but also actually to prevent them from doing so. Thus I moved the pedestal back to the door and slipped a piece of wood under the plinth so Napoleon's statue was about to topple.

Appropriate I considered.

The noise would alert me and the plinth should keep the door shut as surely as any foot pressed against it.

I hastened to meet the challenges posed by the other hidden space. I stood before it and removed the painting to study the shape of the wall. As my examination continued, I removed another painting and exposed a second keyhole. They were symmetrically placed in the middle of two full-height doors. Each door was six feet across. Careful study showed a joint hidden behind beading down the middle.

Mr. Anstruther had drawings of these doors together with a lengthy explanation of how they worked. Without that knowledge I would never have understood the problem. I spent two days and the best part of two nights working in the stable's forge making blanks and cutting them. Making a blank key is not difficult if you can work in bronze or iron and ever since working with von Dreyse, I could. Cutting blanks is easy but time consuming. Suffice it to say that if you want to open a lock without a key, you can either pick it or make new keys.

From the drawings and descriptions we had found in the coach all those years before, I knew the locks had to be opened at the same time. Therefore, picking the locks, one by one, wouldn't work. I had to make new keys. To do that you cover a blank with candle wax and fit it to the lock. Where the wax is indented and where it is not shows where to cut and file. It's a long dull process and one mistake means you have to start all over again.

There are two other tricks to these locks. They are fitted in the doors too far apart for one person to turn both keys at the same time and opening both at the same time is required by the mechanism. The intention of the maker is that two people working together are required to open the doors. To resolve this, I had to make two long handles and braze them to the keys so I could stand between the locks with a handle in each hand.

At length I was ready. I turned the keys and opened the two massive doors. I will admit to some lack of excitement. I knew I could open the safe, so failing to do so would have produced emotion not success. In the wall safe stood a formidable collection of table silver including ornate candelabra and huge table centrepieces including one enormous figure of St. George on horseback slaying a dragon. Finding these was exciting. More exciting was the sight in the middle of this collection. There stood another door on which was written "Chubb, Winchester."

I knew about Mr. Winchester's locks, but I knew nothing of Mr. Chubb's.

However, this door had three keyholes and a capstan wheel. I had seen drawings of it in Mr. Anstruther's papers, so I was quietly confident that I could open it if I was prepared to devote a further two days.

It took longer than that, but I finally turned the capstan wheel. I knew which key to turn first and second and I also knew the trick that the first key had to be turned for a second time before finally turning the third key. It all took a lot of effort, but without the drawings in the Englishman's luggage, I would never have worked it out. I pulled the centre door open.

If this was not the Englishman's fortune, it was a national war chest. I saw a great hoard of gold coin together with gold bars stamped with St George on horseback pinning a dragon to the ground with his lance.

I pocketed a handful of coins as just reward for my effort and noted their surprising weight. They would prove tomorrow morning that it had all been real. I closed the safes and had just replaced the last of the pictures when I heard a crash from the other side of the house.

I made my way to the source of the noise: a mouse possibly, even a rat? A big one? Or had the cat come back?

The passage door to the cellar steps stood open. I had miscalculated. It had been possible for someone to enter the house. The corridor was dim, not dark, but the shadows deep.

I became very still and very quiet. I hardly breathed. I heard a pistol lock being drawn back and leaped to one side as the crash deafened me and the flash blinded me. The ball stung as it punched. I was thrown to the floor stunned and bleeding. A foot trod on me and rolled me over like dead game.

"Brandt! Well you're done now; you jumped up little peasant." It was Dumarque.

"I thought you were dead."

"By whose hand? The Duke's? Certainly not. As soon as Castel heard your story, he sent word to release me. Castel also wrote to beg my urgent return to Berlin to take charge of this house. I can see why. There's no possibility he would leave it in the care of a Russian serf like you."

I moaned and made to rise but thought, *No one ever begged you Dumarque—if they ever did. It won't be repeated now.* I spoke aloud, hissing against the pain, "Like so many things French

261

these days, this house isn't Castel's. It is the property of an Englishman and one day he will reclaim it."

"You talk romantic nonsense, peasant. The English will never be here. It is us, the French, who are masters of all Europe and it is us who will remain so."

I stood clasping my side. I really wanted time to see how bad the wound was. It hurt—it hurt to high heaven—and it was bloody, but it felt like a gash, so possibly not serious. I began to hope. In the gloom I saw Dumarque lackadaisically recharging his pistol. I moaned and stumbled. He made to push me away as though something disgusting had tried to touch him. My tiny dagger entered his body just under the middle of his rib cage and made its way up to his heart, which it found. His blood gushed down the blade over my hand and revoltingly up my sleeve to bathe my elbow. It was quite hot.

Dumarque's eyes rolled upwards. He sank to his knees, fell onto his face, moaned and died.

"I know you cannot hear me, Dumarque, but your death is inadequate recompense for those of Albert, the two foresters and even the poor Fougas."

Holding my hand to my side, I made my way to the stables. There, I pumped icy water to wash away Dumarque's blood and mine. Soaking wet and shivering I returned to my chamber to examine myself by arranging two cheval mirrors. The ball had cut me over the lowest rib on my right side and passed on. I did not think it had broken a bone, but forbore to probe very deeply.

I stared at my reflection and concluded that although I was alone, I wasn't about to die alone. That had been my first fear. I was panting—a bad sign and tried to regain my balance of mind. But I became overwhelmed at the thought of my uncles and remembered that dear Albert was dead and Franz and the others were so far away. I wanted Anna. In fact, I needed her. Rosina would be far more practical, but I longed for Anna in a way that was new to me. I no longer craved the company of Susannah and certainly not Beatrice, but Anna! And that realization made me happy. More than that it made me content—fulfilled almost. This benign mood was enhanced as a voice in my head said, *And you're rich!*

The wound oozed blood. It did not pour it and it throbbed more than stung. There were bandages in the household and I used these to bind the wound having carefully folded a strip of flesh back into place.

Having done the best I could, I dressed cautiously in warm dry clothing all covered under Du Vallois' woollen cloak. With the papers from the ghost office tucked into a pouch and a few gold coins from my purloined hoard in my pocket, I made my way painfully back to von Clausewitz's lodgings. On the way, I considered that Dumarque was correct about one matter. By sending the staff on holiday, I had removed Castel's spies from his own household. He would certainly replace them: hence Dumarque's presence, but how did he know, unless he was still in Berlin? I concluded that, on the balance of probabilities, he was not and that he had sent for Dumarque the same night he had drugged me. It was a clear indication that Castel intended to hold me captive in his home and that he was not ceding it to me. It was time to change that perception.

Chapter Sixteen: I Report for Duty

I entered a brightly lit drawing room expecting to find von Clausewitz alone. But the room was both hot and crowded with military men. In truth, it was ablaze with candlelight that glittered on their braid and flashed on their medals. I recognized some of these decorated officers from that evening after the battle. One or two of them were, actually, quite young: older than me, but young compared to the others, and to my expectation.

I had interrupted a meeting and by the looks I received, it was an important one. My interruption was unwelcome, but necessary.

"This is the young gentleman who came to wait upon you last week, sir," intoned the footman, who bowed and left.

"Oh my God, he's covered in blood," exclaimed Clausewitz. I had entered with such dignity as I could, but my wound had opened and my right side from elbow to hip was sticky and scarlet. Coming down stairs at home had ben excessively painful and I supposed that was when the bleeding had restarted.

"Metzendorff your skills are required," observed the oldest man in the room. I'd seen him at Jena and I did remember his face. Indeed, his was not a face or a moustache to forget. I handed my papers to none other than Graf von Blücher.

"Sir, these are from Bonaparte's Imperial Police."

His eyes opened wide. "And who is this?" he asked.

"This is, without doubt, the Angel of Jena and a month late. But it's him," answered Scharnhorst. To me he asked, "What have you been doing? Were you attacked in the street?"

I nodded and swallowed. "It was Dumarque. He shot me."

"Regardless of who he is or who shot him, step back and let me attend him. Or he'll bleed to death," ordered Metzendorff.

"And on your chair, Clausewitz," observed Gneisenau with a touch of malice.

"It's not my chair. I only rent these rooms as I need them, August."

With that remark Clausewitz turned to the earnest doctor. "Metzendorff please do everything you can to reduce the flow as soon as possible. Regardless that it's angel's blood, the housekeeper will charge me for cleaning it up and my pay is stretched as thin as hope these days."

"With that observation, my dear Clausewitz, I'm in total agreement," offered August Gneisenau.

The good doctor ordered me to lay on the table, which he cleared by sweeping everything on it to the edge.

"Careful, man! Careful." Clausewitz dashed to grab a glass vase, a pair of candlesticks and a china dish full of nuts and moved them out of harm's, or in truth, Metzendorff's way. I felt my feet being lifted and then lowered on to a cushion and realized that Clausewitz was not being solicitous to me, but protecting his rented table-top from my boots.

"Hold him down," Metzendorff ordered his fellow officers and between them they pinned me by knees, ankles and shoulders so that I lay still with my wounded side uppermost.

"Prices are high for all of us," observed Blücher absently. He leaned on my calf with one hand while he flicked through the papers, which he had arranged on the tabletop, with the other.

He laughed. "The Angel of Jena has delivered us a gift from Providence itself, not the Imperial Police. I have before me your file Gneisenau. And, lest you scoff my dear Boyen, I have yours also. Ah! Oh dear! And this is mine."

"It would appear this angel has been flying into dangerous places." It was really a question from von Clausewitz.

"Your concentration is required, Count," Metzendorff instructed Blücher. "Hold his leg steady."

The Count Blücher spread the papers out so he could study them and leaned on me more heavily.

I must have sniggered.

"What's so amusing?"

I looked into the questioning eyes of Scharnhorst who had asked the question. "I know what a fish feels like." I tried to turn my head to speak to Clausewitz. "I'm happy to pay for the damage to your furniture. I'm sure the rightful owner of the coins in my pocket will regard the cost as part of their war effort."

It was at that moment that Metzendorff ripped the seam of my jacket from hem to shoulder. My jacket had been perfectly good. The blood had stained my waistcoat, but that followed my jacket and my shirt followed them. Everything ripped to tatters! Once he had cut my bandages away, Dumarque's handiwork was exposed. I could not help feeling apprehensive. This man was brutal and I was next.

Von Boyen dipped a cautious hand into my jacket pocket, which then dangled on a strip of cloth in front of me. I watched the surprised look cross his face as he withdrew an English gold sovereign. He held it up. "You're in touch with the English?"

"Through circumstance am I able to draw on them."

Gneisenau took the coin and studied it. He flicked it to Clausewitz. It spun flashing and ringing as only gold will do. "It is possible the habit of making gifts at Christmas time will become a tradition. If it does, do not expect the same again, and certainly not from me."

There was a deal of laughter amongst these officers who obviously enjoyed a deep friendship.

I yelped in pain and thrashed like a fish. "Hold him," ordered Metzendorff to no one in particular. To me he added, "This may hurt a little. Do your best to bear it."

I found myself clamped to the tabletop as the officers concentrated on the task at hand. The Count continued with his dialogue on the papers.

"Steady, steady," he muttered and patted my leg.

I was panting but wondered if I was expected to whinny instead.

"You've got a piece of cloth in the wound and I must remove it." To Scharnhorst he instructed, "Hold the candles closer and don't drip wax on the boy. I don't want to deal with burns as well."

Scharnhorst held the candles aloft and said to Clausewitz, "That'll buy new furniture for you let alone cleaning what's already here."

Gneisenau squatted down to look me in the face. "Have you any more like that one, young man? Do they mint them in heaven?"

I was about to answer when the doctor took the laughter as the excuse he needed to hurt me and I exhaled in real pain. "Yes!" I hissed, beaded in sweat.

"All out now," said Metzendorff.

"Can we let go?"

"Oh, no. I have to wash the wound and that will make him flinch a little and then I must stitch him closed. After that you can let him go." Just at the edge of my vision, I saw the good doctor pour something onto a cloth and I smelled vinegar.

"Steady everyone." The good doctor clapped the wet cloth onto the wound and I felt the vinegar run around my body just before the wound exploded in pain. I cried out as hands held me tight.

"These really are files from Bonaparte's Imperial Police, are they not?" asked Blücher.

"Yes, but read the instructions, sir," I whispered. My mouth was dry as stale bread and I felt terribly sick.

Blücher took up the instructions and read aloud. A profound silence followed.

"The point is surely that there will be no Prussian survivors in Bonaparte's army. Surely that's Bonaparte's intention." I rasped as Metzendorff squeezed my torn flesh together.

It was Boyen who spoke, "Prussia is to be stripped of two hundred thousand young men who will be sacrificed as a French spearpoint in a battle against the Russians. Is that correct?"

I nodded and whispered, "Yes, that's the point."

"No, my Angel, this is the point." I felt Metzendorff's sewing needle enter my side.

"I don't need to be trussed." I whispered, hovering on this side of consciousness.

"You're lucky," Metzendorff opined.

"At the moment, I don't feel it." I swallowed, dry and painful and panted like a dog.

The youthful face of Clausewitz came into my vision. "Young man, thank you again for delivering us from doubt. Your papers answer many questions. We can convince everyone our interpretation of the current situation and our plans for the future are both correct."

"Prussia must raise the men though," I added.

"Why, in heaven's name? Why must Prussia raise the men? It will be a great and terrible battle," said David Scharnhorst.

I shook my head, which is a difficult thing to do while lying on your side. "No. There must be no battle. That's why you must raise the men so they can be trained to fight: but for Prussia, not France. No Prussian need die. They only need to know when to turn out of the French column. The French will die whether they fight or not." I wanted so desperately to sleep, to drift away.

"I appreciate you're in pain, Angel, but please try to tell us what you believe and why you believe it." It was Scharnhorst again.

"Napoleon believes Tsar Alexander has an army of one million men."

"That's preposterous. The Tsar doesn't have one tenth part of that number." It was Blücher, leaning hard on my leg.

"It doesn't matter what the Tsar has, Your Grace. It's what Bonaparte believes he has that matters. You can now understand why Prussian soldiers are to be sacrificed in Bonaparte's plan."

"I can understand that two hundred thousand Prussians could be slaughtered by one million Russians, but why does Napoleon believe this when it's so obviously untrue?" asked the Graf.

"He believes it because the French intercepted a letter from the English Lord Mulgrave informing the Tsar that the English agreed with his plan for an army of that size and they would arm it and help pay for it." Being involved in the conversation brought my mind to concentrate and not to drift off.

"And how do you know this?" asked Clausewitz.

"Because I was with Viscount Castlereagh when he forged it. He used me and my family to set his trap with the letter as bait. Bonaparte can never ignore it, whether he believes it or not. He can never ignore it."

"Keep him talking. I'm nearly done," ordered Metzendorff.

I licked my lips, but it was no use. My tongue was as dry as my mouth. "He also believes the English are supplying this army with a thousand heavy cannon."

"A thousand heavy cannon," muttered von Boyen in amazement.

"And that's why Bonaparte is raising this vast army?" asked Scharnhorst.

"Castel, Bonaparte's man in Berlin—or at least one of them—told me Bonaparte will invade Russia with a number somewhere between three quarters of a million and one million men. He'll do that because he thinks he will face a million Russians with a thousand English cannon. That reminds me. Please find a letter in my coat and send it to the address in Hannover immediately. A little more subterfuge is necessary."

"And the English are good at that." Not a question from Scharnhorst this time. "I'll take it. I'm looking to absent myself."

It was Gneisenau who added quietly, "If two hundred thousand Prussian men are killed in battle, Prussia will die out."

The others looked at him.

"That's part of Bonaparte's plan. Prussia and Austria will die in battle but not France. Bonaparte does not want to use French troops in the van of his army because the odds are so bad he knows the van will be destroyed," I said.

"But Bonaparte will crush Russia's army, just like he crushed the Prussian army." It was Clausewitz.

"And every other army he has met," observed Blücher.

"Only if they close to fight, sir," I countered.

"I have advised the Generals Phull and Kutuzov not to offer it."

"Clausewitz, you have to be more specific. If you do not offer battle, what will Bonaparte do?" asked Scharnhorst.

"He'll look for it," answered Clausewitz, "because that's how Bonaparte wins. He fights a decisive battle to crush his enemy and then impose his terms for the political peace he desires. He's good on the battlefield. He has the eye for opportunities and an army that can make fast responses."

"But if he attacked Vilnius, Riga and St. Petersburg, he could destroy the English trade with Russia, which is what he wants. Isn't it?" asked von Boyen. "After all, this looming war with Russia is to enforce the Continental System and its embargo on trade with England. So he should attack the trading ports."

"All done," Doctor Metzendorff announced. "Well done, young man. I'm going to bandage you now. You can let go of him, gentlemen."

They stood away checking their hands to make sure they weren't covered in angel's blood.

"Boyen, I think you may be confusing the reason for this war with the excuse for it," Clausewitz offered, smiling slightly.

"What do you mean, Carl?"

"It's just that Bonaparte either wants this war for conquest's sake, or he wants it for the furtherance of policy. Which do you choose? Because if it's for the furtherance of policy, he'll attack the trading ports. But if it's for conquest, he will seek a major battle to defeat the Tsar and impose peace terms. And he doesn't need three quarters of a million men to attack the trading ports."

Graf von Blücher smiled. "And as the Angel says—and as we have already determined—if Bonaparte is denied his battle, he'll lose the war because he'll run out of supplies. By the way there is good news from Spain. Wellesley is preparing his offensive."

"Thank heavens! But timing is important. If Wellesley defeats Bonaparte's forces in Spain early, he may delay his attack on Russia so he fights on one front only," offered Boyen.

"We have no date for Bonaparte's attack on Russia, but it must be sooner this year than later especially with three quarters of a million men. It's such a giant enterprise that even the Emperor's noted flexibility must be constrained." Scharnhorst ran his hand over his mouth.

"The invasion is set and only Russian capitulation can prevent it." It was Blücher.

"And that capitulation will not be offered?" asked Boyen.

"No. For the Russians this is a Holy War in the making." Blücher clamped his hands behind his back.

"In that case the war will continue until there are no Russians alive or no French alive on Russian soil," concluded Gneisenau.

"Thus Bonaparte must take the bait offered by the proximity of a Russian army he can defeat but never catch up with." Carl von Clausewitz looked at me as he thought.

Metzendorff helped me to sit up, but I felt giddy and faint. Many hands grabbed hold of me even as their conversation continued.

"And the Russian army's retreat must lead away from St. Petersburg," Scharnhorst offered.

"There's a plan that the Russian army would retreat towards Drissa," admitted Clausewitz.

"But not stop there?" I asked.

"The Tsar has yet to make that decision, but he has said the coming war represented 'The last struggle of independence against enslavement and of liberal ideas against tyranny's system.' Thus I agree that this will develop into a Holy War," Clausewitz continued.

"I do not think Tsar Alexander represents liberal ideas as we have come to understand them in the new enlightenment," offered Blücher, "but I do believe that France and the French system offer tyranny and perpetual enslavement."

"It isn't France, sir," I begged as the doctor tied the remains of my jacket around me. "Ordinary Frenchmen want to go home and live their lives in peace. The madness is inside the French government."

"That's as may be. Unfortunately, it's the ordinary Frenchman who stands between us and the French government. And the French government will always manoeuvre so its population shields it against the foes it so wilfully generates."

"Where do you live? We must get you home to bed and rest." The doctor was forceful.

I told the good doctor.

"A French army of between three quarters and one million men will attack an army of less than one hundred thousand Russians. It's obvious how it will end eventually," mused Clausewitz.

I turned to look at Clausewitz. "But it is not an army of a million Frenchmen. Up to half of it will be composed of Prussians, Genovese, Austrians, Poles and a host of others. I told Castel that Bonaparte will lose in Russia and I'm right."

My side hurt terribly and I found it very difficult to decipher the words I heard let alone make a sensible contribution to the conversation. Through watering eyes, I saw their jackets: blue, white, red and green. Their gold braid flickered and flashed in the candlelight as they moved.

"If all the other nations desert the French, as I think you are suggesting, there would still be between a quarter and half a million French against less than one hundred thousand Russians." Again it was Clausewitz.

"I'm not very good at cards, but are the odds improving?" I asked.

"Who will lead the Prussian troops?" It was Blücher.

"General Grawert and he's an admirer of Napoleon." Scharnhorst rubbed his hand on his knee as he thought about the leadership of the Prussian column.

"But General Yorck is his deputy and he hates Napoleon," added Clausewitz.

"That's true and it's something to consider. Do you know Yorck, Clausewitz?" asked Boyen.

"Yes. I know him well."

"If Yorck defects, he will reduce Bonaparte's army by the size of the Prussian force. He also potentially increases the Russian force by the same number," Boyen said. "He might also tempt the Austrians to follow his example."

"The Prussian force must defect early enough to survive and win our freedom from the French. We mustn't fight against the Russians," I implored.

Blücher mused. "A war of attrition between a million men—my God, but it's unthinkable! And what will make our troops defect?" Blücher seemed uneasy with the politics of deceit.

"I suspect that when the time is right and the passage is clear, they will receive a sign from above," Boyen spoke quietly, but he looked at me and pointed to the ceiling.

"Have the odds improved again? But there must be no battle." I moved unadvisedly and I felt I had been penetrated by a knight on horseback with his lance at full tilt.

"It was just a little scratch," offered Metzendorff with remarkable insincerity.

"Liar," I whispered and passed out.

I came around to hear. "Careful man, don't open the wound. I spent good time and thread sewing him up." I felt myself being lifted by men who did not really know what the word 'careful' meant and I moaned.

"Oh, you're awake, are you?" the good doctor asked. "That's a pity because this is going to hurt."

"Your timing is imprecise."

I was carried upstairs to my own bedroom and dumped on my bed to be unceremoniously stripped. The doctor checked the bandages and pronounced in a comforting way, "One really ought to study the science of wounds more, don't you think?"

He looked at me and smiled. "Young man, last time we met I fed you laudanum and I am going to do it again. I hope it doesn't become a habit."

"Could you move his body before the housemaid finds it?"

"Body? What body?" asked Clausewitz.

"The French agent Dumarque."

"You killed him?" Clausewitz exclaimed.

"Young man you really must leave some for us. Where is he?" Scharnhorst asked.

I explained.

The Count von Blücher's eyebrows rose. "Let me understand you rightly. You have finessed this palace from the French who previously sequestered it from the English and you now live here alone. And all this in less than a month?" He shook his head.

Gneisenau chuckled. "You know, Clausewitz, if we all moved in here, we could save the rent you are paying."

"I am not quite sure how it is that we would save the rent I am paying, August. But if the Angel agrees, I think it's a good idea."

The Angel did agree naturally.

"Remarkable." Gneisenau grinned and asked, "Have you found the wine cellar? All this excitement gives me an appetite."

"And you left a dead body on the floor and you would like us to move it? I do feel compelled to write to the Duke. I am sure he has no idea what he's unleashed onto this world," added Blücher.

"But, Graf, possibly it was not the Duke. Perhaps he really isn't from this world," opined von Boyen.

"You are daydreaming," the Graf retorted.

"No. I am thinking what our troops will want to think," von Boyen considered.

"Yes, maybe you're right. But we have a body to move," said Scharnhorst.

"Before the maid finds it!" Gneisenau shook his head.

I drank from the flask.

"Quite, naturally." I think it was von Boyen who spoke, but his pronouncement was followed by a distant mooing noise in my head and that was followed by oblivion.

Chapter Seventeen: Reunion

I must have been afflicted with inflammation again. I remember moments of wakefulness and struggling against hands holding me down and then nothing. I remember calling out and sweating and each time more laudanum. One morning I smelled lavender water and floated to the surface opening my eyes.

There are few things so pleasing to a man than to see the top third of a bosom especially if it belongs to the woman he is coming to love.

"Anna?" I croaked.

"I'm up here."

"I do hope so."

I am biased, or possibly just weakened, but I concluded she was lovely to look at and I was falling quite in love with her.

Anna smiled. "You smell dreadful."

"Then I shall take a Turkish bath!" I made to sit up and managed it at the second attempt.

By noon, I no longer smelled and was freshly washed, bathed and dressed. My wound, which had previously shown the signs of putrescence according to Anna, had begun to heal properly. But it was still very sore and red to look at.

After a light lunch I sat with Anna, Rosina and Franz in the dining room all telling our stories and plans. We spoke of the Duke, of Jerome's steady recovery and of the funerals and the village in winter. I explained about how it was that I came to be living here, but I left out a great deal of the detail.

The imposing group of officers I had recruited as frequent visitors and occasional house guests entered to say they had been summoned elsewhere that evening and would dine there. It should not be wondered that we all rose and either bowed or curtsied. It hurt to bow and I wasn't going to curtsy.

As our family met the officers, we could hear distant hammering and sawing, but at least we still had the dining room free from builders. That would change soon.

I faced Scharnhorst who was somehow the most approachable. "Sir, I do not know how to address you, but this is my family: my uncle Franz and Rosina and Anna who joined us on the road."

"They captured us and held us slaves," offered Anna.

"That is not true!" I exclaimed in righteous indignation.

"Really?" Scharnhorst queried me. His face betrayed the seriousness with a smile.

"Well not all of it," I answered.

"And which road was this?" It was Blücher who asked.

"The road from Russia, sir. We are Russian peasants," I replied.

Anna tossed her lovely head proudly. "That may be the truth for them. But it's not for us, is it Rosina?"

I feared she had learned the secret of her birth and was about to spill it.

"Certainly not. We came from Moscow, near the Kremlin." Rosina stepped into the possible breach.

"Very near the Kremlin," continued Anna.

It was David Scharnhorst who broke the ensuing silence. "I'm the son of a farmer. Von Clausewitz is really a Pole and, if I may speak for him, an impoverished Pole at that. And August Gneisenau also comes from the ranks of ordinary mortals. So treat us as equals. It is not until you consider von Boyen here and, of course, the Graf von Blücher that the situation changes. It is rumoured," he continued as though revealing a secret. "that, in the ancestry of von Boyen, the apostles actually stood and that up in the top branches of Count's family tree, there is no one but Blücher and possibly God himself. So," Scharnhorst became expansive, "rather than calling yourselves Russian peasants, call yourselves the sons of farmers."

"And already we are equals," conceded Clausewitz.

"Next you'll call yourselves landowners like me!" expostulated Blücher.

"No, my dear Count, nobody actually wants to be like you." Only Scharnhorst could dare make such a remark, even amongst friends, and survive without a severe reprimand. He steered the conversation into safer and shallower waters by making small talk about friends and colleagues.

The Count changed the focus by turning to me and stopping Scharnhorst's rambling by announcing, "I have heard from the Duke. He's making his way to Berlin. He's looking for a new pastor, but I think he has other matters on his mind also."

The remainder of the afternoon drifted into early evening and the bottles increased with the volume. The question of food was raised and I suggested the inn. "We could use the tunnel."

"Er, no, not a good idea. It's a bit smelly by now I expect," offered Clausewitz. "I blame Boyen myself. It was his idea."

"What was?"

"You asked us to dispose of Dumarque, so we did."

"In the tunnel?"

"He waits in the sedan chair even as we speak."

"I must arrange to bury him in the garden and have the sedan chair burned." Then I added, "But not in the lavender garden."

"Why not?" Clausewitz asked as he removed the stopper from a fresh decanter.

"It's occupied."

"By whom?"

"Du Vallois tried to horsewhip me."

"So you shot him?" asked Rosina amazed.

"What would you have me do?" I looked at her squarely. "Stab him in the neck?"

"I will see what's in the kitchens. Come, Anna. If we leave it to the men, we'll all starve." Rosina looked at me. "It was self-preservation merely."

The officers rose to leave also.

Franz, who was more out of his depth with the conversation than I, waited until we were alone. He touched my arm and said, "Paul, Rosina and I will marry as soon as we return home after this visit and after that we'll go to Höxter to take a ship for America. We will go to live there."

I completed the sentence in my head, *Leaving Anna alone.*

"Uncle Franz, excuse me a moment. I need to make some plans." I followed the officers into the hall where they pulled on their gloves and wrapped themselves in their cloaks. "May I ask your advice?" I had the attention of all the best military brains in Prussia and, to be honest, probably all of Europe.

"How can we help an angel? This is worrying. We look to you for guidance." It was Blücher mocking me.

"When will I be required and for how long?" Those questions caused a lot of sideways glances.

It was Scharnhorst who answered, "I wish General Yorck was here tonight, but he is detained elsewhere." He thought as he tugged at his gloves. "I think you will be required from approximately May this coming year. Bonaparte cannot delay his invasion much later than that." He flexed his fingers and looked at me squarely. "It seems you must play your part as a member of the French force at the outset."

Carl von Clausewitz continued, "Yes, but remember Angel, the lives of our young men will very largely lie in your hands. You'll face the same dangers we all face from the moment the invasion begins. And depending on how tactics develop, those dangers may not ease for a full twelvemonth, possibly longer. How you act and react will determine if the dangers for our young men are eased." He paused and opened his hands. "I don't know what you require that we can supply, but ask."

"I will attach myself to Prussian cavalry as a scout if you think that's sensible. I speak Russian. I am Russian. I speak German. I am Prussian and I'm also the Angel. I would make one observation if I may. It is the sooner I can turn Prussian troops back, the lower our losses will be."

"You must be commissioned. I will arrange it." Graf von Blücher was adamant and I did not object. "Because you will require a level of authority." The Graf studied me as thoughts worked in his mind. "Young man, the invasion of Russia is the stage on which the monster Bonaparte will meet his first defeat. And it will be total. You have the responsibility of extracting our young men from that fate. Take the greatest care because you face the greatest risks and challenges."

"Yes, sir," was all I could say. But the weight of the Count's words grew as I thought.

"What will you do until May?" asked Scharnhorst after some moments of silence.

"I shall marry Anna."

"An excellent plan." Clausewitz clapped me on the shoulder and with that they stepped into the snow flurries closing the huge door firmly behind them.

I stood alone in the hall. The clock ticked and the fire crackled. The candles blazed and the chandeliers glittered with the great mirrors reflecting and multiplying the light over and again. The builders had found little difficulty expanding their mandate from my original requirement to repair damage, meaning to the fabric of the house, to refreshing the decoration inside it as well. The restored entrance hall stood resplendent and I shrank in awe of what they had created.

The colours on the walls were subtle and although a little dated according to the builder, they represented a restoration of the house as it had been. The Constantinople rugs were newly returned from the merchant who had been most critical of the dirty state they had been allowed to get into. It was no fault of mine. They lay on the marble floor, and glowed with warmth.

I stared down the restored gallery with its candelabra all lit. The builder had suggested that every fire should be lit each evening and all the candelabra as well. In this way the last of the damp would be driven out of the house now that the repairs to the leaking roof and windows had been completed.

I stared at the ceiling. Of course you could not see the roof beams for the exquisite plasterwork and the blaze from the candles. I thought of the barn, our hut and our tent. I thought of the cold, the collapsed back wall and making six bricks a day. I thought of Uncle Albert and I thought of the old man who stood in the freezing mud and admitted he knew how to read but his eyes were so bad that he could no longer do so.

I tried to remember the old man's words. Something like "I shall savour your temptation, but I shall not yield to it." And with that he had splashed onwards into winter and in search of his wife and daughters. I wondered what had happened to him—and them. I concluded, that alone, he stood little chance of success. He would just run out of energy: another death on the road.

I stood in all this opulence and was overwhelmed by sadness. I shivered and stood close to the fire staring into the flames and warmed my hands until the silk of my sleeve became too hot. I concluded my dismal reverie with the notion that I had succeeded. Others might, or might not, succeed, but they had no cause to resent me. I had injured no one. Well, that was not entirely true, but I had only injured enemies. I also admitted that the word "injured" grossly understated what I had done to them.

284

To people I had come across in the normal course of my life I had behaved as I had been taught.

I stood back from the flames and concluded that ownership meant possession because the opposite was also true. Certainly that rule had dominated my past and I had been prepared to fight for what I had.

But then I thought of my current activities. I had lent money, sometimes on a handshake and sometimes on paper pledges and wondered which security would prove superior. I had also become involved in trade because I had to earn something. The Englishman's money would not go on forever especially at my current level of spending.

I concluded, with some suppression of my spirits, that the traders I had become involved with required no paperwork because our business concerned the undocumented importation of unspecified goods. It was usually tobacco and always at night because French Customs officials went home at dusk.

I finally concluded the fringes of polite society were as far as I should venture.

Chapter Eighteen: Weddings and Invasions Are Planned—1812

Neither the Count, nor von Boyen, stayed in my adopted manor house. But Scharnhorst and Clausewitz did for a few days. Rosina, Anna and Franz stayed for longer.

To enable the household to operate, I crept about late at night, but not trying to seduce Anna. She and Rosina shared a room and I have a fear of Rosina in her night clothes or out of them. My purpose was to rob the Englishman's hoard of gold. Thus we filled the house with food, wine and staff.

I was also able to pay the builders who were, by that time, coming perilously close to the sedan chair.

We greeted the New Year of 1812 with a great deal of revelry and a number of guests, including the Duke, who arrived early and requested that Anna speak privately with him in the drawing room. It had just been released by the builders and it spoke of luxury and opulence. There they remained behind closed doors for a considerable time before Rosina, Franz and I were summoned to attend them.

We entered to see the Duke holding the massive curtains apart and staring through the window. Anna sat beside the fire looking demurely at her hands clasped in her lap.

"Close the door." The Duke turned to face us as we entered and the curtains closed behind him as though he just stepped onto a stage. He approached. "I have Anna's permission to tell you her secret. Before I do, however, I must insist that each of you respect it. In the normal course of events, I would not reveal it, but you are all so particularly close and stand together as her family." He paused to look at Anna fondly. "You see before you the daughter of His Majesty, Tsar Alexander I of all the Russias."

Anna looked up. She had been crying and her eyes sparkled blue. "It's true, Paul." She smiled.

The Duke continued, "Anna's mother goes by the name of Catherine de Brunswick. The Tsar planned to marry her, but the courtiers plotted otherwise and it was not to be. On my recent journey, I believe I discovered as much as there is to discover. However, I regret that no one knows of the whereabouts of Catherine de Brunswick, or even if she still lives. Just as no one outside this room knows Anna's true identity. Her very life will be in danger if her connection becomes known. Therefore, guard this secret with your lives." The Duke paused to assemble his thoughts. "While we are together I wish to speak of other matters. The first is that, although I am happy to have met you and to have been of service to you, I have neither authority over you, nor do I have responsibilities to you." He held his hand up. "That means you are not beholden to me. You owe me no allegiance. There is no blood relationship between Anna and myself as Rosina believed when first she came to see me." We all listened, but could not gauge the importance of the Duke's words. He fished in his jacket pocket. "These two crystals are yours Anna. Rosina has the other three and they represent inadequate recompense for her devotion to your safety, I'm sure you agree." He placed the two rather dull brown crystals in her hand. "I also cannot offer you my protection." He smiled. "If you were a relative I could do so, but as you are not, my protection could be seen as a most unflattering reflection on your character, Anna and I would not want to answer to His Majesty for it." He smiled and went on quickly. "It doesn't matter because you are to marry immediately, but it does matter that you understand exactly where you stood, stand and where you will stand."

A tap on the door and a footman entered to inform us that the first of our guests had arrived.

Before we dispersed I managed to take Anna's hand and asked, "Do you still wish to marry me?"

Anna smiled. "With all my heart."

I wanted to hold her—and more—but guests were arriving.

The Duke spent almost an hour at our small gathering speaking with a number of his military acquaintances.

I agreed that any date Anna chose for our wedding would be perfect and the sooner, the better. I could not bring myself to mention my plans from May onwards. Anna looked so happy she might burst, but the recipient of her exuberance was not me but Rosina. Possibly I was not uppermost in her mind.

The Duke's involvement in our marriage plans accelerated everything magnificently. He threw himself into all aspects of the celebrations, from reserving the church, to obtaining the necessary permissions and recruiting a new pastor. His Grace considered that four of us marrying in the same ceremony would be inappropriate and smack of economy. "The English are paying handsomely," he observed. That was all very well, but one day there would be a reckoning and I was mindful of the Duke's own dictum: "If the English help you, you will pay for it." Now it was the English paying, with us helping ourselves.

The plan eventually was, that Rosina and Franz would marry on the Monday, with Anna acting as Rosina's bridesmaid. We were to marry on the Friday, but by that time, Franz and Rosina would have left for Höxter to take passage for America. Our celebrations would last until the Sunday when they would naturally cease for the Lord's Day of prayer and contemplation.

His Grace, armed with a handful of English gold, went out into the town with the two women in search of wedding dresses and finery of all sorts. Wine from France and the southern German states was available in quantity and most of it was delivered to us, it seemed.

In all this frantic happiness and extravagance, I received a letter from Castel and I made my way to the empty study to open his missive with some foreboding.

Brandt,

At the head of this letter is my direction at Paris. I would be grateful if you would send the three cloth-wrapped bundles I left in the study to this address as soon as may be possible.

I understand that you have granted the staff leave of absence for the festive season and that you have paid up wages due. That was astute of you. However, I also understand you have commissioned extensive repairs to the house. I await news, but do not expect me to send you further funds for the extra works you have undertaken.

I find I may be detained by affairs of a pressing nature in Paris. However, I do warn you that the household must be prepared to receive me at a moment's notice. I look to you as my responsible agent to ensure that is so.

H. Castel

Because Castel wanted the three bundles, I deduced he was at large and not being detained in some terrible torture chamber where there were devices of a "pressing nature."

I wrote back to him:

Your Eminence,

I am happy to confirm the three bundles you spoke of have been dispatched to your address in Paris by coach. Although it was considerably more expensive than transport by cart I considered it would be both faster and safer to send them by coach. I hope you will receive them safely in a week or so.

I turn now to the repairs to your home in Berlin. I hope Your Eminence will appreciate that not all the work has been completed because of the festive season, but we have made progress.

As Your Eminence suspected, there is considerable damage in the roof. Although it is widespread, I am happy to tell you that overall it is no worse than you calculated. New timbers and slates have been supplied and fitted. It is, however, proving difficult to obtain enough lead sheeting. I do not know why this should be the case, but there seems to be a general shortage of lead. I have secured some but not enough as yet. I shall continue to search. I have engaged a company of plumbers to oversee the lead work.

It is on this subject that I would like to elaborate. There is considerable damage to the woodwork of the first-floor landing. This is caused by water leaking into the house from faulty flashing near the main chimney. That flashing has been repaired, but major work is required in this area and I regret it will exceed the amounts you have allowed for contingencies. Nonetheless the work is not optional but essential. Thus I have taken the liberty of ordering new timbers with which to make the repair.

The glazier tells me that he has saved some of the windows and only eight have had to be replaced completely. The other five standing in need of repair have been renovated by replacing only part of the woodwork.

As Your Eminence will appreciate, the repairs are more complicated than either of us suspected during our tour of inspection and they will overrun your budget somewhat.

Of far more significance to Your Eminence is the fact that although the repairs will be finished promptly, the vapours from the paint, lye and varnish used by tradesmen will not disperse adequately for some time longer.

I would estimate that your house would not be habitable by a person of sensibility until late string when the windows can be opened to vent stale airs.

I await your instructions.

P. Brandt

Berlin.

I looked out of the window and saw Rolf and one other digging a hole in the furthest flowerbed, hitherto neglected. A sedan chair stood downwind from them. I watched as they finished their digging and tip the contents of the chair, the remains of the late and loathed Dumarque, into the hole. They kicked a bale of straw around the chair and lit it. They stood back to warm themselves in the fading light of a frosty day in January of the year 1812.

I added a postscript to my letter to Castel.

I am happy to inform you that work has also started on the restoration of the gardens with some interesting specimens established therein.

I considered my letter was evidence Henri Castel might leave on his desk if he intended to deflect criticism of his presence in Paris. I hoped he would appreciate my efforts. I also hoped he would appreciate I had not tampered with the bundles, even now on the coach to Paris.

I had a premonition Henri Castel and I would have dealings in future and those dealings would be more likely to prosper if I had behaved honourably in the past.

Chapter Nineteen: Parting of the Ways

My wedding plans grew a life of their own. I was sent all over town to be fitted or rehearsed, or to attest, or to swear allegiances. One evening, I was diverted from domestic matters by a visit from my military friends led by the youthful Carl von Clausewitz.

"Paul, I can inform you that you may wear your uniform that bears your rank at your wedding. He smiled and added, "Which we're looking forward to with almighty thirsts."

"We've worked long and hard and deserve a festivity. Your marriage will be the occasion. Especially as the English are paying for it," added Scharnhorst, who busied himself by stirring the fire logs with his boot.

"If you tread soot over the new rug, Anna will blame me and refuse to continue with the ceremony."

"No need to worry ourselves. The solution is at hand." Scharnhorst hopped to the fireside and tugged the bell pull.

We waited for the footman to return with a cloth and wipe the offending boot as Gneisenau added a serious note, "Afterwards we must all go our separate ways."

"Yes," continued Clausewitz. "And we'll be wearing different uniforms." He looked at me seriously. "And some of us will be on opposing sides."

As his boot sole was wiped clean by a kneeling footman, Gneisenau continued, "You and Graf Yorck will be with the French force and that's not where we want you."

"No, it isn't," added Scharnhorst. "Understand, Ludwig Yorck is a man of high principles and strict morals. In leading the Prussian Auxiliary force of the French army, he's doing his duty to his King Frederick. He is a great Prussian patriot and his duty to his king comes first."

"General Grawert has resigned then?"

"Retied would be more appropriate but no, not yet. But it will happen," answered Clausewitz as he helped himself to another glass of wine. "Yorck was at Jena with us and regrets not having met you as we did. However, his opportunity lies ahead." He drank. "Brandt, this is excellent and it's very cold outside. I do regret that we cannot tarry but must press on this evening. We are to attend an army conference, so I will take my chances with your wine while I may."

"Yes truly, Carl, you have a point. If we don't drink it, it might go to waste and that must not be." Gneisenau smiled as he held his glass forward.

I watched as the decanter was passed between them. There was to be no waste. There would be a drought instead.

Gneisenau sniffed his glass and exhaled in pleasure. He drank deeply and added, "It will help keep the cold out. Have you considered that, Carl?" There was some laughter as the footman who had ensured Gneisenau's boot was clean enough to walk on the rug took the empty decanter away to refill it.

Scharnhorst explained, "Grawert will announce his retirement very close to the invasion date so there's no time to recruit a replacement we do not approve of, or for anyone to question General Yorck's ascension to command."

Clausewitz concluded, "You must report to General Yorck. He knows of you and wants to meet you. I'm sure he suspects a plot, but we haven't told him. He doesn't even know you're the Angel."

"No," Gneisenau added. "He must make up his own mind. We can't do that for him and we don't want to compromise him. So understand this: when the Angel of Jena first appears, he'll be on his own. So far as Yorck is concerned, he may become hostile."

Scharnhorst instructed, "Please appreciate that you must make your own allies within Yorck's headquarters."

Carl took my lapels in his hands and shook me gently. "You know your duty. So many lives rely on you doing it with as much speed as you can apply that we wish you God's help and guidance. We will not talk of this again before your wedding, so you must inform Anna, as soon as may be, that after it you must leave her side and do your duty by going into great danger for a while." He looked me in the eyes levelly and patted my shoulder.

"If I can add one more thing? Yorck is an enthusiast of skirmishers. He knows what they did to the English in the American Revolutionary War and he knows what the Spanish and Portuguese are doing to the French in the Peninsula war."

Gneisenau added, "But you will face guerrilla actions from Russian troops."

Scharnhorst concluded, "Make no mistake: The Spanish are defeating the French and Wellesley will make the result certain. If Soult had been able to deploy his entire force against the English, the outlook would still be in doubt. As a skirmisher yourself, you'll have the opportunity to contact the Russians who will trail you. Do not assume they know of any plan either."

Scharnhorst came closer to me. "Unless you think and plan clearly, you'll be seen as a traitor to one side and prey to the other. You need to reverse those perceptions so that you are seen as salvation to one side and peace to the other. More help we cannot give you."

They drained their glasses having made a deep impression on the contents of the new decanter and wished me good fortune. I embraced Carl with whom I was most friendly and bowed to the others.

Before Clausewitz left the room, he turned and added, "Every Prussian soldier knows the story: how the Angel of Jena saved the lives of Prussian troops when everything else was lost. Don't expose the Angel too soon. At the outset of a campaign, soldiers think only of victory. It's only later that doubts arise."

I nodded my head.

Clausewitz left me with plenty to think on. Anna questioned me about my lack of excitement over our wedding. She chided me that I did not mean to marry her or that I secretly wished not to do so.

I told her the reason, that I had to leave very soon after our wedding, to join the army that was to invade Russia. She wouldn't believe me. All her fears returned. She would be alone in a strange city. Rosina and Franz would be out of reach. There was no one.

"There is me." The smiling face of the Duke gazed fondly on her. "You can always come to the castle and be assured of a warm welcome."

"But it's not the same," she cried. "I don't want Paul to go. I forbid it."

I smiled. "I'm afraid that a lot of Prussian wives will want me to go, because I shall be responsible for bringing their husbands out of danger."

"I don't care about them. I care about you. You are not to go."

Anna sobbed and clung to me just as I clung to her. It was a long debate with periods of argument and even hostility in it. She tried every tactic and variation, but eventually Anna came to realize I had to go and there was no point imputing choice where none existed.

"But Russia! You always said you'd never go back."

"I know, but it has to be done."

Rosina came to the rescue. I had given her a quantity of money to buy clothes for the journey to America and to last for a while after she had arrived.

"Anna, come with me and help me choose." A little thaw became evident at the prospect of shopping for clothes and that turned into full-blown spring when Rosina suggested that Anna should take the opportunity to stock her own cupboards. "It's high time we parted with everything we brought from the forest."

I agreed. Already the green cloak had slunk to the back of my closet and the coachman's boots had gone. I realized I didn't know where and I no longer cared. "You're right, Rosina. Please help Anna stock her wardrobe," I said.

It was fortunate they met the Duke on their first outing, because he advised against the excesses of high fashion or of falling into the trap of mimicking the aristocracy.

"In the coming period, when the army has gone, there'll be a considerable quieting of society and a more restrained tone will be required," he told them.

Initially the two women had been demurely and modestly turned out, but as time passed, their clothes had become more embellished and eye-catching.

Anna twirled in a new dress and asked, "Do you like it, Paul?"

I realized very early on that my approval was not for the dress. It had already been bought. My opinion on it was not necessary. My approval was sought only because I would pay, or already had paid, for it. I also realized that women do not dress to please or even to attract men. That seemed almost incidental and the results sometimes unwelcome. They dressed to compete with each other. Why they did that, I had no idea. A problem was that this competition was continually stoked by the milliners and couturiers eager to dress the fashionable and wealthy.

"Anna, have you enough clothes for your current needs?" I asked.

"You can never have enough."

"Well, that may be true, but it's possible to spend too much."

"Oh, have I done so? You're correct to chide me. I'm so sorry. You should have told me before."

So it was my fault!

It was a pity to draw in the reins just then because Anna had discovered a superlatively expensive designer who had captured her essence exactly. The dresses she brought back made Anna impossibly adorable. So much so that I began to fear I might have competition on our way to the aisle. However, as I had already concluded, her effect on other men was incidental to her—but certainly not to them! I was most grateful for her indifference.

Her spirits had been lifted, because in her new dresses, she could be seen in society as an equal. She was turned out as well as any and looked a great deal better than most. It is a woman's ability to compete, or at least to stand as equal, in the society she chooses that provides her contentment and happiness. It's only a working hypothesis, you must understand.

Even though Rosina was totally occupied with preparations for her winter sea journey to an unknown land, she continued as Anna's mentor and guide. Anna still had a lot to learn. As far as we could discover, America was still a comparatively wild place and not too much should be relied upon. Bearing in mind the long sea voyage in winter, Rosina's clothes were chosen for practicality and not frippery.

Rosina is a strong-minded powerful woman and she is a good leader. We would both miss her when she and Uncle Franz left. I realized with a shock that day was almost upon us.

Their approaching departure caused ripples of qualm in Anna's mind. "Paul, you will come back to me, won't you? You're not going to fight in battles, are you? I mean, you'll be safe?" she clung to my lapels as she demanded reassurance.

"I won't disguise from you that there are risks. No one knows quite what will happen, so no one knows quite what those risks are. Very little is certain, my love, but this is certain: I will come back to you." I prised her fingers from my jacket.

"You promise?"

"I promise."

"This is all I can hope for." She became despondent again. We stood, face to face, holding hands.

"A brave face and a happy face are necessary for Rosina's wedding tomorrow."

"Paul, let's go with them to America!"

I laughed. "Don't tease me, Anna. You know I must go to Russia with the army."

"Are we poor now? Are we poor because I've spent too much?"

I held her very tightly. "No. Possibly I have lent too much. But we must be careful. The future is not clear and times are not settled."

"Do you think Rosina and Franz are right to go to America?"

I thought, holding her to me. "Yes, I do. When this war is over, would you like to go, too?"

Anna looked up. Her eyes were very blue. "That is certainly something to think about."

"Then, when the time comes, we shall."

Anna squeezed me. "It will be exciting."

"Tomorrow will be exciting. Does your dress become you?"

"My bridesmaid's dress? Yes, it's fabulous."

"Can I see you in it?"

Anna giggled. "Tomorrow. You may see me in it tomorrow. And I shall be in church!"

"Now for the last time, you should go to your room. Tomorrow, Rosina will have a different chamber."

I watched her depart along the corridor. There was a great deal in my mind and most of it fuelled by hot blood.

Next day the tiny church rang with singing. The air was scented with incense and the walls stood decorated with ivy. Every place to the front was taken and we watched Franz Brandt and Rosina marry. There was a moment when the pastor asked if both were called Brandt. It was the Duke, who stood in for Rosina's parents, who answered, "Rosina Matraxan."

I had never heard her name before, but it's not a name one ever forgets. She stood, queenly, confident and happy at a great moment in her life. Behind her stood Anna holding a posy and looking divine. She was better fitted to be an angel than me. Franz stood in a new suit of dark-blue finespun. He didn't quite look like a farmer dressed up, but he didn't quite look like a watchmaker or a locksmith either. He is a strong, sinewy man used to hard work and hard times. His hands were those of a man who knew the countryside and its demands. But he gazed on Rosina with such kindness. Her dress was sheer and white with a cream overdress. The effect was ethereal to the point of make-believe, especially compared to our lives in the forest.

I couldn't help thinking about dear uncle Albert and how much he would have enjoyed this ceremony without a tint of jealousy ever entering his mind. I could hear that great laugh, that I remembered so well, echo around the church and I pictured him with his great beard smiling as he stood beside his brother.

Rosina and Franz stood in a church in Berlin. Behind them was Russia with her privation and hunger. Ahead was America with all her promise. I stood in the same church, but Russia was ahead for me as well as behind me.

We celebrated their wedding at the manor until late in the night and well after they had gone to bed. I woke late next morning with a head that spoke of too much wine and little else. It would pass and if ever there was justification for such a celebration, it was their happiness.

I scuffed down the marble staircase to the main hall. The front door stood open and the snow blew in along with an icy wind. A pile of boxes was being moved slowly from the hall to the trunk of a coach standing outside. The four horses blew clouds of steam from their nostrils as the coachman arranged blankets over his team.

Franz checked the boxes as they were loaded, while Rosina, wrapped up in her blue cloak, stood beside the open door.

"You should climb aboard," I said to her. "You'll freeze out here."

"Where's your coat, Paul. If anyone freezes, it'll be you."

"You're right. You won't leave before I come back, will you?"

"Look at the boxes." Rosina smiled.

I was saved the bother of having to fetch my cloak by Luc who arrived with it. As I wrapped myself up, I heard Uncle Franz. "Ah, Paul, a word with you."

He led me around the coach to the other side and out of earshot of the others. "Paul, I am your last relative and it is possible that we shall never see each other again." I was about to protest, but Uncle Franz stayed me. "You must admit it is at least possible." I nodded. "Good. Therefore, listen to me. You have had success early in life. Unless you are careful, failure will follow it. You will become casual. In fact, Paul, you have become casual. You spend too freely and you arouse jealousy. You are not paying attention to your surroundings."

"What do you mean?"

"If you were more circumspect, you would know that envious eyes are cast in your direction: Russian eyes, hungry eyes, and they are attached to gabbling mouths. They know your background and they seek ways to exploit that knowledge."

"What should I do?"

"You must make your own mind up about that. But the first thing you must do is to remember the skills you learned on the road all those years ago. They kept us alive. Today the threat is the same. Only the surroundings are different."

"What would you do?"

Uncle Franz laughed. "I would marry Rosina and leave for America." He put his hand on my shoulder. "But if you mean what would I do in your place? I would answer that you should establish a guild or refuge for Russians in need in this city. Buy an old inn or some such and make it a place where they can eat, sleep, get warm and meet friendly Russians already established. At least you would know if they plotted against you."

"How would I know?"

"Paul, you really are not thinking. The staff would work for you. Now take care. There are too many poor and you cannot be rich and safe amongst the poor."

At that moment the porter reported that all the boxes were on the coach.

Uncle Franz looked me in the eyes, hugged me and kissed me in the Russian manner. "I must go and take my bride away from Berlin and into our future." Then he added the Russian word that tolled like a bell. "Proschaite."

"Proschaite." I replied. It means, forgive me and farewell forever. "Good fortune and God's presence travel alongside you," I added.

We arrived back at the coach to see it standing there with the door open and no one climbing up. Dear Anna was clasping Rosina to her and not letting go. A few flakes drifted down from the flat grey sky to settle on the women's cloaks.

"Either you must set her free, Anna, or you must go as well, because it is already near noon and the weather will not improve." The Duke stood behind Anna and spoke quietly, holding her shoulders. Anna turned around and buried her head in the Duke's cloak.

"They must be gone before I look again." She sobbed into the cloak's folds.

The Duke looked over Anna's head. "Rosina, take this opportunity to escape the temptations of Berlin." He looked on her with true affection tinged with admiration. Franz handed her up into the coach and followed himself. I closed the door as the coachman clambered up to his perch.

"Anna, you must turn around now," the Duke instructed and reluctantly she did. Her face smeared with tears. It was a very sad face made sadder by a dramatic sob.

Uncle Franz and Aunt Rosina smiled and waved from the window.

Calls of "good-bye," "write soon," "I love you," "remember what I said," "take care," "go with God," and "safe journey" all echoed around the coach as the sound of the whip cracked the winter air and the horses started their journey. "Proschaite, Rosina." I called. The coach rumbled towards the open gates and onto the quiet Berlin street. There, it headed towards the Brandenburg Gate, stripped of its Quadriga by the rapacious Bonaparte.

All that was left of Rosina, Franz, my family and my past were wheel tracks in the dusting of snow. I looked up to the sky. They, too, would be obliterated soon.

We filed into the house. Shutting the front door was final.

Anna's sadness was hardly diverted by her own wedding plans. It was not until she stood in front of a mirror dressed in her gown for the first time that she cheered herself. Even so, it was her wish that Rosina could have seen her and she was cast down.

The Duke had taken care to separate the two ceremonies, for he had lavished his influence on ours in the same way that the Englishman, Anstruther, had lavished his money. The church was filled with finery. The officers had brought their wives and their wives represented the aristocracy, or parts of it. There was colour and opulence everywhere. My dress uniform had the benefit of being new and fitting precisely. Anna's dress had the benefit of having Anna in it and if you asked me today what it looked like, I would have to fetch it from its cupboard to show you because I never really paid it attention. But I do remember pearls and tiny green flowers interwoven with gold lace.

Two events are notable. The first was that when the priest asked Anna's name. The Duke, who stood as her parents, quietly answered for her: "Anna Holstein-Gottorp-Romanov."

To my knowledge it's the only time her full name has been given. But even then it was not written in the parish register of marriages as that—but only as "Anna Holstein."

The other was that, at the moment our privacy arrived, a truth struck me that von Clausewitz had omitted to mention. It was that, should the French discover the Angel of Jena was with their army of invasion, they would shoot me, spit me with their lances, or chop me down with sabres, or possibly all three. The realization that I was about to be inserted amongst five hundred thousand deadly enemies left me entirely impotent—for a while.

END OF VOLUME ONE OF THE BRANDT FAMILY CHRONICLES

VOLUME TWO

The Angel Faces Destruction

(Napoleon's disastrous invasion of Russia.)

A traitor is perfidious, seditious, a betrayer and an informer. Paul ticks all the boxes. It is 1812, and Paul Brandt, a Russian by birth, is attached to the Prussian Auxiliary Column conscripted into Bonaparte's French army for the invasion of Russia. But Paul's newest acquaintances, Gneisenau and Clausewitz, have plotted the destruction of the *Grande Armée*. Half a million French soldiers will march to their death, if their strategy works. But Paul must save his column from the fury of his own countrymen and the depths of the Russian winter. From the Neiman River to Moscow is over a thousand kilometres—and they must get back! If Paul can reach the Tsar, can he hatch the plot that opens the escape route?

2016 Oliver Fairfax

www.oliverfairfax.com

Oliver Fairfax has asserted his rights in accordance with the Copyright, Designs and Patents Act 1988 to be identified as the author of this work.

Published in Christchurch New Zealand by Toby Heale

First published in eBook format in 2015

Second Edition 2016 Second, Edition in Paperback 2017

ISBN: 9781545145937

eBook ISBN

Library of Congress Control Number 2016910254

LCCN Imprint name: CreateSpace Independent Publishing Platform, North Charleston. SC.

Made in the USA
Lexington, KY
11 November 2017